Yule Be the Death of Me:

Book Two of The Vivienne Finch Magical Mysteries

J.D. SHAW

To the Loomis family, You guys are the best! Thanks so much!

J.D. S.

Copyright © 2013 by J.D. Shaw

All rights reserved. No part of this book may be reproduced in any form or by any means without the prior written consent of the author, excepting brief quotes used in reviews.

author@jdshawbooks.com

Manuscript Editing by George G. Weiss.

Cover illustrations by Allison Marie for Alli's Studio. Copyright © 2013 All Rights Reserved. No part of these designs may be reproduced without written consent from the artist.

allisstudio@allisstudio.com

DEDICATION

This one is for my entire family. You have all made Christmas Eve one of the most special gifts I have ever received. I will treasure the memories of each and every one for as long as I live.

J.D. SHAW

THE VIVIENNE FINCH MAGICAL MYSTERIES

Book One: *Easy Bake Coven*

Book Two: *Yule Be the Death of Me*

CHAPTER 1

Monday, December 16th

It was supposed to be the most wonderful time of the year, according to the song lyrics. Yet, as she stood in the line with the others, Vivienne Finch certainly wasn't feeling any holiday cheer. In fact, she was pretty sure that her feelings were matching those of Ebenezer Scrooge before his visit by the three ghosts.

Here it was, nine days before Christmas and she still wasn't even close to finishing her list of tasks. It had been such a flurry of activity ever since Halloween had come and gone. She found herself wishing that the calendar could roll back just a few weeks to allow her a chance to catch up. But she knew better than to do such a thing. The elder council of witches had made it quite clear to her that they frowned upon any tampering with the normal flow of time. She had been given a free pass for the last mess, but that was it. She was on her own to fix any future mistakes.

"Ladies, stay in single file please." A stern, yet matronly voice ordered. The line moved forward but she really wasn't all that eager to proceed. She just wanted to leave this nonsense and go back home. No one really wanted to be standing here anyway.

The line led directly into the next room where bright lights forced her to squint. She put her hand up to her face to shield her eyes from the blinding glare. The line came to a stop and the stern voice returned. "Face forward."

She did as they were told and stared at the bright lights. Nothing ruined the holiday like standing in a police lineup as a suspect in a murder. Yet, that was exactly where she found herself and she had very little time to find the real killer.

"Number three, step forward." The voice ordered as a blonde woman that was about Vivienne's height took a tentative step toward the light.

The others in the lineup remained quiet, except for the occasional gurgle of a nervous stomach or someone breathing a bit too heavy through their nostrils.

"Step back please." The voice ordered.

"Number seven, step forward." The stern voice continued.

No one moved. Vivienne began to tap her foot in annoyance that this was taking so long. An elbow poked into her ribs. "What are you waiting for honey, a red carpet?" A brunette with a very short haircut, multiple piercings, and a rather masculine looking body mocked her.

"They called me forward?" Vivienne asked.

"Number seven, please step forward." The voice echoed from the room speakers in a rather unpleasant tone.

She put one foot in front of the other and stepped toward the light. She couldn't see who was behind the glass, but she had a feeling they weren't going to help her out. It was the worst feeling in the world. She fought to keep herself composed as she faced scrutiny from behind the tinted glass.

"Step back please." The voice ordered.

Vivienne let out a little sigh and was happy to rejoin the line.

"Everyone may return to holding." The voice ordered.

They were led out of the room and marched back toward the holding cells. Vivienne had just cleared the doorway when a firm grip took her by the arm. "Miss Finch, I need you to follow me." The officer in charge, a harsh-looking woman who had lips so thin they were almost non-existent, ordered.

She swallowed hard and left the others in the line. "It can't be me."

"Please come with me, ma'am." The officer replied in her husky voice that revealed years of a heavy smoking habit. Vivienne had seen her around the station many times but always forgot her name.

"This is ridiculous." Vivienne countered. "I'm not the killer." She paused awkwardly as the name rolled off her tongue. "Alma." Vivienne gave a little smile, hoping she got the name right to establish a little bit of empathy.

"It's best not to speak unless your lawyer is present." She clearly was not moved by Vivienne's attempt to guess her name. She marched her into Sheriff Rigsbee's office and tapped the chair facing his desk. "Please have a seat, the Sheriff will be right in."

Vivienne sat down and thought it best to keep her mouth closed from this point on.

The officer stood guard at the door, seeming quite bored with her current task. As the heavy footfalls of Sheriff Zeke Rigsbee approached the office, she smiled for the first time which gave Vivienne a glimmer of hope that everything was going to work out. An early Christmas miracle, perhaps? "Since we know each other so well and all, I thought you should know that I like my Christmas cards made out to Selma. That being my real name and all. Happy holidays."

Vivienne felt her sudden hope harden into a lump of coal. It was going to be a holiday to remember, that much was for sure.

CHAPTER 2

Friday, November 29th

"Tommy, don't bite on those." Vivienne snatched the string of miniature Christmas lights away from her grey and white cat that had chosen to adopt her back in late September. He swiped at the string with his paws and gave her a defiant meow for taking away his newest toy. She crammed the lights up into the higher branches of her seven foot artificial blue spruce to keep them out of his reach. "Why don't you play with those catnip mice I bought the other day?"

Opening a blue plastic tote that was labeled 'Tree Stuff' with a piece of masking tape, Vivienne hoped to find all of her ornaments collected over the years carefully packed into cardboard boxes and organized by color and shape. On the contrary, as she had done every New Year's Day since she had moved into her rented Cape Cod on Sunset Terrance, they were haphazardly wrapped in paper towels and crammed whichever way they would fit. A testament to the end of the season when she was sick to death of holly and jolly and rushed to pack everything away with a vow to do it better the next time.

The tree began to sway side to side as Tommy Cat, all sixteen pounds of him, shimmied up the wire branches in a mad race to the top. "Get out of there you crazy beast." Vivienne shouted.

He meowed from somewhere inside the dark green branches and then stuck his head out from the middle section. He blinked a few times and let out a sound somewhere between a meow and a purr.

Vivienne reached over and pulled him free, before he could bring the entire tree crashing down. His front claws sank deep into her shoulder as he held on for dear life. "Ouch, ouch, claws. Watch the claws." She yelped and released him onto the sofa where he proceeded to dance across her new tan slipcover she had purchased to hide the shredding job he had done to the original fabric.

Nora, always ready with her motherly advice, had told her repeatedly to have her cat declawed. "They're like disobedient children." She had said many times. "You can say no a thousand times but they'll keep doing it just to spite you."

What her mother didn't know was that just before Halloween she had wrestled Tommy into the large plastic cat carrier after discovering his first shredding crime committed on the right arm of the sofa. But by the time she pulled into the parking lot of Lakeside Veterinary, she had calmed down and decided she just couldn't go through with it. Even though her veterinarian had assured her the laser procedure was less painful than the old surgery, she couldn't help but feel it was just plain wrong to take his claws away.

So she vowed to deal with the problem by investing in slip covers. About three or four a year would be about right she guessed. Besides, it would give her tired furniture one of those inexpensive but stylish makeovers she had seen on those home improvement television shows and countless magazine covers.

Tommy Cat curled into a ball shape on the sofa and pulled his tail close to his face as he took what was most likely his tenth nap of the day. After his neutering and vaccinations, he didn't seem to miss going outside much anymore. Fabric mice stuffed with catnip and trailing ribbon tails seemed good enough to stalk as prey. Like many cats, he was content to watch the world on a cozy padded perch from the living room window and only occasionally play a game of 'catch me if you can' with Joshua every now and then when he sometimes escaped. Thankfully, the shaking of a cat treat bag proved irresistible to ignore and he could always be coaxed back inside before straying too far into the wilds of suburbia.

Free to decorate in peace, Vivienne continued pulling out the ornaments one by one and set them on the oak coffee table where several packages of green hooks were waiting. Not that she would need to use many hooks, as most of the baubles still had them attached from last year.

Actually, as she stared at the package she had thrown into her cart during her last trip to the Monarch Grocery, they weren't even hooks or made of metal. These days, they were manufactured of thin green plastic and had little loops you squeezed apart to put the ornament on. She imagined that switching over to those would save the inevitable holiday chore of having to dig one out of her bare feet whenever she walked past the tree to get the morning paper. Yet, it would take forever to make the switch. No, she would do that when she took the ornaments down at the end of the season. She wanted the tree up and finished before Joshua arrived at her home for the evening.

She pulled out a set of vintage Jewel Brite brand plastic ornaments that had cutout dioramas of little scenes inside them and smiled. They had graced every tree in the Finch household since she was a little girl. One ornament in particular was always hers to hang. It was the yellow plastic diorama scene of an angel petting a deer.

She would hang it last, front and center on her mother's Scotch pine tree, much to Nora's displeasure at having a cheap plastic ornament in such a visible place on her glorious tree. Her father would then find a way to have one of the large glass light bulbs placed nearby so it would be illuminated. She spent hours lying down upon the tree skirt, gazing at the twinkling lights and inhaling the scent of fresh pine that wafted from the sturdy branches. It seemed Christmas Eve would never come fast enough, but it always arrived on time and usually with her parents protesting it came a bit too fast.

The first Christmas after her father had passed away, Nora had given Vivienne most of the ornaments from the family tree. She had said she was downsizing to a table top tree and only needed a few silver and gold glass balls, but Vivienne knew better. The memories of those ornaments proved too painful to look upon for the weeks leading up to the holidays. Where Nora saw only sadness at what once had been, Vivienne treasured as sweet nostalgia that warmed her heart with precious memories.

Pulling herself away from the memories of the past, Vivienne spent the next hour and a half wrapping the tree with colored lights and suspending ornaments on the wire branches. This year, she had to keep the fragile glass ornaments near the top of the tree and used the plastic along the lower branches should wayward paws choose to play. If the worst-case scenario did occur, she hoped the fluffy red tree skirt she wrapped around the base would help cushion the blow and prevent a shattered mess.

With her work complete, she stepped back to admire the effort and then remembered how she hadn't tested the light strands to make sure they worked. She took a deep breath and then plugged the extension cord into the outlet. The lights on the tree burned bright and flooded the surrounding walls and corner windows with a festive kaleidoscope of color. She exhaled and looked over at Tommy Cat who was stretching from his nap. "Isn't it beautiful?" She asked him. He opened one eye, unimpressed, and returned to snoozing.

The front door opened as Joshua returned from his day shift at the Cayuga Cove Sheriff's office. Dapper in his brown deputy uniform and hat, he announced his presence with an impressed whistle.

Vivienne gestured to the tree like a model on a television game show. "What do you think?"

"I think it looks amazing." Joshua took off his hat and coat and hung them on the wall hooks. "Isn't a little strange though?"

"What's strange?" Vivienne asked. "Using colored and clear lights together?" She put her hands on her hips and stared at the tree again. "I couldn't decide which I liked better so I used both."

"I meant being a witch and celebrating Christmas." Joshua clarified as he pulled off his boots and padded across the hardwood floor in his thick black socks with the bright yellow tips. He wrapped his arms around her waist and gave her a kiss.

"Not really." Vivienne smiled at him. I've always loved Christmas. Just because I'm a witch doesn't mean that I don't enjoy the season of giving."

"I understand that." Joshua agreed. "Part of me expected you to ignore the whole Christmas holiday thing. I figured Halloween was your big celebration for the year."

"Most of the traditions that people associate with Christmas are actually older than Christianity and often have Pagan roots." Vivienne walked over the sofa and sat down.

Joshua followed and plopped next to her. "Such as what?"

"Mistletoe." Vivienne continued. "It was actually a symbol for virility that was sacred to the Druids. I read something once about how early tribes used the plant to try and cure fertility problems."

Joshua leaned closer to her and nibbled on her ear. "Is that why people kiss under it?"

Vivienne shrugged. "I don't know, but it sounds reasonable enough." She enjoyed the way the tree lights reflected off his dark hair. Even more so, she thought that his decision to allow his goatee to grow out into a beard gave him a level of distinction and trust that complimented his deputy title quite nicely.

"Smart people, those fertile Druids." Joshua grinned at her.

"I'm not concerned about you needing the mistletoe. It would please my mother to know that you can provide a pack of grandchildren."

"Let's not tell your mother everything." He stifled a little yawn.

She gently swatted his shoulder with her left hand. "For right now, my mother will have to suffice with a fluffy grand-cat. Isn't that right, Tommy?"

Tommy opened one eye and appeared underwhelmed and uninterested.

"What's for dinner?" Joshua asked.

"I have some chicken noodle soup in the slow-cooker." Vivienne ran her hands through his thick brown hair. "Stephanie and I closed the bakery up early because everyone was out at the outlets for the Black Friday sales."

"I thought you and Nora always go Black Friday shopping?"

"We used to." Vivienne sighed. "But now that I have my own business to run, I just can't stay up all night hunting bargains. She ended up going out with Clara since the diner is closed for the holiday weekend."

"Don't forget to make out your list for Santa to look at." Joshua stretched his arms upward with a little yawn. "He likes to have plenty of notice since his shopping skills aren't as fine-tuned as yours."

Vivienne rolled her eyes. "That's a sexist thing to say."

He shrugged. "I didn't mean it like that."

She shook her head and got up from the sofa. "You're lucky it's the season for peace and goodwill toward men."

He reached over to the end table and grabbed the television remote. "Sheriff Rigsbee approved my personal day for tomorrow so we can go to the holiday parade together."

"I don't believe it. Was he visited by three ghosts the other night by any chance?"

"You're the witch in the family, you tell me." He said with a laugh. "But if they visit again, will you ask them to mention something to him about giving me a pay raise?"

"Absolutely." Vivienne snickered. "Maybe we can get Tommy Cat to play the part of Tiny Tim?"

"Tiny?" Joshua scoffed. "I've never seen such a fat cat."

"He's not fat, he's fluffy." Vivienne protested.

"I've never heard of a cat with sixteen pounds of fluff on it." Joshua turned the television on and started flipping through the channels with furious speed. "So what's the plan with the bakery?"

"Well, the parade route covers all of Main Street so we'll have a great view from outside the bakery." Vivienne smiled. "As we sell cups of hot cocoa and cookies from the table we've set up on the sidewalk."

Joshua stopped on the sports channel that was showing a football game. "Sell things?"

"Yes." She replied. "It's going to be a busy day and I'd be a fool not to take advantage of it."

"I thought this was going to be our day to watch the parade, grab something for lunch, and maybe do a little shopping at the Waterloo Premium Outlets?"

"It still will be." Vivienne did her best to sell him on the concept. "We're only going to have the bakery open from eight in the morning until eleven."

Joshua propped his feet up on the coffee table. "I guess that will be okay."

"Stephanie and I will handle the crowds. All you need to do is keep the thermal pots filled with coffee and cocoa and bring out trays of cookies when we get low." Vivienne explained calmly. "It'll be hardly any effort at all."

"I hope so." Joshua flipped through the channels a few more times before stopping on a rerun of a popular sitcom. "We deserve some quality time before the chaos of the season kicks full into gear."

"I couldn't agree more." Vivienne replied. "Besides, I need to work on the finishing touches on our entry for the Gingerbread Dream House contest on Sunday afternoon."

"How is that coming along?"

"Stephanie finished making the sugar stained glass windows for the upstairs turrets." Vivienne was especially proud of her entry in the town's contest. A few weeks beforehand, she and Stephanie had gone around the town and photographed several of the stately old homes around town for inspiration. After some debate, they chose the Edgar Rothwell mansion, named for the railroad tycoon who built the largest home in Cayuga Cove back in 1864.

Today, it housed the local historical society and their collection of relics and documents sealed up in dusty little display cases scattered throughout the fifteen rooms.

"Can you imagine living in a place like that?" Joshua wondered.

"Not without an army of servants to keep it up." Vivienne laughed. "And even then, who the heck needs fifteen rooms?"

* * *

The morning of the holiday parade proved to be every bit as busy as Vivienne had anticipated. She and Stephanie Bridgeman watched as the little metal cash box filled up with fives and tens thanks to eager parade attendees who guzzled down cups of coffee and cocoa and snacked on iced butter cookies cut out in festive shapes.

Joshua remained inside the store looking complete overwhelmed while standing behind the cash register. Most of the crowd had stayed outside and lined the sidewalk for the best views of the floats, but a few curious shoppers stepped into the bakery and browsed the selections of baked goods from inside the display cases.

"I don't normally work here." Joshua explained to each and every customer the moment they stepped inside the Sweet Dreams Bakery. "But if you want to buy something you can pay for it at the table out front."

Lucky for him, everyone just browsed and then left before the sound of the high school marching band echoed out on the street signaling the start of the parade. Abandoning his post behind the counter, he knocked on the window glass at Vivienne who motioned for him to come outside and watch the festivities.

"This was a great idea, Vivienne." Stephanie remarked as Joshua joined them at the table in front of the display window. "We've made a small fortune in cocoa sales alone."

Vivienne nodded. "Your idea for printing up order sheets with goodies available for parties and holiday gatherings was brilliant. We're almost completely out of them."

"We had almost two hundred." Stephanie grinned. "I hope they come back with orders."

"They will." Vivienne smiled as the high school band approached carrying a red and green decorated banner lettered with 'Cayuga Cove Holiday Parade: 110th anniversary'.

Joshua, with his six foot five height, was able to see quite easily above the assembled crowds as the color guard waved their flags and marched along to

'It's beginning to look a lot like Christmas.' The horn section of the band was a little off key, but it didn't really matter. The holiday spirit made the ears of the parade attendees a little more forgiving.

Vivienne and Stephanie, both petite, were not as fortunate when it came to getting a good view. They stood on their tip toes and craned their necks in an effort to see anything.

Joshua, now aware of their plight, pulled the two folding chairs to each side of him and shouted over the music. "Stand up on the chairs and keep your arms on my shoulders for balance."

Vivienne and Stephanie climbed up and at last were able to view the colorful floats and costumed characters that danced along throwing little wrapped candy canes and plastic trinkets to the kids along the parade route. Several businesses had sponsored various parade floats that were pulled along by riding lawnmowers and small pickup trucks. Colonial Bank had a float with a reproduction of their building. Lily's Pad Day Care had a candy-themed winter wonderland float populated with Miss Lily dressed as Mrs. Claus and several of her center's children costumed as elves. Our Lady of the Lake had a float with a live nativity scene, and the crowd roared with approval as a Chinese Dragon wiggled along the road, operated by several staff members from the Shanghai Sunset restaurant.

The crowd swelled with excited applause as the last float, a replica of a rooftop with Santa and his sleigh perched atop, rolled slowly up Main Street. Santa addressed the crowd from a microphone as children screamed their holiday wishes to him. "Santa wants you all to be very good between now and Christmas." He shouted above the little voices. "I'm getting some good reports from my elves."

As usual, Tony DiSanto from The Leaning Tower of Pizza was playing the part of Santa. His thinning black hair was hidden under a big red cap and curly white wig. His puffy cheeks framed the fake beard quite well and he required no padding to fill out the suit around the middle. "What do you want for Christmas?" He asked the children lining the streets.

The kids squealed with delight as he acknowledged some of the toy wishes shouted out to him. Although he was careful to not make any promises, Vivienne was certain more than a few parents were surprised by what this week's new toy request was. More than likely, they started planning a weekend of frantic holiday shopping to find the treasured item before time ran out.

With the parade over, the crowds dispersed quickly to the designated parking areas around the town. Joshua helped Vivienne and Stephanie back down to the sidewalk so they could pack up the table and return the leftover goods back inside the bakery.

"And so it begins." Vivienne spoke up as she placed the remaining butter cookies back into the glass case display.

"I can't wait." Stephanie counted out the money from the metal cash box. "My cousins from Georgia are coming up for a few days around Christmas. I haven't seen them in almost five years."

"That's wonderful, Stephanie. I'm sure you'll have a great time." Vivienne slid the door on the display case closed and turned off the lights inside it.

"That means a few more presents to buy this year, but thanks to all these hours it won't be a problem." Stephanie remarked as she wrote some figures down on a yellow notepad.

Joshua walked over to Vivienne. "Aren't you giving her a holiday bonus?" He whispered.

"It's tucked into her paycheck this week." Vivienne whispered back. "I just love giving little surprises like that."

Stephanie finished counting and tucked the money back into the metal box. "We made two hundred and fifteen dollars. Not bad."

"Don't forget all those order sheets floating around. I'm sure we'll start getting those back soon."

Stephanie handed the box to Vivienne and grabbed her coat from behind the counter. "I'm ready for them."

Joshua walked over to the gingerbread reproduction of the Edgar Rothwell mansion and admired the hours of hard work that had gone into its creation. Stephanie and Vivienne had even wired battery-powered lights into the back to illuminate the stained-glass sugar windows in the turrets that flanked each end of the stately mansion. "You two are going to win first place with this."

"You think so?" Stephanie put her hands on her hips as she scrutinized the confection. "I'm a little worried my landscaping didn't turn out as good as I hoped. The shredded coconut didn't soak up the green food coloring as much as I would have liked."

Vivienne waved her hands at Stephanie. "The lawn looks perfect and the fondant iron fence is a work of art." She narrowed her eyes at the roof. "But my marzipan roofing tiles could have been a little more angular."

Joshua shook his head at them both. "You both are crazy. It looks just like the real thing."

"You think so?" Vivienne and Stephanie asked in stereo and then laughed.

He reached out with his big hand. "Let me taste."

Vivienne and Stephanie both squealed in protest.

Joshua yanked his hand back with a wicked grin. "I'm just kidding." He winked back. "I'm not an official judge or anything," Joshua admitted, "But even if I didn't know you both made it I'd give it my vote."

Vivienne looked up at Joshua. "Well, I think we can close up and head off for our day."

"Sounds like a good idea to me." He retrieved his jacket that was hung on the back of one of the bistro chairs and locked up the front door.

"Where are you both off to?" Stephanie asked with a coy smile.

"We're heading to the outlets near Waterloo and then grabbing a bite to eat later." Vivienne replied as she turned off the overhead spotlights leaving only the front window display illuminated.

"Let me know if you find any good bargains." Stephanie nodded as they walked to the back door to leave. "I just hate spending the gas money if there isn't anything worth purchasing."

"I'll give you a full report." Vivienne held the door for everyone to leave and then locked it with her key. "See you in the morning."

"Bye." Stephanie hurried to her little green Ford Focus, brushing away the huge flakes of snow that the wind hurled into her eyelashes.

"Is it just me, or is it getting colder?" Vivienne asked.

Joshua studied the dark clouds overhead. "Looks like those lake effect snow bands are getting stronger." His breath condensed into steam and flew away with the wind. "It's going to be an early winter."

"I hope the roads stay clear." Vivienne shuddered and pulled the collar of her black winter coat up.

"You know how bad Route 90 can get with blowing snow from all those open fields."

"If it gets too bad, we'll head back early." Joshua led her to his Jeep and opened the passenger door. "I'm sure we can find ways to pass the time."

CHAPTER 3

Saturday, November 30th

"I can't believe we got eight inches of snow in November." Joshua stared out the living room window of Vivienne's home at the blanket of white covering the cars parked along the street. "We've still got a few weeks until it's officially winter."

Vivienne walked over to where he was standing and admired the thick coat of wet snow that transformed the now barren trees and brown grass into something out of a snow globe. "There's always something special about that first big snowfall."

Joshua reached behind and rubbed his back. He had spent the afternoon shoveling out her sidewalk and spreading some pet-safe ice melt to prevent slick spots. "I know what you mean. It has a way of reminding us we're not kids anymore while at the same time making you want to get into a snowball fight and go sledding."

Vivienne brushed his hands away and took over with a quick massage across his lower back. "Well, the cleanup part I could do without."

Joshua let out a little moan as her fingers loosened some of the knots in his back muscles. "I used to wonder why so many older people went to Florida for the winter. Now, I get it."

"Christmas in Florida just wouldn't seem right." Vivienne reasoned as she moved her arms up his back to just below his shoulder blades. "I just can't imagine opening presents and then going outside for a swim in the pool."

"Boy, I sure could." Joshua sighed. "No more shovels or heavy bags of salt."

"You only have to deal with hurricane winds that blow the roof off and storm surges that pound your house walls away." Vivienne replied with a splash of reality about living in a tropical climate. "No matter where you go, there's always something."

Joshua turned around to face her. "I suppose you're right. But it sure feels good to daydream about it."

She was happy to see the sunlight peeking out from the patches of pale blue where the clouds were breaking up. "We better get ready to leave for the contest. I want to get there early to see what the competition has come up with."

Although the contest award wasn't going to be given out until three in the afternoon, Vivienne and Joshua arrived an hour beforehand at Loft 226 art gallery to see all of the entries.

The gallery, located on Main Street, was sandwiched between LaGreca's Furniture and Aunt T's Toys. Unlike the other building interiors that had plenty of exposed brick, Loft 226 had covered their walls with plain white sheetrock to act as a neutral canvas for the artwork on display. The pine floorboards, also painted white, assured that the space itself disappeared while patrons took in what each artist had created.

The owner of the gallery, Todd York, welcomed Vivienne and Joshua with a firm handshake as they stepped into the warm space that smelled of gingerbread and mulling spices. He was nearly six feet tall and bean pole thin. Dressed in a monochrome black suit, with his light blonde hair neatly parted to the side, he looked every bit the fashionable gallery owner. "I'm so glad you both could come." He leaned close to Vivienne and lowered his voice. "I think you have a great chance of winning today."

Vivienne felt her face blush with pride. "I didn't work solo on this. Stephanie was an equal partner."

Todd nodded. "Is she coming too?"

Vivienne shook her head. "She's finishing a paper for one of her night classes at the college today."

"That's a shame, but education is important." Todd remarked. "May I take your coats?"

Joshua helped Vivienne out of hers to reveal one of the new outfits she had treated herself to for the upcoming holiday season of parties and business functions. The jade-green dress was dressy enough for the occasion, but still felt easy and relaxed.

Todd's eyes focused on her outfit. "I saw that in Kathy's store the other day. I must say it looks fabulous on you." He gushed. "Your red hair really sets it off."

"Thank you so much." Vivienne smiled. She knew that Todd was one of only a handful of men in town who actually shopped at Trade Winds Clothier. Although the menswear section in the store was only a small corner, Kathy was more than happy to place custom orders for styles that would never sell in Cayuga Cove. Todd, along with some of the more fashionable men in town, gave her a steady supply of business.

Vivienne often wondered what functions they wore their more modern clothing to. There certainly wasn't any place in town that had a formal dress code, except for the Bistro Parisian, and that was merely a request not to wear jeans and tee shirts during Friday and Saturday dinner service. She assumed they must have found some more use for them in the larger cities like Rochester and Syracuse, places that actually had dance clubs and four star restaurants. She had to admit, she often wished she and Todd were closer friends so she could experience the more posh side of life every now and then.

Like most of the heterosexual men in town, Joshua had chosen his usual non-work clothing option of a pair of dark denim jeans and a blue flannel shirt. The top two buttons he usually left open at home were done up, which was about as fancy as he or the other men ever went when it came to dressing up for an occasion that wasn't a wedding or funeral.

"Feel free to browse the other entries. We broke the record with fifteen this year." Todd said as he disappeared into a small room off to the side of the reception desk with their coats.

Several people had gathered into the gallery for the annual contest, but Vivienne guessed they were mostly fellow participants who were doing the same thing she was; checking out what everyone else had designed. "Fifteen entries makes quite a bit of competition." Vivienne whispered to Joshua.

"Yes." Joshua agreed as he offered her his right arm. They walked into the east wing of the gallery. "But don't get worried just yet. We haven't even seen the others."

The clattering of high heels announced the arrival of Kathy Saunders. "Sorry I'm late, I had to get an order in before five tonight." She was dressed in a simple black dress that had a scattering of sequins along the low-cut top. "How's the competition?"

Joshua offered her his other arm. "We haven't even started to look yet. Care to join us?"

"You bet." Kathy gushed and eagerly took him up on the offer. She pointed to the first entry that was displayed on a cylindrical pedestal. "Oh, look at that one. Someone made a little cathedral."

Vivienne nodded her approval at the creation. It was cute, but the steeple was tipped a little to the side and one of the sugar windows was coming loose under the heat of the spot lights above. "I wonder who made this one?"

"Doesn't it say?" Joshua looked along the base for an information card.

Vivienne shook her head. "No, you only get a number." She pointed to the small card that had the number one printed on it. "That way the judging panel can be completely impartial."

Kathy pointed to the crooked steeple. "Well, I think you can scratch this off as a winner."

Vivienne shushed her and pointed to some of the other guests browsing the room. "The creator just might be in here."

Kathy's eyes widened. "Oh, right. Sorry." She smiled and raised her voice with praise. "Isn't this little church just darling?"

Vivienne rolled her eyes as they moved on to the next entry, a charming little tropical diorama with gingerbread figures frolicking along a beach. "They used sanding sugar and cinnamon to make the sand color. That's pretty clever."

Kathy nodded and pointed to the girl gingerbread figure. "She's a little too doughy to be wearing a bikini, don't you think?"

Vivienne snickered. "I never thought of doing something atypical like this. A tropical theme like that might stand out more in the judge's minds."

"I like it." Joshua smiled. "It makes me feel warm."

"Are we bringing up Florida again?" Vivienne groaned and pulled him away from the display.

"Florida?" Kathy asked.

"It's nothing." Vivienne steered them toward a gingerbread train engine pulling a caboose.

"Are you two thinking of moving away?" Kathy's voice raised an octave in concern.

"No." Vivienne shook her head. "Joshua just mentioned how nice it would be to spend the holidays in a warm climate like the Florida Keys."

Relief washed over Kathy's face. "Oh, thank God. I thought you were going to leave me here with Nora."

"I wouldn't do that to my best friend," Vivienne answered, "Unless you really did something to tick me off."

"Perish the thought." Kathy quipped.

"I guess I don't have a say in the matter." Joshua raised an eyebrow.

"Of course you do, honey." Vivienne tipped her head against his shoulder. "We women only pay attention when you men say what we would have said anyway."

Joshua scoffed and admired the gingerbread train. "I figured as much."

Vivienne and Kathy shared a laugh that echoed through the gallery as Joshua steered them toward the south wing where some of the other displays were waiting. "Where's the wine bar?" Kathy asked.

Cassandra Pembroke appeared from behind the archway leading to the next room with several members of the city council flanking her. Dressed in a flattering two-piece navy-blue business suit with a tasteful strand of pearls, she managed to appear elegant yet approachable. "Vivienne, Kathy, Deputy Arkins, so very nice to see you."

"Hello Cassandra." Vivienne stopped and corrected herself. "Excuse me, Madame Mayor. It's so very nice to see you too."

Cassandra waved her hands at mention of her formal title. "Please, don't start calling me that or I'll have to start calling you Miss Finch."

"I'm sorry, Cassandra." Vivienne had to admit that it was still hard to think of Cassandra as the town's new mayor. After Richard Clarke resigned his post in late September following the murder of his wife Mona, a special election was announced to fill the vacancy. Vivienne, of course, had helped to solve the murder much to the annoyance of Sheriff Rigsbee.

In the month that followed, Cassandra put her name in for the running along with several other candidates and won by a landslide when Election Day arrived. Her no nonsense style of dealing with sticky situations during her time as a socialite in New York City gave a unique advantage to reigning in the often cantankerous town council.

"I must say that Samantha Charles' gift certainly helped to calm down the situation on Main Street." Kathy added. "The new sidewalks really made watching the holiday parade more enjoyable."

Cassandra nodded. "Yes, her monetary offer certainly took the heat off me coming into this job. I can't wait to see the new building facades and signs next spring."

Vivienne's thoughts drifted back to late October when Samantha had generously dipped into her family's deep coffers and assumed seventy-five percent of the cost for the revitalization project, reducing the burden to the Main Street store owners greatly. Her friend, the New York hotel heiress, was true to her word to make her new summer home location a jewel in the Finger Lakes. "I love the idea of the little park area next to the post office. Dedicating those benches and the new fountain to Mona Clarke will be a fitting tribute when it's completed next year."

"Have you seen Samantha in town lately?" Cassandra asked. "I saw some work crews updating the house she bought."

"A few weeks ago." Vivienne replied. "I know that she's had her hands full buying out Fiona Meadows' publishing company."

"And everyone thinks local politics is tricky to navigate." Cassandra added. "They've got nothing on upper social circles."

A young waiter in a rented tuxedo that had sleeves a tad too long for his arms appeared carrying a tray with drinks loaded on it. "Sparkling cider?" He asked.

They each took a glass as he moved on. Joshua guzzled his down with gusto. "Not bad for non-alcoholic."

Kathy took a sip and sighed. "I'll take a nice blush wine any day."

One of the council members, a gentleman with short grey hair and a hook-like nose spoke softly to Cassandra.

"Well, it was so nice seeing you all again. Good luck with your entry." Cassandra drifted off into the crowd that was steadily filing into the gallery as the afternoon continued.

"She's a good fit for the job." Kathy spoke as she finished her drink.

"Everyone likes her over at the Sheriff's office." Joshua added. "I couldn't say the same thing about Richard Clarke."

"I wonder where he ended up moving to?" Kathy asked.

"Florida." Vivienne sighed. "How many times can that state possibly come into conversations today?"

"Maybe it's a sign?" Joshua raised an eyebrow.

"Now there's a sign I like to see." Kathy pointed to a bar set up in the South wing where several patrons were buying glasses of local wine to benefit the library fund. "Cash Bar." She handed her empty glass to Vivienne and scooted over to get a real drink. Joshua shook his head. "She's your friend."

"Yes she is." Vivienne looked around for a trash can to toss the plastic glasses away. "And I wouldn't trade her for the world."

"There's your entry." Joshua pointed to the gingerbread reproduction of the Edgar Rothwell Mansion that was given a prime spot right in the center of the room. "It's drawn quite a crowd."

Vivienne smiled with pride. "It does seem to be getting quite a bit of attention." She enjoyed watching the people point and smile at the various details, but it also made her nervous. "I'm going to find the ladies room, before the winners are announced."

"We passed them when we came inside." Joshua offered.

"That's right." Vivienne gave him a kiss on the cheek. "I'll throw these glasses away while I'm at it." She took the plastic-ware from him and dashed off to the front reception area.

Along the way she bumped into Suzette Powell who owned The Formal Affair Catering. "Vivienne, it's nice to see you."

"Hello Suzette." Vivienne smiled. "How are you doing today?"

"I'm doing well." She leaned forward and lowered her voice. "I'm really curious to see what people think of my entry for the contest." Suzette confessed.

"I'm doing the same thing." Vivienne whispered back.

"I'm glad you entered the contest." Suzette smiled. "Some years, it's really no competition at all."

"Well, each one is unique in its own charming way." Vivienne tried her best to be diplomatic.

"That's true." Suzette smiled. "I'll tell you mine if you tell me yours."

Vivienne paused for a moment. She liked Suzette and had even helped her out when the police wrongly suspected her in Mona Clarke's murder back in October, but she did have a competitive streak in her when it came to business. "I think it's more fun to guess."

Suzette took a sip of her punch and nodded. "That's true." She gave a quick glance at her wrist watch. "Besides, we'll find out in less than an hour anyway."

"I'm thinking the vintage train is your entry." Vivienne lied. She was quite sure that Tristan and

Nathaniel from Carriage House Antiques had designed the vintage fifties era passenger train, as their shop was filled with memorabilia from the famous Super Chief train that Hollywood royalty rode during the golden age of cross-country travel. It was an elegant display and she was sure it would stroke her ego to think it was created by her two hands.

"You think so?" Suzette played along. "I think that little cathedral has your name all over it."

'The little gingerbread piece with the lopsided steeple and loose window?' Vivienne thought to herself and almost guffawed in response. "Well, you just never know." She gave a weak little laugh. "I really must pay a visit to the ladies room."

"Oh, I didn't mean to hold you up. Good luck." Suzette gave a little wave and drifted into the crowd.

Vivienne scooted past a new surge of people who were working their way toward the bar area and arrived at the front reception desk. She was relieved to see the restroom sign next to the little room that Todd had turned into a coat check.

She pushed open the door, and as luck would have it, one of the two stalls was open. She stopped by the sink and dropped the plastic cups into the trash can when she suddenly heard a loud sob erupt from the closed stall.

Looking into the mirror, she could see a pair of plain black flats under the door. Not wanting to appear rude, she pretended not to hear it and stepped into the open stall. Closing the door and latching it, she was just about to sit down when a pair of thick heels clacked into the ladies room.

"Damn, they're both taken up." A woman with a throaty-smoker's voice said.

"I bet the men's room has a dozen stalls." A softer voice added.

"Did you see that God-awful gingerbread church?" The smoker asked.

"I've seen abandoned ruins with more charm." The softer voice laughed. "What a mess."

"They ought to have some kind of minimum standard for entering these things. It's a disgrace to have that eye sore next to some of those others." The smoker agreed.

Another sob erupted from the stall next to Vivienne.

"Honey, pee or get off the pot will you?" The smoker rapped on the stall door where the distraught woman was holed up. "Some of us have small bladders."

Vivienne felt angry at the callousness of the pair outside the stalls. After she finished, she pulled the toilet paper roll off the holder and put it in her purse. She then flushed and opened the door. "This one is open ladies." She smiled.

"It's about time." The smoker voice turned out to be a woman who looked like she was in her late fifties. Tight black curls, a face drawn with wrinkles around the mouth from years of smoking, she appeared as dour as her voice sounded. Dressed in a pair of tan pants and a red sweater, she hurried past Vivienne and closed the door without so much as a nod of thanks.

Her friend, the softer voiced one, turned out to be a petite woman with a bun of white hair and wore a pair of glasses that were a shade of hot pink with gaudy fake diamonds embedded on the temples. She waited patiently by the sink, seeming slightly embarrassed by her companion's behavior, as Vivienne washed her hands and left the restroom.

She held the door open for just a moment and then heard the smoker curse a blue streak that there was no more toilet paper. She let the door close and giggled to herself at her own little version of swift justice. She was about to walk away when a young woman with straight black hair that could desperately use a cut and style slipped out and nearly ran into her.

"Are you okay?" Vivienne asked.

The woman was young, looking to be in her mid-twenties at best. She had soft brown eyes that were red and puffy from crying in the stall. Dressed in a plain green tee shirt and a pair of faded jeans that had ragged bottoms, she didn't look like someone who had much good fortune in this life. "Were you the one in the other stall?"

"Yes." Vivienne nodded. "I didn't want to intrude."

"Oh, that's okay." The young woman replied. "I just wanted to thank you for what you did."

"What did I do?" Vivienne asked.

"Taking all the toilet paper?" The young woman gave a little smile. "She's still in there swearing up a storm."

Vivienne smiled back. "She deserved it."

The young woman opened her purse, a rather beat-up fake leather piece that had seen better days and produced a second roll. "Great minds think alike, I guess." She smiled a little more.

"If you don't mind me asking, why were you crying in there?"

The young woman was about to answer when a portly man with greasy brown hair, thin lips, and a scraggly goatee approached them. He looked exactly like what her mother Nora would call a 'mealy mouth.' "Natalie, what the hell took you so long?"

The young woman, now known as Natalie, shook her head at Vivienne. "Oh, it was nothing."

"When are they going to announce the winner of this thing? I've got to be at the bar ten minutes before the fight starts to get a bet in." The mealy mouth whined.

"We can leave because I'm not going to win." Natalie answered. "You were right. It was a stupid idea to start with."

"You wasted your money making that, not mine." Mealy mouth took hold of her arm. "So that's just less presents for Connor this year. After all, he's not really my kid."

"I'm sorry, Eddie." Natalie apologized and followed him toward the exit. "I thought maybe I could win and we could put some money in the bank for once."

"You'll never win because all your ideas are stupid." Eddie replied.

Vivienne stepped between them. "She has just as much chance as anyone else to win tonight."

Mealy mouth's beady brown eyes squinted, which Vivienne thought made him look like some sort of nasty-tempered overgrown rat. "Who the hell are you?"

"Vivienne Finch. I run the Sweet Dreams Bakery shop in town."

"Well, la dee da." Mealy mouth's voice dripped with sarcasm. "Why don't you go back to baking cookies and mind your own business?"

"Eddie, please don't be rude." Natalie reached out and touched the elbow of his rather expensive looking winter jacket. In fact, all of his clothes were designer labels and in good shape. It was quite the opposite of Natalie who was in head to toe in clothes that practically screamed thrift store.

"I don't go sticking my nose into other people's business." Eddie sniffed. "That's what's rude."

Vivienne really wanted to punch him something good. Get a good solid hit right into his smug face. But, as much as it pained her to think it, he was right. She didn't know them or their situation at all. She of all people knew that outward appearances were frequently deceiving. "I didn't mean to start any trouble."

"Then leave us alone and go back to your kitchen, sweetheart." Eddie pushed his way roughly through the crowd with Natalie in tow. "You better hope my bet pays off tonight. Otherwise, we're going to have to tell Connor that Santa got lost this year."

They disappeared into the crowd leaving Vivienne by the door to the ladies room. She wanted to pursue after Natalie and explain that there were services she could sign up for to help out. There was even a toys for tots fund run by the Sheriff's office where families under the poverty line could have a few donated gifts dropped off on Christmas morning. At the very least, the nuns at Our Lady of the Lake offered hand-made mittens and hats for the children who needed them. But it was too late.

"Thanks for using up all the toilet paper." The smoker complained as she exited the ladies room with her friend in tow. "Not a very Christian thing to do."

"Wasn't there another roll in there?" Vivienne replied with as sickening sweet tone as she could muster. "I better inform the owner about it."

The smoker rolled her eyes in response. "Come on, Mavis." She tugged on the arm of her friend and pulled her into the crowd of people.

She waited a few moments before she returned to the rest room to return the toilet paper. No need for everyone else to suffer. Besides, her bladder was petite and she was sure she'd need room for the delicious drinks Kathy was going to buy her at the bar.

CHAPTER 4

When she finally caught up with Joshua and Kathy again, they were standing in front of her and Stephanie's entry. Kathy, as she had hoped, had a sparkling green appletini with some cherries garnished on the sugared edge of the glass waiting for her. She handed the drink to Vivienne. "This is called a 'Holly Jolly'."

Vivienne accepted the drink and took a sip. It was sweet and had the unique danger of going down far too easy to keep track of how many one imbibed.

"Just be careful. Those creep up on you faster than anything." Joshua nodded and sipped from a bottle of beer from Ithaca Beer Company. It was one of the seasonal winter brews aptly named 'Cold Front.'

Vivienne recalled one of her early dates with Joshua where they had polished off two bottles of Glen Harvest wine. They had both fallen asleep, lulled by the sweet white wine and the warmth of the crackling fireplace in his apartment. It seemed ages ago now but the lesson had been learned. "I remember it quite well." She smiled at him.

Kathy glanced at her watch. "They should be making the announcement anytime now."

Vivienne took hold of Joshua's hand with hers. "I'm really nervous now."

"You shouldn't be." He tried to soothe her. "Your entry is great."

"He's right." Kathy agreed. "Even if I didn't know you made it, I'd have cast my vote because of the local landmark connection. You were the only one to go that route."

Vivienne thought of the sad little church and Natalie again. "You know, we're so lucky to have what we have, when you think about it. So many others aren't so fortunate."

Joshua gave her hand a reassuring squeeze. "Yes, we are."

"I can't argue there." Kathy agreed. "Have you watched 'Mister Magoo's Christmas Carol' on television again?"

"I saw something tonight that just broke my heart a little." Vivienne replied and then took a small sip of her drink.

"What did you see?" Joshua wondered aloud.

"When I went to the ladies room there was a young woman crying in the other stall. She was the one who made the little church with the crooked steeple." Vivienne explained. "Some other women came in and were bad mouthing the entry and she really got upset."

"So what happened?" Kathy asked.

"I left and she came out less than a minute later. I asked her if everything was okay and she thanked me for getting even with them for their nasty remarks."

"How did you do that?" Kathy's eyes lit up with enthusiasm.

"I took all the toilet paper out of the stall." Vivienne felt a little childish admitting it out loud.

"Well, let me be the first to say touché." Kathy laughed and took another sip of her drink.

Joshua failed to keep a little grin from emerging on his face. "You never fail to surprise me."

Vivienne waved off their levity. "So right afterwards, this low life comes in and sort of berates her for wasting money on the entry."

"Is he still here?" Joshua looked around the room quickly.

"No." Vivienne was quick to answer. "He took her by the arm and said that he had some sort of bet to make on a fight and that if they didn't win he was going to cancel Christmas for her son." Vivienne felt tears building up in the corners of her eyes. "Isn't that terrible?"

"What a creep." Kathy added. "Sounds like father of the year to me."

"Did you catch their names?" Joshua asked.

"Her name was Natalie and her son's name is Connor." Vivienne recalled. "I think the guy's name was Eddie, but I never did catch a last name." She took another sip of the drink in her hand. "He said something about Connor not really being his son and cancelling Christmas. What a creep."

"I can check at the station to see if their names are listed for the Toys For Tots program." Joshua put his arm around her shoulder. "He might still have a nice Christmas after all."

"I hope so." Vivienne swirled the liquid around inside her glass. "I just hate to think of a little child crying on Christmas morning because he thinks Santa doesn't care."

Kathy sniffed a little. "Stop it Vivienne or you're going to make me start crying."

Vivienne nodded. "Okay. No need to worry about it yet until we find out if their names are on the list."

"Can I have you attention please?" The voice of local radio host, Bryce Starr, crackled over the ceiling speakers. "We are about to announce the winner of the gingerbread contest."

The conversations died down to a soft murmur as the gathered crowd awaited the news.

"We have three prizes this year and the judges would like everyone to know it was difficult decision to make because there was so much talent on display. Please, let's give everyone a big round of applause." The room erupted into a fair amount of applause.

Vivienne gripped Joshua's hand tightly. "Here we go." She whispered to him.

"Third place and the winner of a twenty-five dollar cash prize is entry number four, Gingerbread Paradise by Suzette Powell."

Vivienne, Joshua, and Kathy applauded with the rest of the room. The tropical beach scene was a cute idea and they all agreed it deserved recognition.

"Second place and the winner of a fifty dollar cash prize is entry number ten, Gingerbread Express created by Nathaniel Schroeder and Tristan Carr."

Once again, the room erupted into applause and Vivienne scanned the room to see if Nathaniel or Tristan were anywhere to be seen. Sadly, they were not.

"Finally, the grand prize and one hundred dollars is awarded to entry number three, the Edgar Rothwell Mansion created by Vivienne Finch and Stephanie Bridgeman. Congratulations to all our talented winners. Prizes can be picked up at the front desk." Bryce finished as the crowd erupted into applause. "Thank you for making this year a smashing success and happy holidays."

"You won!" Kathy danced with excitement, nearly spilling her drink on the floor.

"Congratulations honey." Joshua kissed Vivienne and smiled. "I never doubted it."

"Wow." Vivienne felt her face flush with pride. "We actually did it."

"Now you've got something to brag about when it comes to awards." Kathy noted. "Trust me. This will really bring in some business."

Vivienne nodded back. "Yes it will, but I have an even better idea."

"What?" Joshua asked her.

"I'm going to ask Todd to give the hundred dollars to Natalie and tell her she won a special prize for most creative entry or something. That way, she'll have money to buy Connor some presents."

"That's awful nice of you." Kathy agreed. "But what if her boyfriend just uses the money to gamble with? Maybe we could buy some toys and then have Todd give them to her?"

"That's so obvious." Vivienne countered. "She seemed like she might be a bit too proud to take charity like that."

"But it's for Christmas presents." Kathy argued.

"What do you think, Joshua?" Vivienne looked up at her handsome boyfriend.

"I think both your ideas are good, but we need to check that list before we go too far with this." Joshua answered.

Todd York pushed his way through the crowd and reached out to Vivienne. "Congratulations, you're so very talented." He handed her a white envelope. "Here's the prize money."

She shook her head. "No, that's not for me."

"But you won it fair and square." Todd protested.

"I want to give it to Natalie, the girl who made the cathedral." Vivienne replied.

"That's awful nice of you. She could use it I'm sure." Todd smiled.

"Do you know her?" Joshua asked.

"Well, I got to talking with her when she brought her entry in this morning." Todd glanced around the room quickly before continuing. "She didn't seem like she had two nickels to rub together."

"Tell him what you heard." Kathy prodded Vivienne.

"What did you hear?" Todd asked.

Vivienne sighed. "Did her boyfriend come in with her?"

"You mean Eddie?" Todd smirked. "Yeah, he carried the entry like it was sack of potatoes. I thought he was going to just throw it down on the floor."

"That wouldn't have surprised us to hear." Kathy added.

"Actually, I think it's because he's uncomfortable around me." Todd confessed.

"What makes you say that?" Vivienne asked him. Todd shrugged. "It's just a feeling I got. He looked really uncomfortable, like I was going to expose a dark secret about his past or something."

"Oh, I love dark secrets." Kathy interjected. "Have you got dirt on him?"

"Kathy." Vivienne shook her head at her friend. "That's none of our business."

"It's okay." Todd smiled at them both. "I don't know anything about the guy. It was just that sense of weirdness you get every now and then with someone."

Joshua finished his beer. "I can check to see if he has a criminal record. Do you know his last name?"

Todd shook his head. "Not that I recall."

Vivienne raised her hands in protest. "We're getting off the topic. This is about Connor getting a nice Christmas not investigating Eddie's shady past."

"You're right." Kathy nodded.

"Was her little boy with her?" Vivienne asked Todd.

Todd paused for a moment in thought. "No, but everything was so busy it's all kind of a jumble right now. You know how it is during the holidays."

"Do you have her phone number from the entry list?" Joshua asked.

Todd nodded. "It's in my office with all the others."

"Let me copy it down and I'll reverse search it back at the station." Joshua explained.

"Just hang onto the prize money and we'll call you after we find out some more details about what kind of home life little Connor has." Vivienne explained.

"No problem." Todd nodded to Joshua. "You want to come into the office to get that phone number?"

"Lead the way." Joshua fished his keys out of his front pocket and handed them to Vivienne. "It's pretty cold out there, would you mind warming up the Jeep?"

Vivienne nodded back. "I'll see you out there."

As Joshua followed Todd back to the office, she took one last look around the gallery. "I wish I felt better about this."

"What do you mean?" Kathy asked as they followed some of the crowd toward the coat check.

"I think it's all too easy to get caught up in the commercial madness of gift purchasing these days." Vivienne summed up as the retrieved their winter jackets.

"I can't think of a better way to kick off the holiday season than helping little Connor keep the magic of Santa Claus alive another year." Kathy added as they left the warmth of the Loft 223. She bundled up her black woolen pea coat and turned her back to the cold wind that was blowing harder than ever. "I'd say winter has arrived ahead of schedule."

Vivienne's hairstyle threatened to fly apart as a gusty wind blasted her with some puffy snowflakes. "I was thinking I might ask Sheriff Rigsbee if I can add on something nice with the Toys For Tots presents this year."

Joshua pushed hard to open the front door against the wind and stepped forward to shield Vivienne with his broad chest. "Did you start the car yet?" He asked.

Vivienne pressed the start button on the key fob and nodded. "Uh huh."

Joshua groaned. "Thanks."

Vivienne blew him a little kiss and turned back to face Kathy. "What about baking up some nice gingerbread men and maybe some sugar cookies? I was thinking of filling little stockings with some baked goodies for the kids to enjoy on Christmas morning."

"That's a great idea." Kathy smiled. "I know the nuns are knitting mittens and hats for the kids, but what if I donated some warm scarves for them to use to?"

"I'm sure they'd appreciate anything with our harsh winters." Vivienne agreed.

"Then I better go back to the store and put in an order. I saw a special on fleece scarves that I can order by the gross. I'll see about ordering some little stockings for you to use." Kathy waved goodbye. "Call me later with the details."

"Bye." Vivienne and Joshua said in unison and then walked the opposite way toward the Jeep which was emitting a cloud of hot exhaust in the night air.

Vivienne took hold of Joshua's right arm. "This is what I love about the holiday. The spirit of giving is so strong."

"I just wish the goodwill lasted longer than a month." Joshua added. "After New Year's, the crime picks right back up to normal levels again."

"Well, we can't have everything." Vivienne replied as they crossed the street. "But I'll enjoy the holidays a little more knowing the children have something to look forward to."

"Well said." Joshua replied as he opened the passenger door and helped her inside.

CHAPTER 5

Monday, December 2nd

When Vivienne drove past the front of her bakery, her eyes locked onto a single piece of red paper that was taped to the front door. She had seen several of the same bright red papers attached to utility poles, trees, and a few tucked under the wiper blades of cars parked along Main Street. Someone was papering the town with a new marketing campaign and they certainly were doing a thorough job.

Once she turned on the ovens and lights to start the day, she decided to take a look at whatever it was that someone wanted to drum up business for. She thought the town codes had forbidden such tactics. As she pulled the paper off her glass door, she almost felt sorry for whoever was going to get hit with the nasty fine and the scorn of the town council for defying their directive. 'Thank goodness it's not me.' She thought as she studied the paper in her hand.

'You better watch out!' That's what the paper said with bold green lettering and a large size font that commanded attention. Vivienne had to agree that it certainly was catchy and she was eager to read the rest of the contents. *'Santa is not happy with you, Eddie Robertson. You are a chronic gambler who spends far too*

much time in the bar and not enough time trying to be a father to Connor.'

Vivienne couldn't believe her eyes. This certainly wasn't an advertisement for a holiday special in town. She continued reading. *'I've been watching and keeping tabs on all the bad things you do. You've been a naughty boy, hitting Natalie whenever those silly and illegal bets fail to pay off or threatening to cancel Christmas because you don't want to spend any of your own money on gifts. Find the true spirit before yours is set free. You have been warned. Sincerely, Santa Claus.'*

Vivienne reached the end of the paper and turned it over to see if there was anything more. There wasn't. She walked outside to one of the cars that had a flyer under the wiper and removed it to check if said the same thing as hers. It did. Everywhere she looked there were little flashes of red. Someone had a wicked sense of humor and wasn't afraid to take action. She stepped back into her bakery when her telephone rang.

"Vivienne, you won't believe the note I found taped to my door this morning." Kathy's voice eagerly explained from the phone.

"Eddie Robertson is on Santa's bad list." Vivienne replied. "So now we know his last name."

"So does someone else." Kathy replied.

"Who would do such a thing?" Vivienne wondered.

"I wonder if Natalie took matters into her own hands." Kathy replied. "If so, I have to give her points for originality."

"Natalie." Vivienne worried. "Oh my God, what if Eddie sees this and thinks the same thing?"

"Should we call Joshua?" Kathy asked.

"I'll call him and find out what to do next." Vivienne stared at the paper in her hand in disbelief. "I just hope Natalie and Connor are okay."

"Keep me posted about this." Kathy ordered. "You always forget to do that and I end up hearing the news from your mother."

"I promise." Vivienne answered.

"You better or you might end up on Santa's bad list too." Kathy joked.

Vivienne hung up and dialed the direct line to Joshua's office. He answered on the second ring. "Hi honey." She said.

"I already know about the Santa note." Joshua interrupted.

"I figured as much. They're all over town." Vivienne explained.

"We're on top of it. We've got a unit dispatched to their home to make sure everything is okay." Joshua informed her. "I can't say anything more."

"Just let me know that Natalie and Connor aren't hurt." Vivienne asked.

"I'll let you know as soon as I find out. I better go now." He replied.

"Love you." She finished.

"Love you too." He hung up.

Vivienne stared at the note on her counter and wondered if Natalie really did make them up to shame Eddie into becoming a better man and father to Connor. It would be a bold move to say the least, but sometimes people did bold things when backed into a corner.

* * *

She had just placed her second batch of blueberry crumble muffins into the oven when two police cruisers sped down Main Street followed by an ambulance.

"Looks like they're in a hurry." Stephanie quipped as she dropped a new roll of thermal paper into the credit card printer.

"They sure are." Vivienne closed the oven door and set the timer. She didn't like this one bit.

Stephanie ran an inch of the paper and then tore it off. "I'm sure you'll hear all about it after work tonight." She crumpled the scrap paper in her hand into a ball.

The sound of crinkling paper reminded Vivienne of the Santa note from earlier. With the morning rush over, she knew Stephanie was perfectly capable of running the store for an hour or so. Just enough time to see what was going on. "I'm going to go take a little drive."

Stephanie hurled the little ball of paper into a nearby trash can. "Better bundle up. That wind is still pretty nasty out there."

Vivienne walked into the back room and pulled her coat and purse off the wall hooks. "I'll have my cell phone on if you need me."

"I'll be fine." Stephanie called back from the counter. "If you think of it, you might want to pick up some more holiday sprinkles from the Monarch. We went through most of our supply last week."

"I'll pick up a few to get us by until the delivery comes Wednesday." Vivienne buttoned up her coat and slung her purse over her left shoulder. "Anything else you think we need?"

"I think we're okay with the rest for now." Stephanie tied on her baking apron and moved into the kitchen area. "You want two dozen cranberry orange muffins this morning too?"

"Yes, but be sure to set aside six for Mrs. Fell. I think her bridge club meets this afternoon."

Stephanie nodded. "No problem."

Vivienne hurried out the back door and stepped into the brisk morning air. The wind was still quite strong, even in the alley, and it made the temperature feel well below the freezing mark. She hurried to her car and climbed inside.

As she drove along Main Street, she had to pull over the side as another police cruiser roared past with its blue and red lights flashing. She quickly pulled back onto the road and gave chase to follow along.

She felt guilty for speeding a good ten miles above the posted limit of thirty miles an hour through town, but it was the only way she could keep up with the police car as it hurried toward its destination. Besides, she was quite certain there were no officers parked at the usual speed trap locations this morning.

They were a good two miles outside of town when the police car made a sharp turn onto Old Cemetery Road, which was one of those country lanes which was rarely plowed. She fishtailed slightly, as the road was slick with packed snow. They passed the ruins of the Fitzpatrick farmstead which had burned down last year after a lightning strike ignited the dry wood of the abandoned property. The vegetable stand was still perched near the edge of the road, now leaning and covered up to the counter with large snow drifts.

As they came upon the old Cayuga Union Cemetery, she found the scene hauntingly beautiful. The aged stones were tipped this way and that, some broken and in pieces on the snow-covered ground. There were several civil war veterans buried in the center, between two large cannons that were tilted skyward, along with a stack of cannon balls welded together. It hadn't been used for decades, as most of those who came to mourn the dead had passed on themselves. Yet, as they passed by the front entrance her gaze fell upon a simple green wreath with a red bow tied to the front gates. It was comforting to think that someone still cared for the property.

As they rounded a rather sharp corner, Vivienne could see the small collection of double wide trailers that were clustered along the empty fields. It was intended to be Tall Pine Grove, a planned community that never materialized when the housing bubble burst back in 2008.

After a few years, the developer gave up and decided to use the utility hookups for trailers. The natural gas boom had started and many out-of-state workers were in need of cheap housing.

The police car joined a throng of other emergency vehicles alongside a blue doublewide that had a rusty metal swing set in the front yard.

Vivienne pulled off to the side and felt her heart sink in her chest. She wasn't sure, but she had a feeling this was where Eddie Robertson lived along with Natalie and Connor. She stepped out of her car and joined a small group of neighbors who were gathered in front of a single green trailer that had a gaggle of faded pink plastic flamingos stuck all over the yard.

A woman dressed in a rather-worn looking jacket, pulled over a pair of pink fleece pajama pants and a faded tee shirt with a beer logo approached Vivienne. "Are you a reporter for the news?" She asked as her hands went up to her hair, where pink curlers were poking through a thin blue scarf she had tied atop her head.

Vivienne had never thought of that. She was just going to gawk and try to hear what was going on with everyone else, but if they all thought she was a reporter she'd be able to get people to talk easier. She decided to go with it, fishing around in her coat pocket and pulling out a small pad she kept for writing down grocery lists. "I'm Vera French.", she lied.

"From the local news station, I knew it." The woman with the curlers gave her a big smile. "You look better in person, does anyone tell you that?"

Vivienne shook her head. "I work for the newspaper."

"Oh." The woman's smile faded. "I must have seen your picture in the paper that I line the bird cage with."

Vivienne was glad she didn't work for the paper as a verbal slap like that would be quite painful. She kept a smile on her face and pressed further. "But if the story is big enough, I can get it picked up for the local news station. I have some connections." Vivienne winked.

The woman's face brightened. "Really?"

"Sure." Vivienne leaned forward. "Bryce Starr, the local radio personality is a good friend of mine. He might even ask for a radio interview."

The woman reached out her right hand. "My name is Sally Rollins. Do you need me to spell that?" Vivienne pulled the cap off her pen and scribbled the name down on the pad. "Two L's, right?"

"Yep." Sally continued. "Well, I was inside wrapping up some Christmas presents for my grandkids when I heard a woman screaming."

Vivienne pointed to the trailer where the emergency vehicles were gathered. "From over there?"

"Yes." Sally nodded. "It was something awful, just like out of those horror movies."

"Who lives there?" Vivienne asked.

"That would be Natalie Burdick and her son Connor." Sally waved her hand to the trailer two away from hers.

"Was she injured?" Vivienne began to worry.

"No, but she had blood all over her so I thought she was at first." Sally shook her head. "She must have got it smeared on her from Eddie."

"Who's Eddie?" Vivienne pretended not to know.

"He's her boyfriend. They moved in about six months ago." Sally shook her head. "I never did trust the guy. He just had a real mean look about him."

"What happened to him?" Vivienne pressed further.

"I don't know for sure, but Gus Holt who lives on the other side of them said he thought he was shot. He went in to help when Natalie started screaming."

Vivienne scribbled her description down. "You didn't hear any gun shots?"

"No, it sounded like a clap of thunder to me." Sally folded her arms against her chest. "Weird, huh?"

"So, Eddie was conscious when Gus went in?"

Sally shrugged. "I wish I knew." She clucked her tongue at the scene. "That Eddie was a mean cuss, that's for sure. I'd hear them fighting and screaming at each other all the time." She glanced warily at Vivienne. "Ain't you going to write any of this down?"

Vivienne blinked and nodded. "I'm sorry. I guess I was just processing the whole story in my head." She started writing some of the names down on the paper for her own use.

"So are you going to call the news station? Because if you are I've got to change clothes before they interview me." Sally's eyes widened.

Vivienne shrugged. "I'm going to need more to go on before I can make that call."

"What about talking to Connor? He's inside with my grandkids right now." Sally asked.

"He's in your home?"

"Yes, Gus brought him right over after he calmed Natalie down and called the police. I usually babysit him during the day when they're working anyway."

Vivienne heard some of the assembled neighbors gasp as the emergency workers emerged from the trailer with Eddie strapped to a gurney. They were performing CPR as they climbed into the ambulance and sped away. "Mind if I park my car in your driveway?"

"Go ahead and I'll meet you inside. You want some coffee?" Sally asked.

Vivienne nodded. "That'd be great." She hurried back to her car to park it in the driveway just in case Joshua was at the scene and saw it along the road. She was fairly certain he wouldn't pay attention to it if it were parked at one of the trailers.

The crowd of gawkers began to break up as Vivienne pulled into the driveway and hurried inside the double-wide that Sally Rollins called home. It was neater than she had envisioned, but there were several children's toys scattered along the floor that she had to step over carefully to avoid tripping.

"You like cream and sugar?" Sally asked from the kitchen, which was divided from the living room by a half wall.

"Neither." Vivienne called back.

"You reporters are some tough cookies." Sally stepped out of the kitchen with two mugs of coffee.

"Must be hard seeing all those horrible murders and such."

Vivienne took her mug and sipped the coffee. "You develop a thick skin after your first encounter." She wasn't lying this time. Having dealt with murder when her bakery first opened, she was starting to feel like a seasoned veteran.

Sally walked her through the living room, past a bathroom, into a large spare bedroom where three children were happily playing restaurant with a plastic kitchen set. Sally pointed to a blond girl with pig tails who looked to be about four or five years old. "That's my granddaughter, Hannah."

Hannah looked up at them from the play stove where she was flipping plastic eggs with her spatula. "You want some eggs Grammie?"

Sally shook her head. "Not right now, sweetie." She pointed to a little fair-haired boy stood next to Hannah waiting to use the stove. "That's Mason, her twin brother. Aren't they just precious?"

Mason stomped his feet on the ground. "Grammie, Hannah is taking too long with the oven." He pouted.

"Am not." Hannah raised her spatula up at him.

"Am too." Mason stuck out his tongue.

"Stop fighting or I'll put it away." Sally sternly put her hands on her hips.

Vivienne guessed that the brown haired boy in the denim overalls had to be Connor. He sat at the little table playing with a teapot and some cups. "So that's Connor?"

Sally nodded. "That's him."

Connor looked up at them for a moment and then when back to pretending to pour liquid into the cups.

"How old is he?" Vivienne asked.

"He's four."

She smiled and knelt down to the table where Connor was sitting. "Hello Connor. My name is Vera and I'm a friend of your babysitter, Mrs. Rollins."

Connor looked up at her and then over to Sally.

"She's a good friend of mine, Connor. She wants to talk with you."

Connor studied her with his deep green eyes. He set the teapot down and handed her a little cup. "Wanna drink?"

"You two share a drink while I go freshen up my clothes." Sally smiled and hurried away.

Vivienne sat down on the floor and folded her legs. "That sounds wonderful. Is it tea?"

"Hot cocoa an' marshmallows." He replied.

"That's my favorite." She smiled and accepted the little cup. "Do you like whipped cream in it too?"

He nodded and took a sip out of his cup. "Mommy doesn't buy it cause it costs too much money."

"It can be, yes." She agreed.

"Do you work for Santa Claus?" He asked her.

"Why do you ask?"

He sniffed the air. "You smell like cookies."

Vivienne shook her head. "I don't work for Santa, but I spend a lot of time at a bakery where cookies are made. Do you like cookies Connor?"

He nodded back. "I like chocolate chip with lots of chips."

"How many chips do you like in your cookies?"

He held up his hands and spread his fingers. "This many."

She whistled. "That's a lot of chips."

"Can you make me some?"

"I'm sure Hannah and Mason will let us use the oven."

"I'm not done yet." Mason protested from the oven.

"Yes you are." Hannah interrupted. "You hafta' share."

Mason started to cry. Hannah walked away from the oven and sat down at the table next to Connor. "He's such a baby."

"Am not." Mason shouted back between tears.

Vivienne felt completely out of her element. She looked at Connor. "We better wait on those cookies until Mason is finished."

At that, Mason suddenly dried his tears and went back to shoving pans in the little plastic oven. "I can make cookies."

Connor sighed and went back to pouring more imaginary cocoa from the little teapot. "I wanted real cookies."

Vivienne felt her heart break a little. "Next time I come to visit I'll bring some real ones. I promise."

He looked at her with his expressive eyes and nodded. "Okay."

The doorbell rang twice and Vivienne could feel Sally's footfalls on the floor as she hurried to the door. "Who is it?"

"Sheriff's office." A familiar voice sounded back through the door.

Vivienne pulled herself up and stepped out to the living room just as Sally opened the front door and let Joshua and Sheriff Rigsbee inside. She had changed into a holiday sweater of glittering red poinsettias pulled over a pair of black stirrup pants. Vivienne was quite certain the festive outfit would take top honors at an 'Ugly Christmas Sweater' party. The curlers and scarf were gone, replaced with curled salt and pepper hair that had a bit of a static frizz problem.

"Oh, I thought you had the news crew with you." Sally's voice dropped with disappointment.

"We were told you were babysitting Connor Burdick." Joshua stepped past her. "Vivienne?"

Sally shook her head. "No, this is Vera French from the newspaper. She's writing a story about what happened to Eddie Robertson."

"Is that true, Ms. French?" Sheriff Rigsbee eyed her warily.

Vivienne gave a little smile. "I was just checking out the facts to see if there was a story here."

Joshua bit down on his lower lip which was a sure sign that he was quite annoyed.

"I don't think the media needs to be involved at this stage of the investigation." Sheriff Rigsbee gave her a stern look. "Wouldn't you agree?"

Vivienne nodded meekly. "You're right, Sheriff. I apologize for the intrusion."

"Deputy Arkins, will you please escort Ms. French back to her car?"

Joshua nodded to him. "Yes sir." He gestured for Vivienne to follow him outside.

Vivienne smiled at Sally. "Thank you for your time this morning, Mrs. Rollins."

Sally nodded. "If you have any more questions, I'll be happy to answer them."

"Please come with me." Joshua spoke to Vivienne and opened the front door.

Vivienne followed him outside. As soon as they were out of earshot, he exhaled and shook his head. "Vivienne, what the hell are you doing?"

"I was just checking on Connor to make sure he was okay." Vivienne answered.

"Why are you hanging around a crime scene telling everyone you're a reporter?" Joshua pressed further. "Shouldn't you be at the bakery?"

"It's kind of a funny story actually." Vivienne tried to lighten the mood.

"I don't have time because I have to work." Joshua snapped back. "You masquerading as someone else isn't making that any easier."

"I'm sorry, Joshua. I didn't mean to get in the way."

"Sheriff Rigsbee is going to rake me over the coals about you being here."

"I wasn't poking around the crime scene or anything. I really was just here to make sure Connor was okay."

"We've called in a social worker to take care of that." Joshua continued.

"Is Eddie going to be okay?" Vivienne asked.

Joshua shrugged. "He looked pretty bad when they took him away. Wasn't responsive and he lost a lot of blood."

Vivienne thought about Connor and lowered her head. "The poor little kid has no idea. He wasn't upset or anything."

"Kids are tougher than you think." Joshua reminded her. "Now please, just get in your car and go."

"Okay." Vivienne moved to kiss him but Joshua pulled away and walked back toward Sally's trailer.

She climbed into her car and leaned back against the head rest. "So much for good will toward men."

CHAPTER 6

Tuesday, December 3rd

Clara Bunton, the proprietor of Clara's Diner, held the nozzle of the whipped cream dispenser just above a mug of her famous 'Dark Of The Moon' hot chocolate. "Heavy on the whip?" She asked in her usual matronly tone to Vivienne.

"Absolutely." Vivienne nodded back.

Clara sprayed a hefty mound of the whipped cream onto the surface of the hot chocolate. "You haven't had one of those days in quite some time. Want to talk about it?"

Vivienne unwrapped the spoon from her paper napkin and stirred the quickly melting whipped cream into her drink. "Let's just say that I sort of stuck my nose where it doesn't belong and Joshua is going to take the heat for it."

Clara smoothed out the creases along her soft pink uniform top and smiled. "Men always want women to think that. It makes them feel better because it saves them the trouble of having to admit they've probably missed something obvious."

Vivienne smiled and took a sip from her mug. "It's not like I go out looking for trouble. It just sort of has a way of finding me."

Clara aimed the whipped cream at the hot chocolate and sprayed another puffy cloud. "Funny, I always thought that more about your mother."

"Whoa." Vivienne joked. "It's hard enough

keeping a trim figure when you work with sweets all day."

"Vivienne Finch, as I live and breathe, you do not have an extra ounce anywhere on that body." Clara scolded her with her hands on her hips.

"I'm just saying I'd like to stay that way, at least until the wedding." Vivienne interrupted.

Clara's pencil-thin eyebrows shot upwards. "A wedding? Did he propose?"

Vivienne shushed her with a wave of her hands. "No. It's much too soon for that anyways."

Clara did the math in her head. "You met in September, so I can see your point."

"We're still living in separate homes." Vivienne reasoned. "We haven't even tried to move in together yet."

"I envy you young people." Clara spoke as she wrapped flatware in paper napkins and tossed them into a plastic bin. "We never had that option in our day."

"Was it easy for you and Jake to move in with each other?" Vivienne asked.

Clara shrugged. "We actually had to move in with his parents for about a year before we saved up enough to buy a house."

"That must have been awkward." Vivienne took another sip of her cocoa.

"Not really. His parents owned a duplex and we rented the other side of their house. It wasn't a bad place, but having your mother-in-law so close wasn't ideal." Clara smiled.

"I'll bet." Vivienne smiled. "I've never met anyone in Joshua's family."

"Where do they live?"

Vivienne cupped her hands around the warm mug. "Indian Lake."

"I've never heard of it. Is it in the state?"

"Yes, up in the Adirondack region." Vivienne mused as her thoughts drifted back to Natalie and Connor. "It's so easy to take family for granted."

Clara finished wrapping up the flatware for the dinner rush and tucked the big plastic bin under the counter. "How do you mean?"

"Well, I guess when you have nice relatives you sort of forget what it could be like to live with the opposite." Vivienne sighed.

"There are always some nasty ones in everyone's family." Clara wondered. "My Aunt Sarah had quite the tart tongue whenever she came to visit. Always running her white gloves over my furniture and clucking her tongue."

"If that's the worst that his family dishes out I can live with that." Vivienne tried not to spill what had happened but she just couldn't keep it in any longer. She tapped her fingers on the counter nervously. "If I tell you something, you need to promise it goes no further until I say so."

Clara leaned close to Vivienne. "There's no one here except you, me, and Harold in the kitchen." She cast a wary eye back toward the kitchen order window. "He's too busy studying the scratch sheets from Off Track Betting to hear anything. I think we're safe."

Vivienne took a breath. "Well, the reason Joshua was upset with me was because of a family situation here in town. Do you know a woman named Natalie

Burdick?"

Clara paused for a moment in thought. "Can't say that I do. Is she new in town?"

"She and her family moved here about six months ago. They live out at the trailer court where Tall Pine Grove was supposed to build."

"I don't know anyone who lives out there." Clara sniffed. "Nor would I really want to."

"It's not that bad, actually." Vivienne continued. "Not everyone can afford a home here in town."

"Which is why things are so nice." Clara reasoned. "It only takes a few weeds to ruin a perfect lawn."

Vivienne knew this was how many of the locals in Cayuga Cove felt. When someone moved into town, they were considered an outsider for months. They were judged on how well they maintained their new home, how they conducted themselves at public functions, and how deftly they steered clear of the gossip train. Once a reasonable quality of character had been established, they were welcomed into the fold with open arms. "Well, a certain weed named Eddie Robertson was shot out there today."

Clara blinked in response. "Eddie Robertson?"

"You know him?"

Clara reached into one of her large apron pockets and pulled out a red sheet of paper. "The subject of this Bad Santa note?"

Vivienne nodded. "They were all over town."

"I found this one taped to the diner door this morning." Clara's eyes narrowed. "This is why we need to keep people like that out."

"Well, Eddie looked to be in pretty bad shape

when the paramedics took him away. I was talking with one of the neighbors who lived nearby and then Joshua and Sheriff Rigsby found me."

"So what?" Clara sniffed. "Is it against the law to talk to people anymore?"

Vivienne lowered her head a bit. "And, I sort of told the neighbor I was a newspaper reporter named Vera French who was chasing the story about what really happened."

Clara let out a little laugh. "Why on earth would you do something like that?"

"Because the other night at the gingerbread house contest I had a run in with Natalie and Eddie. He was so mean to her. I just felt like I needed to find out what was going on."

Clara clucked her tongue. "As a Christian woman I must say that I'm shocked and appalled at this sort of behavior."

Vivienne nodded. "I know."

Clara leaned closer. "Now that God's heard that, please continue with all the juicy details."

Vivienne did her best to explain the rest of the situation to Clara who was more than happy to be the first to know the real story of what happened at Tall Pine Grove.

It was well after lunch when she returned to the Sweet Dreams Bakery. Stephanie, as she had never doubted, had everything working like clockwork.

"Thanks for holding down the fort." Vivienne said to Stephanie as she tied on her apron and pulled out some chilled butter cookie dough from the refrigerator.

"You just missed Eunice Kilpatrick." Stephanie

washed some red sprinkles off her hands. "She kept nosing around looking for you, but pretended she was shopping for gifts."

"She's not the most subtle creature." Vivienne laughed.

"I kept pestering her until she bought a candy cane whoopie pie and left." Stephanie yanked a paper towel off the spinner and dried her hands. "She knows something is up."

"Well she's not going to hear anything from me." Vivienne began to work the cold cookie dough with her hands. It always felt good to knead and press the stress away. "It seems pretty quiet today. If you'd like to go home early and study that's fine with me."

Stephanie nodded. "I could use a little extra study time after the past few days."

"Oh, and before you leave be sure to take your paycheck. I left it under the register drawer." Vivienne reached for her marble rolling pin and began to flatten the dough on the worktable.

Stephanie grabbed her coat, purse, and hat from the back room and marched over to the register. "If you get busy, give me a call."

"I'll be fine." Vivienne appreciated how much Stephanie cared about the store. She had heard from other business owners how unenthusiastic and apathetic their young adult employees could be, but she had lucked out. Here was a young woman who took her job as seriously as her schooling. Vivienne sometimes felt guilty when she thought of the day that Stephanie would finish college and leave for her own career. Would she ever find someone like her again or would she become one of those owners who had to watch every move their young employees made?

Stephanie opened the envelope to sign her paycheck when two crisp hundred dollar bills fluttered to the floor. "What's this?"

Vivienne played dumb as she ran her rolling pin across the cookie dough. "What's what?"

Stephanie knelt down and grasped the hundred dollar bills in her hand. "Some of your store cash wound up in the envelope with my check."

Vivienne shook her head. "I didn't do it. Must have been one of those Christmas elves you hear about."

Stephanie's bottom lip began to quiver. "You really shouldn't have."

"You deserve all that and more." Vivienne smiled brightly. "I couldn't have come this far without your help."

Stephanie rushed over and embraced her. "You don't know how much I needed this." She fought back tears of joy.

"You have family coming from Georgia. Go out and buy them some nice things." Vivienne set the rolling pin down. "Or use it to treat yourself to something nice."

Stephanie nodded. "You're like the best boss ever."

Vivienne felt her cheeks blush. "Now go enjoy the rest of the day."

The brass bell over the front door rang as Todd York stepped into the shop. He rubbed his hands together and blew on them, as his gloves had the tips missing for texting on his phone.

"Hello Todd." Stephanie waved cheerfully as she walked past the counter. "How are you doing?"

"I'm just fine, Stephanie." Todd smiled back and studied the bakery case where a batch of white frosted cupcakes were lined up for sale. "Why do I feel like I gain weight just breathing the air in here?"

Stephanie shrugged her shoulders. "I pack little baggies of cut veggies to munch on when I'm working here."

"I wish I had your will power." Todd joked and waved to Vivienne.

"I was just on the way out, but I can help you before I leave." Stephanie gestured to the bakery case.

Todd shook his head. "I'm just here to see Vivienne, not buy anything."

"Good to see you again." Stephanie gave a final wave to Vivienne and exited the front door as a gust of cold wind swirled the glass ornaments that were hung with fishing line over the display windows.

Vivienne stepped out to the counter. "What's up Todd?"

He reached into his coat pocket and pulled out the check from the gingerbread contest. "This is yours."

"I thought we were setting it aside for Natalie and Connor?"

Todd shook his head. "I tried calling the number that we have for her but I just get a message that the phone isn't in service."

Vivienne shook her head. "I'm not surprised they're having trouble paying the bills. Most of those trailers are heated with propane."

"My apartment above the gallery has oil heat,

but there's no way I can afford to use that. So I bought some of those little electric space heaters and use those instead." Todd revealed.

"My place has natural gas so the bill isn't too terrible." Vivienne reasoned. "But my windows are quite old and drafty. I'm sure more heat escapes than I'd care to know about."

Todd glanced longingly at the cupcakes. He admired the perfect swirls of white frosting, the red and green sprinkles, even the retro little plastic figures of snowmen, angels, and Santa's stuck on top of each one. "I really shouldn't have one."

Vivienne slid the door of the case open and pulled out a cupcake. "We deserve to indulge this month." She set it on top of the case as she closed it up. "It's small anyway."

"I'll probably burn the calories up walking back to the gallery, right?" Todd asked as he took the cupcake in his grasp.

"Of course!" She reasoned. "Christmas calories are magical, don't you know?"

Todd smiled and took a small bite. He moaned with pleasure as the sweet vanilla buttercream melted on his tongue.

Vivienne thought for a moment about her words. She hadn't really done much with her magic in a few weeks. She had done some intensive studying with Nana Mary leading up to Halloween, but then she sort of let it fall to the back burner as the holidays appeared on the calendar. "I found a sealed box of those little retro plastic cake picks at Carriage House Antiques not too long ago."

Todd pulled the snowman out from the cupcake

and licked the frosting from the base. "They're so cute."

"I remember having those at school when I was a kid." She smiled. "I used to have a whole jewelry box full of them in my bedroom because I thought the silver and gold paint on them was real."

Todd finished the cupcake and tossed the liner into a small trash bin that was near his feet. "I used to think my grandparents were millionaires because all of their doorknobs looked like big diamonds." He laughed. "I told everyone at school much to my parent's dismay."

Vivienne cringed. "I can top that. I once brought a 'devil dog' to school for show and tell."

"Those little chocolate cakes?" Todd raised an eyebrow.

"No." Vivienne laughed. "A skull from a devil dog."

Todd's eyebrow went up higher. "Say what?"

"So, my Uncle Joe was a big deer hunter when I was growing up and he spent lots of time scouting out places for tree stands in the woods around here."

"Okay." Todd nodded back. "And you're saying he found a devil dog skull?"

"It was the skull from a small deer, with just little nubs for antlers." Vivienne recalled. "It really looked like a dog with devil horns and he brought it over one day and told me it was a 'devil dog.' Naturally, I believed him."

Todd burst out with a hearty laugh. "Of course."

Vivienne continued. "So, unbeknownst to my parents, I snuck it into my backpack and brought it to school the next day for show and tell. They got a call from the teacher that afternoon."

Todd wiped some tears that formed in the corners of his eyes from laughing so hard. "Oh my God, that is the funniest thing I have heard in a long time."

"These days if a kid did that, they'd have her shipped off into therapy for mental instability." Vivienne laughed. "But back then, the teacher had a good laugh and my parents had a chance to be mortified at how gullible their daughter was."

Todd looked at his watch and shook his head. "Let me pay up for the cupcake and get back to work."

Vivienne waved him off. "It's on the house."

Todd opened his wallet and slipped two dollars onto the bakery case. "I insist."

Vivienne took his two dollars and dropped it into a collection box for the local food pantry that was sitting next to the register. "I'm so terribly clumsy these days."

He winked at her and pointed to the check. "I'm sorry I couldn't be more help with getting the money to Natalie."

Vivienne took the check and tucked it into her register drawer. "That's okay. I found out where she lives so we can just drop it off in person."

Todd snapped his fingers. "I'm going to be filling out one of those order sheets for a party I'm having at the gallery the week before Christmas. When do you need them in by?"

"The sooner the better." Vivienne answered.

"It's an Ugly Christmas Sweater party and you and Joshua are going to be invited."

Vivienne groaned. "I don't own one and trying to

get Joshua into one is going to take nothing short of a Christmas miracle."

Todd made a little pouty face. "You have to come."

Vivienne took a deep breath and sighed. "I'll see what I can do."

Todd's face brightened. "So I can count you in?"

"I'll see what I can do." Vivienne repeated.

Todd nodded and waved as he sailed out the front door. "I'm glad you both can make it."

"I may need that spell book after all." Vivienne spoke softly to herself and returned to the workspace to finish her butter cookies.

* * *

When she arrived home just after sunset, the house was dark. She parked her Toyota in the driveway and carefully navigated across the blacktop in case the ice melt missed a few spots. She stopped at the mailbox and pulled out a wad of junk mail along with a few red and green envelopes that heralded the start of the great neighborhood Christmas card exchange.

Once inside the front door, Tommy meowed loudly to let her know he wanted dinner served as soon as possible. He darted between her legs, curling his tail around her knees with a loud purring sound that one could almost mistake as a snow blower engine.

As she unbundled her winter coat and hung it on the wall hook, she noticed the red light flashing on her answering machine.

She dropped the mail onto the small end table and pressed the message play button. It was Joshua's voice. "I won't be making it over for dinner tonight. Eddie Robertson is in critical condition over at the hospital and we're hoping to get some answers about what happened."

Vivienne could tell from the sound of his voice that he was still quite unhappy with her. She reached down to her knees and ran her hands along Tommy's back as he arched it upwards with another meow.

Joshua's message continued. "I'll see you tomorrow." There was a rather long pause before he cleared his throat. "Love you. Bye."

Vivienne hated that pause. It felt like someone had stabbed her in the heart. He had said the words, but they sounded almost forced. She took a deep breath and tried to convince herself that she was genuinely trying to do a good thing. True, she could see where it might seem she was getting a little too nosy.

Tommy Cat had grown tired of her standing still and gently batted at her legs with his front paws to herd her toward the kitchen.

"Yes, yes." She replied. "I'm running late with your dinner."

He meowed back at her with excitement as she opened a pouch of chicken and gravy cat food and shook it into his food dish. With a gentle nudge he pushed her hand out of the way and eagerly gobbled down his supper.

She pulled out one of her kitchen chairs and plopped down. She had hoped that Joshua would have been up for bringing home some takeout from

Shanghai Sunset on his way over from work, but she was on her own for dinner.

She closed her eyes and decided she really wasn't all that hungry after hearing the message on the machine. She'd resort to her usual 'standby' recipe for nights like this. Cereal and milk followed by some trashy reality show television in her comfy sweats.

The wind picked up outside with a roar and the house creaked in response as a strong gust battered the little cape cod. From the kitchen window, she watched the branches of the small sugar maple in her back yard sway back and forth as wisps of snow sparkled in the darkness outside.

The wind almost sounded like a moan. A very long, drawn out cry that was almost human. It made her feel chilly and she brought her arms up across her chest wishing that Joshua were with her on such a cold and dark night.

As she got up from the kitchen chair to make sure the back door was locked up tight, she paused. The moaning now sounded like crying and she could almost make out a name being carried on the wind.

Tommy Cat suddenly backed away from his food dish and gave a little growl in the direction of the kitchen door.

"Eddie." A mournful voice carried along in the cold night air. "Eddie Robertson."

Vivienne crossed over to the kitchen window and peered out from the café curtains. In the night sky, the moon was only a slender crescent, yet it seemed brighter than usual. A stray cloud moved in front of the moon, creating the appearance of an enormous illuminated skull.

The wind picked up and battered the thin glass against the window panes as the moaning grew louder. "Eddie Robertson." The spectral voice called louder.

For a moment, she could have sworn she saw a shadowy figure flailing up in the sky, moving toward the skull moon. Arms and legs kicked as it fell into the mouth and then disappeared altogether as two large black clouds closed around like two stage curtains, plunging the sky into complete darkness.

CHAPTER 7

Wednesday, December 4th

The next morning, Vivienne had left for work extra early in order to meet Kathy at Clara's. She had texted her last night with the details of what had happened with Joshua. Kathy, in turn, demanded a before work breakfast meeting to talk things out as texting just wasn't up to this type of task.

"I would have done the same thing." Kathy confided as she gave her Greek yogurt a stir to mix up the strawberries from the bottom. "You have nothing to apologize for."

Vivienne munched on a buttered cinnamon toast point and swallowed before answering. "I don't know. I sort of feel a bit guilty for sticking my nose in."

"We're doing a good thing here." Kathy reminded her as the new waitress, a young college student named Alexis, poured a refill of coffee as she sauntered by the booth. Unlike former waitress, Stephanie Bridgeman, Alexis had the grace of a runway model and the looks to go along with it. Kathy smiled at the pretty girl. "Thank you so much. Would you be a love and get our checks ready?"

Alexis nodded, as she brushed her expertly trimmed blond bangs to the side of her face. "Sure thing." She swayed her hips back and forth as she walked to the cash register where Clara was busy signing paperwork for the truck driver who had dropped off her weekly food delivery.

"I'm almost done, Frank." Clara flipped to the last page of the manifest. "I know you're always in a hurry."

"Take your time, Miss Clara." Frank smiled as Alexis moved past, causing him to suck in his stomach which spilled over his belt. "I'm not complaining."

Clara cast a wary eye at him. "There's a first time for everything I suppose."

"Ah, to be that young again." Kathy pointed with her index finger at the scene taking place near the cash register. "Like he'd even have a chance with her."

"I just hate it when someone is mad at me." Vivienne replied as she took a sip of coffee. "It just throws my whole day off."

"You're not even listening to what I say, are you?" Kathy said with a hint of annoyance in her tone.

"I'm sorry." Vivienne took a deep breath and shook her head.

"He'll get over it soon enough when he realizes that he's wrong." Kathy smiled back. "So, I haven't heard anything about Eddie Robertson's condition. Bryce Starr mentioned that he was in critical condition at Cayuga Memorial Hospital on his radio show this morning."

"I heard it too. They're describing it as an 'incident'." Vivienne used her fingers to make air quotes.

"Do you think Natalie shot him?" Kathy whispered.

Vivienne shrugged. "I don't know. I didn't get to see the actual crime scene."

Kathy finished off the last of her yogurt and dapped a napkin across her lips. "Well, I don't think there will be many people shedding a tear if he doesn't make it."

"Don't say that." Vivienne interrupted. "I don't ever want to get involved with a murder again. I've barely recovered from the last time."

Kathy shook her head. "Look on the bright side. At least he didn't end up in the dumpster behind your bakery."

"That's the bright side? Really?" Vivienne scoffed.

Alexis returned with two checks and placed them face down on the table. "Have a good morning, ladies."

"Thanks hon." Kathy grabbed Vivienne's check.

"I can afford to pay for toast and coffee." Vivienne protested.

"It was my idea to come here." Kathy opened one of her many designer Coach purses and pulled out a ten and a five. "That Alexis sure was a good waitress."

Vivienne nodded. "She's very quick and polite."

Kathy slipped the five under the sugar container. "She has a figure most women would die for."

"Where is this going?" Vivienne asked.

"Whatever do you mean?"

Vivienne pointed to the five. "Our breakfast couldn't have been more than seven dollars. Why the huge tip?"

Kathy sighed. "Okay, you've got me. There's a

spring fashion show coming up in Syracuse and I want her to model for my store."

"So why don't you just ask her? "

Kathy pursed her lips together. "Because I don't want her to have the power in this deal. I know kids these days and they all have such an air of entitlement about them. I ask her to do this and the next thing you know she has a contract drawn up with some crazy modeling fee."

Vivienne exhaled at her friend's response. "Aren't you putting the cart before the horse a bit?"

Kathy shrugged. "Could be. But I'm just a few big tips away from becoming her favorite customer. Then, when she's fawning over me I casually mention I have this big fashion show spot coming up and how much press the young models are going to get by participating."

Vivienne nodded back in response. "So, she then asks for a favor to put her in the show?"

"Now you're getting it." Kathy stepped out of the booth and straightened her outfit.

"Care to fix my mess with Joshua?" Vivienne eased out of the booth and gave a few stray crumbs a quick brush off her pants.

"I've got my hands full at the moment." Kathy smiled. "If you're so unsure, why don't you try that New Age store on the corner of Weyer Place?"

They stepped out the front door into the cold morning air. "I didn't think they were open yet." Vivienne buttoned her coat up.

"Not until after the first, but the owner stopped in my store the other day and introduced herself." Kathy hurried to her car. "She gives psychic readings too."

"Maybe I'll stop by for a friendly visit." Vivienne waved goodbye as she climbed into her car and slammed the door. Their breakfast meeting had taken much less time than she thought, so she still had over an hour before she was due to open. She turned the engine on and cranked up the heat. As she pulled out of the parking lot, she headed for Weyer Place which was just a few blocks down the road from her current location on Spruce Street.

Traffic was light and parking places plentiful along the less busy section of motley businesses which lined Weyer Place. Unlike Main Street with its uniform look, this area had buildings which were well overdue for facelifts and overhauls. The sidewalks were broken and narrow, the tree branches overgrown and snarled in the remains of shredded awnings. Less-than-savory landlords rented the buildings out to whoever could come up with the rent fast enough. Of course, they evicted them even faster when the rent check bounced which created a revolving door of failed small business attempts.

Vivienne had a hard time making out the names of most of the businesses as makeshift signs were crammed into small display windows, most with 'Store closing, everything must go!' signs nearby. A few very lucky businesses had a stroke of luck and were able to relocate to Main Street after a few months, but most just locked the doors one night and never came back.

As she reached the corner of Weyer Place and McCann's Avenue, she was surprised to see a warm light emanating from a red brick building that was in better shape than most. She pulled into the nearest parking spot, her daytime running lights reflecting off the display window which was partially filled with geodes, crystals, tarot cards, spirit boards, and other curious items associated with modern Paganism and metaphysical practitioners. Further in, she could make out a few rows of shelving where it looked like herbs, bulk food barrels, and other grocery-type items would be displayed.

There was a small sign above the door which identified the business as Mother Earth Mercantile. The words were framed on each side by the triple moon characters which Vivienne recognized as a symbol Wiccans used to represent the Goddess. Below that, was a handwritten note that the grand opening was to be January 2nd.

Vivienne stepped out of her vehicle and admired the items in the display window. The owner had done a good job with the shelving which had been left behind from a former pawn shop that had closed almost five years ago. Richly colored swaths of cloth had been laid out to give some visual pop from behind the old window glass that was discolored from age and pollution.

She nearly jumped out of her skin when a slender hand rapped on the window glass from inside the store. "Oh!" She gasped in surprise as the hand pulled back to reveal a woman in a purple blouse and faded denim pants who smiled and motioned for her to come inside.

Vivienne walked over to the door and gave it several good yanks, but it failed to open.

The owner helped push from the other side and soon the door swung outward with a rusty-gate type sound that was as grating as nails on a chalkboard. "I'm sorry if I scared you. Please come in." The woman had light cocoa skin that was well moisturized and glistened with a bit of sparkle from blush on her cheekbones.

Vivienne stepped into the shop, noticing immediately the spicy scent of incense burning in the air. It was one of the more spicy scents, something like cinnamon mixed with patchouli. "I didn't think you were open for business yet."

"I'm not officially, but sometimes the Goddess sends people to me regardless." Her voice was soft and melodic, with the hint of an accent from one of the Caribbean islands.

Vivienne smiled. "Thank you for allowing me in to see your new business."

The woman yanked the door closed and rubbed her hands together from the cold. "I've talked to the owner three times now about getting this door fixed, but he's always busy. But then again, aren't men always saying the same thing to women when there is real work to be done?"

Vivienne nodded. "These buildings are very old."

"We never had cold like this in Barbados." She winked playfully and extended her right hand. "I'm Miss Octavia." Her slender fingers were bejeweled with various rings of all kinds of metal and sparkling gemstones. Along her wrist, a small crescent moon tattoo was visible.

"Vivienne Finch, owner of Sweet Dreams Bakery over on Main Street." Vivienne shook her hand. "You're doing a wonderful job with this place."

Octavia whistled back in response. "So you're the

one everyone's talking about."

Vivienne cocked her head slightly to the side. "All good I hope."

"The winner of the gingerbread house competition." Octavia clarified as she fiddled with a floral-print scarf wrapped around her short afro-styled hair that had come loose.

"Did you have an entry?" Vivienne asked, recognizing the scarf as one that was currently available for sale at Kathy's store.

"Oh Goddess no, I have zero talent when it comes to baking." She laughed. "So what brings you down here today?"

Vivienne picked up a small wooden rod that was wrapped with copper wire and topped with an amethyst crystal from a nearby shelf. "I was curious to meet the owner of the newest business coming into town."

Octavia's brown, almond-shaped eyes narrowed. "Well, here I am." She walked over to a small round table that was set up in the center of the room. It was covered with a silver cloth upon which rested a large crystal ball on a brass pedestal shaped like two dragons "But I think you'd rather talk about your troubles."

Vivienne set the wand down and followed her to the table. "My troubles?"

"With your man." Octavia pulled out a chair and sat down at the table. "Isn't that why you're really here?"

"I'm not having trouble with my man." Vivienne protested.

Octavia shrugged. "It wasn't all directed at you.

There are other circumstances in play that are making him edgier than usual."

"Did Kathy tell you about what happened?" Vivienne put her hands on her hips. "She probably posted a status about it on Social Butterfly too."

"I did meet Miss Saunders the other day, but she did not betray your trust." Octavia clarified. "I picked that up all on my own."

"So you're a psychic?" Vivienne asked, her posture refusing to relax from its defensive stance.

"I get visions from time to time, but they're just fragments really. You need to put them together to make them meaningful and change your fate."

Without thinking, Vivienne found herself compelled to sit down at the table. "You had a vision about Joshua?"

Octavia nodded. "He's a fine looking man, but he's hiding something from everyone. There's a darkness very close to him."

Vivienne nodded. "We all have our secrets in a small town."

"True, but this is something like I've never felt before." Octavia shuddered. "It's something that doesn't want to be discovered."

Vivienne felt her heart flutter a bit. "You can't tell what it is?"

"Not yet, but it's getting closer to being revealed." Octavia warned.

Vivienne knew that it was still some time before the full moon when Joshua would take up his wolf form for the night. That had to be what Miss Octavia was seeing in her vision. Would she keep quiet about it if she discovered the truth? Would she expose him to the townsfolk and the world for fame and fortune?

"Are you okay sweetie?" Octavia asked with concern in her voice.

Vivienne glanced at her watch. "I really need to get going and open up shop for the day."

"I didn't mean to scare you off." Octavia responded. "I can sense you know your way around magic pretty well."

Vivienne forced a polite smile. "Well, I'm not an expert by any means." She pushed back the chair and stood up. "But I'm aware of certain things."

Octavia nodded back. "If you want to know more about the situation, I'll be happy to do a card reading for you. Or perhaps you'd like me to read your aura?"

Vivienne nodded back. "Thank you, but I don't think that'll be necessary." She turned to leave. "It was very nice to meet you."

Octavia rose from her chair. "Likewise, my dear." She placed her hand upon the crystal ball and yanked it back with a startled gasp.

Vivienne whirled around, fully prepared to deal with a carnival-style side show performance when she noticed that her brown eyes were fading into pure white. Not rolling back, but losing all color in a matter of seconds. "Miss Octavia? Are you ill?"

"Beware the cold moon. It is still hungry." Octavia's voice was low and foreboding.

Vivienne took a tentative step toward her. "What about the moon?"

"It is not finished. It will strike again. The voice in the wind gives warning." Octavia finished and then slumped onto the table.

Vivienne rushed forward and pulled her back

against the chair. "Miss Octavia?"

Octavia's eyelids fluttered and her brown eyes returned to their normal hue. "What happened?"

"I wish I knew." Vivienne patted her gently on the arms. "You started to say something about the moon and then you passed out."

Octavia took a deep breath and shook her head. "I did?"

Vivienne nodded. "You mentioned the cold moon."

"That's what the December moon is called on the witch's calendar."

"I'm aware of that." Vivienne replied. "You said it was hungry and going to strike again. What did you mean?"

"I have no idea. I just remember feeling dizzy and then you asking me if I was okay." Octavia groaned and put her hands on her temples. "But I've got a nasty headache all of a sudden."

"Would you like me to take you to the urgent care center to get checked out?"

Octavia waved her off. "No, my dear. It's fading away now." She shook her head a few times and then gave a little smile. "Besides, I've got plenty of natural remedies that cost far less than a trip to the doctor."

Vivienne glanced at her watch and knew she couldn't afford to stay much longer. "I'd be happy to take you."

"Go and bake your goodies." She smiled and stood up from the chair. "I've been working so hard trying to get this store together and skipping meals. My blood sugar is probably all over the place."

"Are you a diabetic?" Vivienne asked.

"No, praise the Goddess." Octavia gave her a wicked little grin. "But making friends with the town baker isn't going to do me any favors."

Vivienne glanced at her watch once more. "Well, it was nice to meet you. I'm making apple doughnuts this morning if you'd like to stop buy and try a complimentary sample."

"Isn't that sweet of you?" Octavia beamed with a warm smile. "I just might do that."

"See you later today." Vivienne rushed off to open her bakery.

CHAPTER 8

Joshua stepped into the Sweet Dreams Bakery still dressed in his uniform. His steel-blue eyes looked heavy and sleep-deprived as he walked up to the counter where Vivienne was busy transcribing a telephone order onto a notepad. She thanked the caller and hung up, clipping the order to a large magnetic board that had 'New Orders' labeled in bold letters on top.

"You look like you haven't slept in days." Vivienne spoke softly, trying to gauge his mood.

He nodded. "This case has been keeping us all on edge."

Vivienne stepped around the counter and faced him head on. "Before we say anything else I just want to apologize for snooping around like that and making trouble for you. I'm planning to go down and tell Sheriff Rigsbee it was all my idea and you had nothing to do with it. I'm so sorry."

Joshua reached out and placed his hands on her shoulders. "I know you are and you don't need to do that because I'm not in any sort of trouble."

Vivienne exhaled. "Good. Heaven knows I'm probably the last person he wants walking into his office right now."

"Sheriff Rigsbee wanted nothing more than to toss you in a cell for being a busybody, but you haven't broken any laws so that's not an option."

"I promise I won't go near Eddie, Natalie, or Connor." Vivienne held her right hand up as if taking an oath. "I learned my lesson."

Joshua swallowed hard and looked away from her. "Yeah, about that."

"You don't believe me?"

He shook his head. "No, I believe you. It's something else."

Vivienne couldn't take the agonizing silence that followed. Her thoughts drifted back to her conversation with Miss Octavia. Could he feel that she was close to figuring out his secret? She reached up to his chin and turned his head toward hers. It was then that she saw the tears in the corners of her eyes. "You're starting to scare me here. Whatever is wrong, we'll deal with it together."

"I just came from the hospital. Eddie Robertson died this morning."

"What?" Vivienne gasped.

"I was there for the whole thing and it was awful. Natalie was in the room right up until the end and she had Connor next to her the whole time. Poor little guy was so upset and confused." Joshua reached up and swept a tear away that had run down his right cheek.

Vivienne guided him over to one of the bistro tables and sat down directly across from him. She was slightly relieved his news didn't concern Miss Octavia, but the alternative was almost as bad. "So I take it Natalie isn't a suspect in the shooting?"

"He wasn't shot." Joshua continued. "He had something else going on and was bleeding out. I know the doctors were pretty stumped."

"That's very strange. The next door neighbor told me she didn't hear any gun shots, but one of the other neighbors claimed he did." Vivienne cupped her hands over his. "I'm sure the autopsy will shed some light on what happened to him."

He lowered his head. "The whole time Connor was in the room he kept telling Natalie that Santa could keep all his toys if he made his Daddy better."

Vivienne's eyes clouded up with tears. "Bless his little heart."

Joshua nodded back. "I've never seen anything like it. He was like this little soldier just standing at attention next to the bed. Didn't make a fuss or whine that he wanted to go play with the toys in the waiting room."

"This is terrible." Vivienne sniffed as she pictured the image in her head. "To lose his father so close to the holidays."

"Eddie was conscious right up until the end. He was crying most of the time." Joshua revealed. "He just kept saying how sorry he was ."

"What did Natalie say happened?" Vivienne asked.

"I've already said too much." Joshua straightened up in his chair. "You can't say anything about this to anyone until it hits the media."

Vivienne nodded back. "You have my word."

"The whole department wants to find out what happened for Connor's sake." Joshua continued. "When he's old enough, he deserves to know the truth."

"Of course." Vivienne agreed. "I wouldn't want to jeopardize that."

"I'm sorry for acting the way I have lately." Joshua glanced around the bakery at all the colorful decorations. "This whole thing has just taken the joy right out of the holidays."

"Any progress figuring out who penned that Bad Santa note?" Vivienne asked.

He shook his head. "Not that I know of. But whoever wrote it probably had something to do with Eddie's death. It's being analyzed at the crime lab in Rochester."

"Let's hope that's the end of it then." Vivienne added. Although the Cayuga Cove sheriff's department was competent, she knew they lacked the sophisticated equipment that could yield the critical break in a case.

"Let's hope so." Joshua agreed.

"Is there anything I can do to help?" Vivienne asked.

Joshua looked around the bakery. "Are we alone?"

"Stephanie isn't in until this afternoon." Vivienne assured him.

"Is there some kind of spell you could cast to figure out what happened? Something to put us on the right path?"

Vivienne shook her head. "I'm not even close to those kind of heavy duty spells. Nana Mary told me it will take years of practice before I reach that level."

"Damn." Joshua frowned. "I was hoping we could solve this fast."

"I'll bet she can put me on the right path."

Joshua gave her a little smile. "I'm all for any help that solves this case as fast as possible."

"There might be a way, if I can get to see Natalie in person." Vivienne pondered. "If my power kicks in, that is."

"You can't fully control it yet?"

Vivienne sighed. "Nana Mary says that the more I utilize it, the more control I'll gain. Unfortunately, I've been a bit lax in practicing magic lately."

"We still have the problem of you losing consciousness after your power kicks in too." Joshua felt a little shudder at how close Vivienne came to having her life taken away a few months ago when she was investigating the murder of Mona Clarke. Her power had revealed the awful truth, but she had almost taken it to the grave. "I can't have you put yourself in danger like that again."

Vivienne took a deep breath. "It really sucks being a new witch sometimes. You have all these spells and powers, but you have to wait years to use them."

"Well, I guess we learned the danger of someone getting power too early." Joshua agreed. "So, it makes sense to hold back while you learn the fundamentals."

"So, that leaves Nana Mary and her advice."

"Won't Nora find it odd with you two talking about magic and spells?" Joshua asked.

"She doesn't listen to a word we say. Whenever she comes over she spends the whole time cleaning and organizing the apartment according to the latest *Martha Stewart* magazine article while getting the latest tips on television from *Doctor Oz*." Vivienne chuckled. "I'll call Nana Mary beforehand and make sure she really leaves a mess to keep her extra occupied.

"I love you." Joshua leaned forward and kissed her fully on the lips.

* * *

A little past noon, Stephanie arrived for her afternoon shift. Vivienne had tried to focus on crafting the perfect apple donuts, but she kept overcooking them when her mind wandered off concerning Eddie's death and Octavia's vision. When she amassed a rather full baker's dozen of ruined treats, she had to resort to casting the minor time-reversal spell she had re-named 'Oopsie Doopsie' to fix the problem. It had been a few weeks since she used magic, and it felt good to be able to actually practice it again. Plus, she'd be able to say she'd been practicing her magic when Nana Mary asked.

"These look amazing." Stephanie commented on the glistening fried donuts cooling on the marble slab table. "What's your secret?"

"Magic, naturally." Vivienne told the truth with a little twinkle in her hazel eyes.

"I believe you." Stephanie smiled and tied her apron on. "I was going to knock out those three dozen ginger snaps for the VFW ladies lunch order tomorrow. Was there anything else you wanted me to take care of?"

"Would you mind finishing off another two dozen donuts?" Vivienne stepped away from the fryer. "I've just about had a full shower of hot oil this morning standing here." She smiled.

"No problem, but don't expect them to turn out quite as nice as yours."

Vivienne chuckled. "I have complete faith in you."

Stephanie walked over to the fryer and glanced at the temperature gauge. "Wow, you really must be working magic."

"What do you mean?" Vivienne asked as she loosened the apron strings from around her waist.

"This oil is at almost four hundred." Stephanie turned the dial down to the standard three hundred and sixty degree setting. "I can't believe you didn't burn them to a crisp."

"So that's why I was having so much trouble." Vivienne fibbed. "What you don't see is a garbage bag filled with charred donut cinders out back."

Stephanie grinned. "I won't tell if you don't."

Vivienne sighed. "I guess I should play a lotto ticket given the lucky streak I've been on."

"Would you get me a winning ticket too?" Stephanie joked. "I'd sure love that jackpot for Christmas shopping."

Vivienne winked. "Wouldn't we all?" She dropped her dirty apron into the hamper along the side wall and gave her appearance a once over in the small mirror mounted on the stockroom door. "I won't need to do any hot oil treatments on my hair this month." She tossed her shoulder-length auburn locks with her fingers.

An hour later, after a quick shower and a change of clothes, she hopped into her Toyota Matrix and drove over to pick up her mother.

As usual, she was standing on the curb with her trusty L.L. Bean canvas tote bag at her side. Vivienne didn't have to look inside to know the contents. It was filled with her usual weekly visit supplies. Cleaning products from double coupon day at the Monarch

Grocery, small plastic storage containers that were color-coordinated and pre-labeled for easy access, and several magazines she had read and was passing on to the Whispering Pines residents. When it came to schedules and consistent efficiency, even the United States military could learn a thing or two from Nora Finch.

"Hello, Mother." Vivienne said cheerfully as her mother opened the passenger side door and tucked the bag in the back seat.

"You're ten minutes late." Nora climbed into the front passenger seat and put on her seatbelt. "This blasted cold goes right to your bones."

"I'm sorry about that." Vivienne checked her mirror and pulled out onto the road to head for Nana Mary's. "I wanted to change clothes after working this morning."

"Be careful of icy patches." Nora warned as she placed her hands on the dashboard. She tapped her fingernails across the plastic as if preparing for the airbag to inflate at any moment.

Vivienne suppressed a grin and eased off the gas, even though she was doing the posted speed limit of exactly thirty miles an hour. "The roads are dry as a bone, mother."

Nora relaxed as their speed dropped to a more leisurely twenty-five and allowed her hands to rest upon her lap. "Well, you just never know with these town services today. Not many people take pride in their work."

"I do." Vivienne added as they turned onto Cayuga Circle and headed for their destination.

"Well, you're my daughter so that's a given."

Nora commented. "I meant with the younger generation."

"Ouch." Vivienne grimaced. "I guess I walked into that one on my own."

"I didn't mean you were old, darling daughter." Nora was quick to reply.

"Oh good." Vivienne was surprised.

"But you really should make an effort to get married and start a family while you still have a few prime years left." Nora added with her usual sweet sting.

Vivienne stepped on the gas pedal a little more, just for good measure as her response to the barb.

Nora cleared her throat. "My, the snow certainly is bright when the sun is shining like this."

"It reminds me of the sand reflecting on the beach in Ogunquit. Those were the best family vacations."

"Except for you always ordering a lobster roll and then refusing to eat it." Nora added. "Good gracious, you pulled that little stunt every vacation until you were almost sixteen."

"It took me some time to get used to cold seafood." Vivienne defended herself from the very old battle. "Besides, Daddy always ate my entrée anyway."

Nora nodded. "Which probably didn't help his cholesterol levels with all the heavy mayonnaise and extra bread."

"You're right, Mother. I'm sure it didn't help matters." Vivienne spoke as she admired the well-kept homes that lined both sides of the street. Most were decorated with tasteful holiday wreathes, gold and silver ribbons, and the occasional menorah.

White lights, of course, were the standard and each home was modestly illuminated, yet they could not chase, blink, or flash in any sort of pattern. The Residential Association kept strict guidelines for approved outdoor decor along the street and the homeowners followed it to the letter as hefty fines were given out at the slightest sign of defiance. Vivienne had to admit the tasteful displays of holiday cheer were something to be admired, but part of her missed the tacky blow up snowmen and the light up flamingos and pigs that gave a certain unexpected gleefulness to the holiday.

"I hope Nana isn't confused today. She can get into moods when I start to organize." Nora broke the silence between them.

"I'm sure she'll be happy to see us." Vivienne slowed the car down as they passed over a speed bump and turned into the parking lot of the assisted living facility. "She loves the holidays."

"Let's hope so." Nora replied as they pulled into a spot between two mini vans that had stick figure families plastered to the back windows. "Those are so cute. I can't wait until you get to put some on your car."

Vivienne took a deep breath and smiled. "I can put the woman and the cat on right away."

Nora frowned. "I wouldn't do that, dear. It'll make everyone think you're just some crazy cat lady."

A few minutes later as they stepped into Nana Mary's apartment, Vivienne was pleased to see that her grandmother had gone out of way to keep Nora busy while they chatted about magic. There were piles of clutter scattered everywhere except for the living room which was surprisingly quite neat. Her Amish-made wooden rocking chair that faced the picture window anchored a tranquil island of order around a sea of chaos.

"I'm so glad that you both came to see me today, I decided I wanted to get organized before the holiday craziness hits." Nana Mary hugged Vivienne and Nora as she gestured to the clutter. "What do you think?"

Nora did her best to smile. "I think we have a lot of work to do." She set her canvas bag down by a vintage wooden umbrella holder that was filled to the top with empty water bottles.

Nana Mary scratched her short white hair, which looked to be styled and curled quite recently at the beauty salon downstairs. "I thought we could divide and conquer, that way the work will go faster."

Vivienne smiled. "Sounds like a good plan, Nana. Where do you want us to start?"

"Why don't I start by finding a better place to store your recyclables?" Nora offered. "It's a sin to use this lovely umbrella holder like that."

Nana Mary waved her hands. "What fool needs that many umbrellas in the world? I think it's better off holding empty bottles, at least then it has a useful purpose."

Vivienne caught Nora's eyes widen in shock at the remark. Her mother had given the expensive holder as a Christmas present last year along with a stylish Vera Bradley umbrella. "Didn't someone give you a beautiful umbrella to display in that?"

Nana Mary scratched her chin. "Oh, maybe they did. Haven't seen that umbrella around her lately.

Flora Rogers, down the hall likes to borrow things and keep them. She's even been known to pull name labels right off whatever she's using. Can you believe that?"

"I'm sure she'll return it soon." Nora was quick to add. "Then we can display it in the holder."

Nana Mary winked at Vivienne. "You're right, Nora. Why don't you go down and talk to her today and while you're there see if she has a red KitchenAid coffee grinder in her apartment? Agnes McCarren loaned that out almost six months ago and she'd really like it back."

Nora walked over to the small coat closet to hang up her jacket. As she opened the door, a pile of magazines spilled onto the cream carpet. "Good heavens."

"I was saving those to put down in the lobby." Nana Mary smiled. "I'll leave that job for you too."

"Thanks, Mother." Nora winced and bent down to sort the magazines into piles according to date and subject.

"Vivienne, you come and help me sort through these boxes from the hall closet. I put them all in the living room to make it easier." Nana Mary wandered off toward the kitchen. "Would anyone like something to drink?"

Nora and Vivienne declined as they assumed their work stations in the apartment. Nana Mary poured herself a cup of hot ginger-spiced tea and sat down in the rocker that was surrounded with cardboard boxes.

Vivienne opened the first box only to discover it was quite empty, save for a few glass ornaments.

"This one doesn't look too bad." She peered further into the box and found everything wrapped carefully in bubble wrap and tucked into empty Styrofoam egg containers. "Actually, it looks perfectly packed."

"They're all organized and ready to be labeled." Nana Mary whispered with a twinkle in her blue eyes. "I thought we could focus on the important things instead."

Vivienne nodded. "So, where do I begin?"

"Right at the beginning, of course." Nana Mary smiled and took a sip of her tea. "Don't leave anything out."

"Okay." Vivienne spent the next half hour telling Nana Mary everything that had happened with Natalie, Eddie, Connor, and lastly Miss Octavia. She was careful to keep her voice low and look busy as Nora wandered into the living room from time to time to give them tips on how to separate trash from treasure, how to group items to make labeling easier, and an occasional health tip from the *Doctor Oz Show* that was airing on the small television mounted above the kitchen counter where she was re-arranging the cabinets to make things easier to find.

"I'll die of thirst before I ever find a drinking glass again." Nana Mary joked to Vivienne as Nora disappeared back into the kitchen.

Vivienne laughed. "At least she only spends an afternoon organizing your place. I get two days at the very least now that Joshua is spending most of his time there."

Nana Mary chuckled and rocked back and forth in her chair. "Things are going well with you both?"

Vivienne nodded. "I'd like to think so."

"That doesn't sound too terribly affirmative." Nana Mary watched a red cardinal perch upon the bird feeder outside her window and peck at the seeds stored inside. "It's not easy trying to live with someone."

"We're figuring all that out. We still have our own places, but we've been testing out having him stay more at my place." Vivienne pulled out a simple glass ball of silver and held it in her hands. It reminded her of a miniature version of the crystal ball Miss Octavia used in her store. "I've been so used to doing things on my own that I sometimes forget to compromise. We've had a few arguments here and there."

Nana Mary smiled. "You'll both work it out. I'm sure of it." She let out a little sigh. "Back when I was your age, it just wasn't acceptable in polite society for a woman to test the waters. We had to put a ring on the finger and keep them crossed that we didn't want to kill each other the next morning."

Vivienne felt lucky to have that chance. "I do love him and I know he loves me."

"Then you're very lucky." Nana Mary smiled back. "Not everyone in this world gets that chance."

"I know I am." Vivienne agreed. "That's why I love coming to talk with you Nana. You always make me see what I'm taking for granted and that gives me a chance to set things right."

"I'm glad I can help, my darling granddaughter."

Vivienne pulled herself up from the floor and wrapped her arms around Nana Mary. "I love you so much."

"We witches need to stick together." Nana Mary

chuckled as Vivienne pulled away.

"We sure do." Vivienne stared at the silver ornament in her hand. "Especially whenever someone is murdered in town."

"So, you've got quite the mystery on your hands again." Nana Mary rocked slowly back and forth in her chair. "Do you suspect there was magic involved?"

Vivienne carefully set the ornament back in the egg container and shrugged her shoulders. "There doesn't seem to be any evidence of that nature, but then again I didn't get a chance to go to the crime scene."

"Ah." Nana Mary answered. "But, you don't need to go to the crime scene to get a chance to see what happened now, do you?"

Vivienne's jaw went slack. "Goddess, I feel so stupid. The viewing will be probably be at Fritz and Candor Funeral Home. "It'll be the perfect time to touch Natalie's hand and maybe see what really happened that day."

"Well, except for the passing out part." Nana Mary laughed. "But given you'll be inside a funeral home, I suspect that happens from time to time. It shouldn't raise too many red flags. Just don't let them stick you in a casket."

"I can warn Joshua ahead of time so he'll keep me from tumbling to the floor or ending up in the casket." Vivienne reasoned.

Nana Mary nodded. "See, you're a smart girl. You didn't need me to find the next step."

Nora's voice echoed from the kitchen. "I hear lots of chatter but not much cleaning." A clattering of pots and pans followed for emphasis.

Nana Mary rolled her eyes. "We're almost done in here, Nora. We're busy little bees."

Vivienne reached into a nearby box and pulled out a mess of tangled extension cords. She knelt down on the carpet and sorted them by length on the floor. "Wait until you see what progress we made." Vivienne shouted back with a wicked little grin.

"Doing things legally to make them stick, that's the biggest challenge you're going to face." Nana Mary spoke softly. "It always is with magic."

"What about Miss Octavia? Is she a witch?"

Nana Mary shook her head. "It sounds like she's quite skilled working with energy and reading people, but she's still limited by her non-magical human genes. Besides, the Elder Council would have informed me if another witch moved into town. They've got this place on their radar."

"Then how does she know that Joshua is a werewolf?" Vivienne wondered.

"She's gifted with some sixth sense, that's for certain. But, she can't harness it like one of us. She has to fumble around with the power and occasionally it works out in her favor."

Vivienne shook her head. "Something magical took over her body." She began to loop the cords around her wrist, tie them off with large garbage bag twists, and place them in a storage bin Nora provided. "It wanted me to know that whatever killed Eddie was still out there and going to strike again."

Nana Mary nodded. "When Missy Collins began casting her rituals and spells here in town a few months ago, she inadvertently opened some portals to other planes of existence. Those portals don't just close up afterwards. They're like sign posts to other beings that lead into this world."

"Can't the Elder Council close them up?"

"Missy worked with some very dark magic, communed with beings who feed upon the innocent." Nana Mary warned. "Those portals can never be fully closed off." She folded her arms across her chest as if she were suddenly cold. "You already know that Cayuga Cove is a magnet for the supernatural. But, with these portals opened it's practically a lighthouse drawing all sorts of strange beings from the darkness. They're curious and craving the chance to get a foothold in our world."

"That sounds dangerous."

"It is." Nana Mary agreed. "But if anyone can fix this, it's you."

Vivienne finished with the last power cord and snapped the lid on the storage bin. "I hope you're right, Nana."

"I'd bet every last dollar in my savings on you, my darling granddaughter." Nana Mary spoke just as Nora wandered into the living room and surveyed the scene like a general on the battlefield.

"I thought you said you made progress?" Nora asked.

"We did." Vivienne gestured to the boxes around them. "Everything is wrapped, labeled, and ready for storage."

Nora eyed them both suspiciously. "Is that so?"

Nana Mary smiled at her daughter. "Did I ever tell you how much you remind me of Martha

Stewart?"

"It doesn't look like you've made much progress at all." Nora started to open one of the boxes and then paused when the flattery kicked in. "You think so, Mother?"

Nana Mary smiled. "I was just telling all my friends at Bingo how much you remind me of her. Ida Purnell was asking if you'd consider coming in next week and having a workshop for the residents here."

Nora closed the box. "Why, I'd love to."

Nana Mary winked at Vivienne. "Now that's real magic."

CHAPTER 9

Friday, December 6th

Kathy gripped Vivienne's right arm as they steeled themselves from the bitterly cold wind that was coming off the nearby shore of Cayuga Lake. "I really hate funeral homes."

"Joshua is stuck at work and might not be able to make it." Vivienne reminded her. "Besides, I'm not a fan of these places either."

"So why exactly are we here, other than morbid curiosity?" She asked as a strong gust of wind nearly blew her maroon knit beret off her blond hair.

"To pay our respects." Vivienne spoke as she guided her into the front entrance of the Fritz and Candor Funeral Home. "Plus a chance to speak with Natalie." It was pleasant, at least as pleasant as one could hope for when it came to funeral homes in general. The owner, James Fritz was, in fact, one of the most happy men in Cayuga Cove, according to most residents. He always had a smile, a joke, or just a pat on the back whenever anyone ran into him outside of his work. But more importantly, he genuinely cared about his work and made sure that the family and friends of the dearly departed always felt as if they had his complete and unwavering attention.

"I could have been home right now, curled up on the sofa with a blanket and the remote." Kathy moaned.

"Trust me, it'll be worth it." Vivienne whispered back as one of the attendants, a bearded man in a nice suit, took their coats for them and hung them on a wall rack nearby. "When I stopped into Hummingbird Floral, Brian Amberry told me that Bistro Parisian is donating the food after the memorial service. How can you resist that?"

"Oh." Kathy's tone brightened. "Do you think they'll have their famous French Onion soup?"

"It sure would be a nice way to counter this blasted cold spell." Vivienne whispered back and felt her stomach rumble slightly. She had skipped lunch earlier because she had completely forgotten about the four dozen brownies for the library bake sale she had promised earlier in the week to Harriet Nettles, the town librarian.

She managed to get it done without magic, which made her proud. According to Nana Mary, using magic too much made one lazy. Lazy often brought along careless, which usually invited chaos for the ride. Vivienne was all about order, these days. She had never liked surprises and she liked them even less when they were of the magical variety.

As they waited in line with Cayuga Cove's fellow residents to comfort Natalie and Connor, Vivienne admired the collection of antique clocks that were displayed on tables and shelves throughout the many rooms leading to the viewing atrium where the family greeted guests. There were Black Forest German Cuckoo clocks, complete with little diorama dancers that circled at the top of each hour in the room nearest the entry hall, Versailles-style mantle clocks with over-the-top gilt décor in the following room that had several fancy stuffed sofas for holding hushed conversations, and in the narrow hallway right before the atrium a duo of early-American Grandfather and Grandmother clocks. She wondered if perhaps James, being a funeral director, was slightly obsessed with time? Surely, he had seen many who an accident or cruel twist of fate seemed to cheat.

Kathy signed her name on the guest book resting just outside the atrium. "James must keep Nathaniel and Tristan in business. Those clocks are worth a small fortune."

Vivienne signed her name under Kathy's and quickly scanned those who were listed above. She recognized a few downtown business owners, such as Tony DiSanto, but most were unfamiliar to her. She guessed quite a few were from the trailer park where Natalie, Eddie, and Connor had resided for the past few months.

"Vera?" A familiar voice called out as she stepped into the atrium with Kathy.

Kathy scowled at the woman who approached them with open arms. "Is she talking to us?"

"Vera French." Sally Rollins pushed past Kathy and wrapped her arms around Vivienne. "I had a feeling you'd be here. What a sad day."

Kathy's eyes narrowed as she remembered Vivienne explaining to her how she impersonated a journalist on the day of Eddie's attack. "Here we go again."

Vivienne cringed slightly in response to the hug. She hadn't seen Sally since that day in the trailer park and she felt incredibly guilty for not going back to explain her little white lie. "It's good to see you again."

Sally was dressed up in a simple black sweater and skirt combo that looked right off the racks of the bargain section at one of the outlet stores due to ill-fitting proportions. The shoulders still had little points from the plastic hangar that poked out like horns, and the skirt stuck together in strange spots thanks to static cling. From her neck, dangled a simple gold chain with the figure of an angel knelt in prayer. "Isn't this just tragic?" She asked. "Are you doing a follow up story?"

Vivienne wanted to come clean but this wasn't the place to do it. If Sally raised a stink, it could ruin her plan to speak quietly with Natalie and perhaps get a glimpse into what happened that dreadful day. "Well, I'm just here to give my condolences to Natalie and little Connor."

"Of course." Sally nodded. "But, if you need any more reactions from neighbors, I'd be happy to oblige."

"Thank you, but I won't be needing that as I'm not writing a story." Vivienne politely turned to face Kathy. "Have I introduced you to Sally Rollins?"

Sally ignored Vivienne's attempt to change the conversation. "I've had offers from other news stations and papers to give my story, you know. But I wanted to save it for you because you were first on the scene. I think that's only fair."

"That's very generous of you, but I can assure you I'm not here on assignment. I'm just here to offer comfort to Natalie and her son." Vivienne tried once more to explain, but she could see the stars in Sally's eyes and she wasn't going to be pushed aside so easily.

"I understand." Sally winked at Vivienne. "You'll get a better story if you don't have the notepad and cameras around. I've been interviewed for stories before, you know. I have the tapes at home if you want to review them. One was at the gas station last year talking about high prices around the holidays and the other was about natural gas drilling around the lakes."

Vivienne noticed that some of the other people in line were starting to look at them and that was last thing she wanted. "I appreciate the offer, Sally, but I don't think this moment is about us. This is to mourn the loss of a husband and father."

Sally nodded back eagerly. "So you want me to talk about Eddie in a nice way for the story? I can do that. He wasn't an upstanding citizen in any way, but I can put a spin on it. Is that the right term you people use?"

Kathy shook her head and stepped in to stop the momentum of the conversation. "Excuse me, we haven't been properly introduced."

Vivienne cast a look of desperation at Kathy. "I can't believe how rude I've been."

Kathy extended her hand to Sally and shook it vigorously. "Karen Monroe, I'm so pleased to meet you."

Sally smiled. "Do you work at one of the television stations? You look sort of familiar. Are you an anchor for the Syracuse news?"

"Oh, people say that all the time but I'm not in the media." Kathy smiled back. "I'm Vera's lesbian partner."

Sally pulled her hand back quickly. "Oh, my."

Vivienne felt her face flush red with embarrassment. "Karen," she spoke through a forced smile, "you really needn't be so forward."

"Why not?" Kathy played back with glee. "Isn't this one of your ex-girlfriends? There are so many I just can't keep track. I thought you dated a Sally in the past?"

Sally stepped back, clutching her necklace. "Heavens no. Why would you think that? I'm a good Christian woman."

Kathy shrugged. "I know her type and you fit it perfectly, sister."

"I'm not a lesbian." Sally could barely get the words out of her mouth. "I'm normal."

"Oh, then I beg your pardon." Kathy grinned and batted her eyes at Vivienne. "I'm ashamed to admit that I'm kind of the jealous type."

Vivienne looked down at the floor, playing along with the ruse. "Yes, you really need to work on that when we're out in public."

Sally glanced down at her watch and let out a little gasp. "I've got to hit the road." She reached into her purse and pulled out an obnoxiously long keychain that had a pink-haired good luck troll dangling off the end. "The kids will be hollering like little banshees if I'm late getting dinner on the table."

"It was great meeting you." Kathy waved with a huge smile. "Maybe we can all meet sometime soon for drinks?"

Sally hurried toward the exit as fast as her scuffed flats could carry here. "I don't think so. The holidays are so hectic and all." She opened her mouth to say something else, but changed her mind and disappeared into the cold wind outside.

"That was brilliant." Vivienne marveled. "I really should have taken you with me to the trailer park that day."

"She wasn't going to let you out of her sight in here." Kathy reasoned. "I had to come up with something that would make her uncomfortable enough to leave."

"Well, that worked like a charm." Vivienne replied. "I wish I could lie so casually."

"That's why I'm here." Kathy grinned and wrapped her arm around Vivienne's waist. "Stick with me, babe. I'll have you up to speed in no time." She winked.

The line slowly wound around the edge of the room where an open casket holding the body of Eddie Robertson was flanked with two rather lackluster displays of black and white carnations that said 'bereaved on a budget' quite noticeably.

Natalie was standing off to the side, wearing a simple black dress and a pair of sensible heels that she had kicked off to side to be more comfortable on the carpet. She looked pale and gaunt, her fine black hair pulled back into a simple pony tail. Seated on the floor near her, Connor, dressed in a little navy blue suit, was engrossed in a game of chase with a pair of toy cars that he pushed around the legs of the folding chairs nearby.

Kathy reached out and offered her hand to Natalie. "I'm sorry for your loss."

Natalie barely seemed to notice her. "Thank you." She spoke back, her voice barely a whisper.

Kathy stepped aside and allowed Vivienne a moment to share with Natalie. "Your son is just precious."

"Thank you." Natalie repeated.

"I'm sorry for your loss." Vivienne felt awkward using the standard opening line as she faced Natalie.

Natalie squinted as she tried to place Vivienne. "Thank you." She spoke softly.

"How are you holding up?"

"One day at a time." Natalie answered. "I wish we had the innocence bliss of children, though." She gestured to Connor.

Vivienne paused for a moment before the casket. The conservative suit that had been a burial staple for years was missing. Eddie was dressed in a light blue bowling shirt and a pair of dark denim pants. In the front pocket of his shirt, a photo of Natalie and Connor embracing was sticking out. "He was so young."

Natalie's eyes widened as recognition set it. "I remember you now. You were at the gingerbread house competition."

"Yes. We met outside the bathroom." Vivienne confirmed. She reached into her purse and pulled out the envelope with the prize money in it. "You won a prize that night."

Natalie accepted the envelope and looked inside of it. "I did?"

"I'm sure you could use it now." Vivienne added.

"You are so kind." Natalie's eyes filled with tears that began to run down her cheeks. "I'm sorry I didn't recognize you sooner but all this has been such a shock."

Vivienne opened her arms for a hug. "That's perfectly okay."

"It's all been such a blur since we left the hospital." Natalie dabbed at her eyes with a crumpled tissue that was nearly soaked through. "I keep thinking it's just a bad dream I'm going to wake up from."

"I can't say that I know what you're going though because I haven't." Vivienne tried to comfort her. "But, you have my deepest sympathies for your loss and if you ever need someone to talk things over with, my bakery is right on Main Street. It feels like I spend more time there than at my actual home."

"You're the Deputy's girlfriend, aren't you?"

"That's right." Vivienne smiled. "He wanted to be here too, but he's been held over at work tonight."

Natalie glanced at Eddie's body in the casket. "He was very kind to both of us during the police questioning."

"He's very good at his job." Vivienne added. "The town is lucky to have him."

Natalie nodded and sniffed back some tears. "Eddie was never a great man or even a good boyfriend." She placed her hand on the simple polished wood edge of the casket. "He did provide for us when he had to, though."

"I'm sorry to hear that." Vivienne felt a bit uneasy at the turn the conversation was taking. "I'm sure he cared for both of you deeply but was one of those guys who just couldn't show it."

"No." Natalie countered. "He was just Eddie. What you saw was what you got. He wasn't particularly deep."

"I've taken up enough of your time." Vivienne gestured to the line of people waiting behind her and Kathy.

Natalie leaned in with her embrace and Vivienne felt an ice-cold chill seize her chest. The room began to swirl and then everything faded to black.

She next felt a hard slap belt her across the face. The room was dark, but could make out a simple wooden table and some chairs as her eyes began to adjust.

"You think I don't know what you did?" A man's voice growled at her. "Do you think me that naïve?"

Vivienne instinctively put her hands up toward her face to ward off another blow. "Stop it."

Her hands were pulled away and she was twisted sharply so her back was to her captor. "You stupid woman, I've risked everything for us. He's not even my son."

Vivienne tried to look at her captor, but she was unable to move. She could see now that she was in a rather large kitchen in an older-style home.

She felt something like a belt twist around her wrists. "What are you doing?" She asked.

"I'm taking care of this myself." The voice replied and pulled the straps tight. "Stupid woman."

Vivienne dropped to her knees with a thud and then was kicked in the rear so that she pitched forward to the floor, banging her nose against the wooden boards. She heard his heavy footfalls trail off as she lay there in a daze.

She could taste the salty tinge of blood in her mouth, as she rolled over to her side and saw what looked like the scattered remains of a breakfast all around her. Shattered plates smeared with egg yolk, silverware, and a red-hot skillet that was scorching the wooden floor. As she craned her neck, she could see Natalie's reflection in a large serving spoon that was upended. Her eyes were blackened from bruising, her lips caked with blood and swollen.

The heavy footfalls returned and she tried to free her arms. She could hear the cry of an infant in the distance as she tried to pick herself from the floor without success. "Please don't hurt me." She pleaded.

She was struck on the back of the head and everything went black. "Vivienne?" A kinder sounding male voice sounded out. "Can you hear me?"

She grunted in response.

"I think she's coming around now." The kind male voice returned.

"She's getting her color back." A female voice joined in.

Vivienne opened her eyes and everything was so bright she forced them shut with a groan.

"That's it." Kathy's voice appeared. "Come on, girl, climb out of it."

"Is she diabetic?" The friendly male voice asked.

Vivienne groaned once more and opened her eyes. "I'm not diabetic."

Kathy smiled at her from above. "There you are. You gave us quite a scare."

The visage of James Fritz suddenly swooped into view next to Kathy. "I called the paramedics just to be safe." His brown eyes were kind, his receding black hair groomed into a pleasant style that displayed the slight graying around his temples.

"I don't need them." Vivienne was surprised to find herself reclined on one of the fancy sofas in the funeral parlor. "I just pushed myself too hard at the bakery today and skipped lunch."

Kathy and James reached out and pulled her upright. "You should probably have them check you out." Kathy added with a touch of concern in her voice.

"I'm fine, honest." Vivienne shook off the fuzzy feeling from her experience and gave a weak smile. "I just need a few minutes and maybe a glass of water."

"I'll get that." James patted her gently on the hand and rushed off.

"So much for not drawing attention." Kathy spoke softly.

"Where is everyone?" Vivienne asked as she looked around the empty room. With the crowd dispersed, she could hear the rhythmic ticking of all the antique clocks.

"They're at the memorial service at Bistro Parisian. James thought it best to move everyone over there in case the medics needed room to work on you."

"How long was I out?"

Kathy looked over at one of the clocks. "For about a ten minutes at least. You were so still we thought you had dropped dead. But then you started mumbling gibberish and James had you moved into here and called the paramedics."

They could hear the front door open with a bang. "Kathy? Vivienne?" Joshua's voice called out.

"In here." Kathy shouted back.

Joshua flew into the room, his eyes wild with a

mixture of adrenaline and fear. "Are you okay? Selma heard the call go out over the radio and told me you were in trouble." He rushed over to her side and plopped next to her on the sofa.

"I'm fine, Joshua. I don't need the paramedics." She motioned him closer and whispered in his ear. "I saw Natalie getting beat up. She was hurt pretty bad."

Joshua raised an eyebrow. "So Eddie really was a bad guy?" He whispered back.

"I think so. It was hard to see what was really going on."

Kathy folded her arms across her chest. "They'll be here any minute. Just let them check you out to be sure."

The sound of the siren could be heard echoing off the buildings on the street outside. Joshua nodded to her. "I think that's a good idea."

Vivienne sighed and shook her head. "Fine, they can check me out but I'm telling you both it's nothing."

"Let the medicals guys decide that." Kathy added as James stepped back into the room with a glass of water.

She took the glass into her grip and sipped generously. The water soothed her throat, which was a tad sore. "Thank you, James."

Red and blue lights lit up the windows around them as the ambulance arrived. "I'll bring them in." He said and rushed off.

"You certainly know how to pep up a deadly slow evening." Kathy joked.

"Really?" Vivienne groaned at the pun.

"I'm sorry I wasn't here." Joshua added. "But I've got some rather distressing news."

"What now?" Vivienne asked.

Joshua reached into his pants pocket and pulled out a green paper. "Looks like the bad Santa notes are back. I found this stuck to my car windshield when I rushed over to see you. Looks like they're appearing all over town again."

"Oh, great." Kathy spoke up. "Just what we need after this."

"Who is the note about this time?" Vivienne asked.

Before he could answer, James rushed into the room. "The paramedics just got called away on an emergency call. Eunice Kilpatrick was just struck down by a car in front of the Bistro Parisian."

Joshua handed the note to Vivienne where Eunice Kilpatrick's name was written with a flourish.

CHAPTER 10

Saturday, December 7th

Y*ou better not cry! Eunice Kilpatrick, you are a mean-spirited old woman who delights in the misfortunes of your fellow friends and neighbors.* *You pretend to care, you give a shoulder to cry on, yet you are counting the minutes until you can spread gossip and add your spin. Santa is watching you. He sees you when you raise your nose in the air, as if you are so far above the other folks in town. The trouble with keeping your head held so high is that you fail to see what's coming right before you. You've been warned. Santa Claus.*

Vivienne read the note for a third time, as she sipped her morning coffee at the kitchen table. Tommy curled around her ankles, wrapping his tail around her legs as he bumped his head against her for more treats. "Not right now. You've just had breakfast." She warned him.

He meowed back at her, one of his lower tones that informed her that he was a little annoyed that she wasn't catering to his needs.

"Go play with that paper bag I gave you last night." She reached down and stroked the top of his furry head.

"Yes, ma'am." Joshua spoke as he stepped into the kitchen wearing only his blue plaid boxers and a plain white tee shirt.

Vivienne looked up and smiled at him. "Not you." She teased.

He sat down in the chair facing her and pointed to the green note in her hand. "Please tell me you found out something that is going to help."

"I'm at a loss." Vivienne conceded.

"In your vision, you're positive it was Natalie being attacked?" Joshua asked.

"Yes." Vivienne shuddered as she recalled the terrible feeling of being attacked. "I saw her reflection." She paused for a moment as she replayed the terrible vision in her mind. "There was the sound of a baby crying in the background, so it had to be a few years ago when Connor was an infant."

"Was she with Eddie back then?" Joshua wondered.

"I don't think so." Vivienne scratched her chin in deep thought. "The voice of the attacker was male, but it deeper and more nasty." She recalled the feeling of his hands as he grabbed her and began to bind her arms. "The hands were rough, very worn. Like someone who'd done lots of manual labor during his lifetime. That definitely wasn't Eddie."

"That's for sure." Joshua agreed. "So perhaps it was an ex-husband or boyfriend?"

"We need to find out some information about Eddie's background." Vivienne agreed. "Can you run a check at the station?"

"I think Sheriff Rigsbee already did during the early part of the investigation. I'll go take a look at it and see what I can find out."

Vivienne stared at the letter on the table again and scowled. "We still have the mystery of these bad Santa letters to solve too."

"I think we can rule out Natalie because she didn't even know Eunice." Joshua added as he began to thumb through the morning paper. "So there's a start."

"Eunice certainly has made more than her fair share of enemies over the years in Cayuga Cove." Vivienne agreed. "But I don't think any of them would want to run her down."

"She's a tough old bird." Joshua replied as he pulled out the sports section. "Run down by a car on Main Street and she ends up with two broken legs and a sprained wrist. It could have been much worse."

"I still can't believe no one saw the car that hit her." Vivienne set the note down on the table and stared at it some more. "Whoever is doing this knows exactly when to strike. They must keep close tabs on their subject."

"The preliminary autopsy report is due to come in this morning from Rochester." Joshua reached out and gently held her hand across the table. "Maybe we'll have some answers from that."

"I hope so. These notes are really starting to terrorize the town."

"Don't worry." Joshua reassured her. "I'm not going to let anything happen to you."

"It's not me I'm worried about." Vivienne added.

Joshua pulled her hand up to his lips and kissed it gently. "I love you."

"I love you too." She smiled back and then looked at the wall clock. "I better get a shower and go in early. Stephanie and I have a wedding cake to start today."

The telephone rang, piercing the quiet of the house with a shrill tone. Vivienne jumped up from the table and wandered over to the base where the caller information was displayed. It was Kathy. She picked up the receiver. "You're up awful early."

"What can I say? Having a psychopath wandering the streets of Cayuga Cove has got me a little nervous these days."

"I slept pretty well last night." Vivienne smiled at Joshua and made a little kissy face.

"That's because you had a big strong man with you, Vivienne Finch."

"Yes, I did."

"Some of us aren't that lucky. On behalf of the sleep-deprived, I say this." Kathy replied with coarse sound of blowing a raspberry into the phone.

Vivienne laughed. "Was there another reason you called?"

"Actually, yes. Do you want to swing by the hospital today and visit Eunice?" Kathy wondered.

"Well, this is a change. I thought you couldn't stand her?"

"Don't get me wrong, she's a miserable old wretch who has cheated me at the bank more times than I can count." Kathy countered. "But, given the season, I still feel the need to see how she is doing."

"Did you get visited be three ghosts last night?"

"If I did I would have paid them to stand guard so I could get some descent shut eye."

Vivienne laughed. "I have some extra whoopie pies. Stephanie mentioned she stopped in the bakery the other day and bought one. Why don't we bring her a few in a little basket?"

"That sounds good." Kathy replied. "I'll tuck in one of my floral print scarves too."

"I really need to shower and get to the bakery.

Want to meet at the hospital snack bar for a quick lunch and then visit?" Vivienne asked.

"Sounds good. See you around noon." Kathy finished and hung up.

"What was that all about?" Joshua asked.

Vivienne set the phone back on the receiver and shook her head. "She'd never admit it, but I think Kathy feels sorry for Eunice."

"Are you serious?" Joshua wandered over to the counter and poured himself a mug of coffee. "She can't stand the woman."

"I know it sounds crazy, but I think sometimes Kathy sees Eunice as a cautionary tale of what her life could become in a worst-case scenario."

Joshua opened the fridge, pulled out a carton of milk, and poured in a generous amount that threatened to spill over the rim of the mug. "They're nothing alike."

"Kathy is pretty forward and she sometimes gets away with outrageous things because of her uncanny knack for flirting her way out of some tricky situations. But she knows, eventually, that defensive measure isn't going to always work. Then she'll just be another bitter old woman mad who is mad at the world. That's where the whole psychology of how her possible future fits in." Vivienne reasoned. "Why didn't I go to school to become a psychologist?"

"Because you hate all the red tape and paperwork that goes along with the medical field." Joshua surmised. "I mean, you were just complaining about changing insurance and having to fill out a new medical form at the dentist last month."

Vivienne thought for a moment and nodded in

agreement. "You're right."

"I wish this case were as easy to crack." Joshua grumbled as he stirred his coffee with a spoon.

* * *

"We're here to see Eunice Kilpatrick." Kathy smiled at the volunteer who was working the front desk at Cayuga Memorial Hospital, a pleasant looking woman with a bun of grey hair and a nametag that identified her as 'Helen'.

"Are you friends or family?" Helen asked back.

Vivienne was happy to see that the lobby of the hospital was decorated with seasonal cheer. Garland, white lights, and silver and gold ornaments were strung up around the many windows facing Peddler Parkway, where traffic raced by at the higher speed limit of forty miles per hour. "We're friends." Vivienne replied.

Helen glanced at computer screen and then back up at them. "I'm sorry, Ms. Kilpatrick's family has requested no visitors outside of family. Would you like me to have that basket delivered?"

"Family?" Kathy was shocked. "She has family?"

Helen grimaced. "I'm not allowed to say anything without authorization. Privacy rules and such."

Vivienne glanced at Kathy, the basket heavy in her grip. "Well, we had a good lunch at least."

"Can you call up to her room and tell her that Kathy Saunders and Vivienne Finch are here to see her? I'm sure she'll want to see us in person."

Helen shook her head. "I'm sorry ladies. I really can't help you any further."

"Well, bah humbug to you too." Kathy grumbled and stomped over to the exit.

Vivienne rushed to catch up with her. "She's just following the rules here. She could lose her job if she tells us something that's not authorized."

"This is just another example of how screwed up the world is today. I mean, lawyers have got everyone so paranoid about every little detail of their lives, you can't even visit a sick friend without getting the third degree." She fumed.

"Wow. I didn't realize not seeing Eunice would be such a tragedy." Vivienne set the basket down on one of the hard plastic chairs that lined the lobby. "What's going on?"

"Nothing." Kathy snapped quickly. "I'm just on edge with all this nonsense."

"Why don't we tuck a note in the basket and leave it reception? If Eunice wants to see us, she can call down and put us on the visitor list."

"I guess so." Kathy seemed to calm down. "Just when you think…" Her voice trailed off.

"What did you say?" Vivienne asked.

"Stay right here." Kathy raised a finger and then dashed off toward the elevators and tapped a young blonde girl who was dressed in a soft-pink volunteer uniform on the shoulder. As she turned to talk to Kathy, Vivienne recognized that it was Alexis, the new waitress at Clara's.

Kathy engaged the young girl in conversation, used a few hand gestures toward the volunteer desk, and then reached into her purse and pulled out something she kept hidden in her palm. Alexis quickly stuffed whatever it was into the pocket of her uniform and then strolled briskly toward the reception desk.

Kathy sauntered back over to Vivienne with a grin on her face. "So the old saying was right. A window just opened." She practically cooed.

"What did you do?"

Kathy leaned close and whispered. "It turns out that she volunteers here a few hours a week to earn her community involvement program credits from the college."

Vivienne knew about the credits. Lakeshore Community College had put into place a program to offer a tuition discount to any student that volunteered at least four hours a week at various agencies throughout the community. Stephanie assisted at the local animal shelter as part of her credits. She often brought pet adoption posters in to the bakery to try to help place pets in family homes. "So why is she helping us?"

"I asked nicely and she remembered all the big tips I have left for her lately." Kathy smiled.

"What if she gets caught?" Vivienne worried.

"She's a smart girl." Kathy smiled. "I wouldn't worry about that."

"Did you pay her off?" Vivienne began to worry about her friend's ethics.

"Of course not." Kathy seemed genuinely insulted at the question.

"I saw you give her something." Vivienne folded her arms. "What was it then?"

"My business card." Kathy replied flatly.

"What else?"

"I promised her fifty percent off an outfit or

accessory at my store of her choosing." Kathy finished.

Vivienne picked up the basket and stared at the whoopie pies inside. "I sure hope this doesn't create a scandal. If the college found out, they could expel her."

"No money changed hands so it's not a bribe." Kathy explained. "We're not breaking the law."

"I think we are bending it a little." Vivienne watched nervously as Alexis talked with Helen at the front desk and then accessed the computer database. She then wrote something on a piece of paper and walked away toward the gift shop.

"Looks like she didn't have any luck." Vivienne sighed. "Let's go."

Kathy put her hand on Vivienne's arm and held her in place. "Just a second."

Alexis walked over to a trash can and carelessly missed throwing the paper into the bin. It tumbled off to the side as she disappeared into the double doors that led to the pediatric ward.

"Come on." Kathy pulled Vivienne along as they hustled past the reception desk where Helen eyed them suspiciously.

They reached the trash can where Kathy opened her purse and began to toss a few scraps of paper into the bin, missing two or three pieces which tumbled onto the floor. "Oh, drat." She knelt down and grabbed the paper Alexis had left for them. After a quick glance she slipped it into her purse and whispered to Vivienne. "She's in room 508."

"So how do we get there?" Vivienne looked over at Helen who kept them in her field of vision.

"She's suspicious of us already."

"Just play it cool." Kathy added. "When she gets swamped, we just slip by."

Vivienne looked at her wrist watch. "It's almost quarter to one. I told Stephanie I wouldn't be late today."

"She'll be fine." Kathy hushed her and sat down in one of the chairs.

Vivienne sat down beside her. Some soothing orchestral music played softly from speakers in the ceiling above them and for a moment, she relished the peace. "Why are you so certain that there's going to be a sudden crowd?"

Kathy pointed toward the windows where two large vans pulled up slowly along the curb, each packed to the gills with the faces of boy and girl scouts. "How's that for a reason?"

The children began to file out of the vans in neat lines, heading for the automatic doors. "Oh, I see." Vivienne remarked as the first wave of excited faces stomped their feet on the rubber mats, knocking clumps of dirty snow out of boots and shoes.

Vivienne tried to look casual, but she could feel her cheeks reddening. She didn't like all this sneaking around and hoped that she wasn't setting up another situation where Joshua was going to have to explain to the sheriff why she was somewhere she shouldn't be.

The children hurried into the lobby carrying homemade paper ornaments and cards. Several chaperones were trying their best to keep their conversations down to an acceptable level, but the excitement of a field trip just proved too much.

"Go for the elevators." Kathy ordered like a general directing troops on the battlefield.

Vivienne could see that Helen was suddenly overwhelmed with the group of children and was soon surrounded on all sides by a colorful horde of puffy jackets, knit hats, and woolen mittens. She pressed the call button three times as Kathy waited impatiently behind her.

Just as one of the scout leader's raised his voice to quiet the group down, the elevator chimed and the doors slid open. Vivienne and Kathy rushed inside and pressed the five key.

Once on the fifth floor, it was a simple matter to find Eunice's room. As they neared the nurse's station, they were relieved to find it unmanned. "This way." Kathy led them both down a hallway and stopped outside room 508. From inside the double room, they could hear a television program squawking from one of the bedside speakers. Kathy popped head into the room and noticed a petite member of the blue rinse crowd crocheting happily away on the first bed. "Hello there." Kathy said sweetly.

"Are you looking for me?" The little lady smiled hopefully.

"No, I'm here to see my friend Eunice." Kathy glanced around the room.

"I'm Delores." She replied. "Your friend is on the other side of the curtain."

"Thank you." Kathy replied as she walked slowly toward the other side of the curtain divider.

"Are you here to see me?" Delores asked Vivienne as she followed behind Kathy.

"Well, I'm here to see our friend Eunice too." Vivienne replied. "But I can visit with you if you'd like for a few minutes."

Delores' face brightened and she reached over with shaky hands to turn off the television. "Really?"

Kathy peeked around the curtain and then looked at Vivienne with concern. "She's asleep."

Delores pointed to the basket in Vivienne's hands with a metal crochet needle. "Is that for me?"

"Do you like peppermint?" Vivienne asked.

Delores nodded. "My Leroy used to buy me peppermint sticks when we were teenagers."

"Eunice." Kathy spoke softly trying to rouse her. "Eunice?"

Vivienne reached into the basket and pulled out a chocolate peppermint whoopie pie. She set it on the bedside stand. "I don't know if the nurses would agree with this for your dietary plan, but I won't tell if you won't."

Delores smiled and picked up the dessert. She gave it a quick smell and closed her eyes. "I never get tired of that. I can almost see Norman's Malt Shop if I think hard enough."

"Are you from Cayuga Cove?" Vivienne asked.

Delores took a small bite of the confection and shook her head. "I was born and raised in Rhode Island. I didn't move here until my husband died about fifteen years ago."

Kathy re-appeared from behind the curtain. "It's no use. She won't wake up."

"How does she look?" Vivienne asked.

"Bruised and battered." Kathy's voice was low. "But alive."

Delores swallowed and looked up at Kathy. "She hasn't been awake at all."

Kathy looked at Vivienne. "The whole time?"

Delores set the whoopie pie down on the bedside stand and cleaned her hands off with a tissue. "They brought her in the other day but she just sleeps all the time. Haven't heard a word out of her."

"Has she had any visitors?" Vivienne asked.

"Just her brother. He's tall, with salt and pepper hair and is always dressed very conservatively in a suit and tie. Very proper looking." Delores explained.

"Did he tell you his name?" Kathy asked.

Delores thought for a moment. "Pastor Kilpatrick. He said he drove all the way from West Virginia."

Vivienne shrugged at Kathy. "I didn't even know she had a brother."

Delores took a sip of water and then licked her lips. "He seemed nice and all, but he kept pestering me about saving my soul. Asking me if I walked in the light with Jesus."

"Has he been in to visit today?" Kathy asked.

"Not that I remember." Delores smiled at Vivienne. "It's easy to lose track of the time in here."

"What are you here for, Delores?" Vivienne asked.

"My heart, dear." Delores wrapped the rest of the whoopie pie in another tissue and set it off to the side with a small stack of magazines. "It's been filled with joy, it's been broken by sorrow, and now it's winding down." She gave a little sigh. "Leroy and I never did have children so everyone I ever loved is gone now."

Kathy's eyes blinked a few times as she fought back tears. "You're all alone?"

"When I was a little girl, I remember wishing on many a star to live to be a hundred." Delores spoke softly. "I shouldn't complain after ninety-five years, but I really wish I had added in a part about having someone with me until then."

Vivienne reached out and took Delores' hand in hers. "I would be happy to call you a friend, Delores. My name is Vivienne and I run a little bakery downtown."

"I wish I could see it." Delores smiled.

Kathy reached into her purse and pulled out her cell phone. "I have pictures on my phone if you'd like to see them."

They sat with her for almost an hour, before leaving with the promise to return every Monday for a visit. As Eunice dozed quietly in the next bed, she remained unaware of the circle of friends around her. Like most blessings, they didn't announce themselves with great fanfare or trumpets. They just happened during the routine of an ordinary day.

CHAPTER 11

Joshua set a thick folder down on the marble topped table in the kitchen of the Sweet Dreams Bakery. "You're not going to believe this. Eddie Robertson died of hydroxybenzene poisoning."

Vivienne set the bowl of wet sugar cookie ingredients down onto her large stand mixer with a thud and locked it in place. "I have no idea what that is, but it sounds an awful lot like murder to me."

Joshua opened the folder with the autopsy report and proceeded to recite what the medical examiner had written. "Trauma to vascular and respiratory centers suggests paralysis due to oxidation. Blood of exceedingly dark color with poor coagulating factor. Severe damage to esophagus, stomach, and intestinal lining suggests acute gastroenteritis due to long-term duration of exposure to phenol." He scanned the next few lines and shook his head. "There's more technical terms here that I don't even want to attempt to pronounce."

"Someone poisoned him for a few weeks." Vivienne turned the mixer on low. "So that means that the killer has been here in Cayuga Cove for some time now."

"Yes." Joshua agreed.

"Can you write some of that down on my notepad?"

Joshua looked over the table where sheets of recipes were scattered and pulled a yellow tablet out from under a stack of wire-bound cookbooks with vintage pictures of holiday cookies from the 50's and

60's on the cover. "Sure thing." He scribbled down the basics and did his best to make it legible.

"Did you find out why Natalie was ruled out as a suspect?" Vivienne asked him as he scanned the report with his index finger and copied more information down.

"She cooperated fully with an investigation of her home right after the incident. Nothing was found that suggested foul play." Joshua explained as he finished his brief notes. "You've got the basics now."

As the mixing paddles churned the butter, sugar, eggs, and vanilla extract, Vivienne added the dry ingredients in small increments. "Did anyone suspect poisoning during the initial investigation?"

"No."

Vivienne raised the speed of the mixer up one notch as the dough began to form. "Is Sheriff Rigsbee going to re-examine the scene again?"

"They're doing it now. That's why I was able to sneak this report over to you." Joshua added. "Speaking of which, I need to get back to the station." He closed the report and tucked it beside his hip. "How's Eunice doing?"

"She's stable but has been unconscious the entire time." Vivienne replied as she turned off the mixer and tipped the paddles back to inspect the cookie dough. "Did you know she has a brother?"

"I did not." Joshua leaned forward and gave her a kiss. "But then again, she and I barely spoke."

"Well, he just came into town after the accident. Her roommate at the hospital met him briefly. Said he was a Pastor."

"I'm glad she has someone to watch over her after

the accident."

"Me too." Vivienne agreed. "I'm looking forward to meeting him soon." She stared at his deputy uniform for a moment and then brushed away a few crumbles of flour. "Can't have you looking a mess going back to the station."

"Are you going to be working late tonight?"

She glanced at the stack of slips that were waiting to be started on the order board. "I'll have Stephanie for a few hours this afternoon so not too terribly late. I should be home no later than six thirty or seven. Why do you ask?"

"Late dinner? I was thinking of takeout from Shanghai Sunset."

"Sounds perfect. I'll shoot you a text when I'm about a half hour from locking up. That way the food will be nice and hot when you bring it over."

"Our usual order?"

Vivienne thought for a moment and nodded. "Could you add some spring rolls in too? I've been craving them lately for some reason."

Joshua waved goodbye and strolled out the door just as two customers pushed their way in with holiday order forms in their hands. 'It's going to be a long day.' Vivienne thought as she greeted them from behind the counter with a smile.

* * *

As the sun slipped lower on the horizon, Vivienne couldn't help but stare at the information Joshua had written on the notepad. Giving in to her inquisitive mind, she asked Stephanie if she would mind closing up alone as she could use the last hour to conduct some research at the public library to find out more information about this hydroxybenzene poisoning that had been Eddie's ultimate undoing.

Harriet Nettles was thrilled as Vivienne stepped into the front entrance and stopped at the circulation desk. "Vivienne Finch, I'm so glad you stopped by today." She gushed. "The bake sale was a huge success and I wanted to personally thank you for your help with the tea selections. The library board was so impressed, they want to start a monthly afternoon tea and book discussion club."

"That's wonderful, Harriet." Vivienne loved the smell of old books that filled the air. There was just something about it that made her feel so at ease and eager to soak up knowledge.

"I'll be stopping by after the New Year holiday to talk more about it when the board comes up with a budget." Harriet adjusted her gold wire-rimmed glasses so that the bifocals were properly lined up in her field of vision. "What brings you here today?"

"I was wondering if you could point me in the right direction to look up some medical information?"

Harriet straightened her back and pivoted her office chair toward the desktop computer that was in front of her. "Sure. What do you need?"

Vivienne pulled out the notepad from her purse and set it on the desk. "Hydroxybenzene poisoning."

"Could you spell that?"

Vivienne handed the yellow notepad to Harriet. "This will make it easier."

Harriet typed in the name and then scanned the screen as information scrolled down. "There's quite a bit of information here. Did you want to add anything else in with your search to narrow it down a little?"

Vivienne thought for a moment. "Could you cross-reference Cayuga Cove?"

Harriet nodded back. "This new system has made finding information so much easier these days." She waited for the query to yield the new results. "Everyone just hops onto the internet and finds things on their own these days. But the problem is, not everything on there is factual."

"I agree." Vivienne thought back to her days in school having to write a paper on some random subject. Having to learn to use a card catalog and understand the Dewey Decimal System.

"Here we go. It looks like I found quite a few cemetery records that match your query."

"So, other people have died from this?" Vivienne leaned forward to try and read the information on the screen.

"Not recently. Most of these records are from the late 1800's. Let me print you a copy." Harriet sent the information to the printer. "Do you want a medical encyclopedia for symptoms and signs of this type of poisoning?"

"That'd be great." Vivienne smiled, finally feeling as if she were getting somewhere. "I knew you'd be able to find what I needed."

Harriet pulled the paper from the printer.

"Okay, the cemetery records are stored on disc up in the genealogy section on the second floor. You can use the terminals up there to find and print what you need as the actual books are not stored here."

Vivienne nodded. "I can do that."

Harriet printed another document and handed that to Vivienne. "Now, the medical encyclopedia is on this floor. If you want to head upstairs, I'll locate it and bring it up."

'That'd be great."

"We're only open for another half hour, so I thought I'd save you some time." Harriet glanced at the clock on the wall which read four-thirty.

"Thanks. I'll get right on it." Vivienne hurried to the staircase that led upstairs, forgoing the elevator ride and figuring the extra burned calories would help offset the extra holiday calories that invaded her hips every winter.

Upon reaching the top level, she caught movement out of the corner of her eye as another patron pulled a book off a shelf and disappeared into the long rows of bookcases that lined the carpeted floors. The roof of the old building had been retro-fitted with modern skylights to allow natural light to fill the space, saving money on the electric bills. But, in the winter months, the sunlight was weaker and it gave a rather dim pallor to the upper level that made one want to gravitate to one of the nice walnut tables where brass reading lamps glowed softly.

The genealogy department was walled off with office partitions that could easily be converted to cubicles in a different setting. Here, they simply were arranged around a cluster of four computer terminals that were much less modern than the sleek touch screen at Harriet's desk. Basic metal shelving was installed where sleeves of data discs were arranged by years and grouped by cemetery. Vivienne set her purse down at the nearest computer and stared at the paper in her hand. Most of the records were located at the Cayuga Union Cemetery, which was not that far from the trailer park where Natalie, Connor, and Eddie called home. The earliest death linked with her search was 1856, but there appeared to be many more associated with the years 1872 and 1873. She decided to start with those discs and see what information she could find.

After locating and loading the discs into the computer, she scanned through the records. All of the deaths were listed as carbolic acid poisoning, but she saw no mention of hydroxybenzene. Rather than write them all down, she selected a bunch of records and sent them to the printer. She was about to ask Harriet if there had been a mistake when there was the sudden clap of a heavy book hitting the floor nearby. Vivienne nearly jumped out of her chair, turning around to see who had caused the commotion. She expected to see the patron whom she had glimpsed a few minutes earlier, red-faced and apologetic, but the upstairs was quit empty.

"Are you okay Vivienne?" Harriet called out as she ascended the stairs and appeared at the top of the landing with a rather thick book in her hands.

"I was going to ask you the same thing." Vivienne felt relieved to see Harriet.

"What'd you drop up here?"

"It wasn't me." Vivienne shook her head and pointed to the fiction area several feet away from them. "It must have been the other person up here."

Harriet walked over and set the book down on the table next to Vivienne's purse with a thud. "Other person?"

"Yes, someone was up here when I first came up." Vivienne shrugged. "I only saw them from the corner of my eye."

Harriet shook her head. "There's no one else here but the two of us. It's been empty all afternoon."

"I could have sworn I saw someone else up here." Vivienne squinted in the dim light.

Harriet smiled. "It can get a little spooky up here in the late afternoons. Sometimes I think I see people moving amongst the shelves too, but it's just a trick of the light."

Vivienne scratched her chin. "Was whatever fell a trick of the light also?"

Harriet shook her head. "People shove books back on the shelves in the wrong spots all the time. It was probably just waiting to fall and when you walked up here it finally did."

"If you say so." Vivienne felt a little chill pass through the air.

"Vivienne Finch, don't tell me you think it's a ghost."

Vivienne wanted to tell her it was entirely possible, but she knew better than to do that. "Well, I'm guessing probably not."

"Now that woman opening that peculiar store downtown, I'd expect her to think that."

"You mean Miss Octavia?" Vivienne asked.

Harriet snapped her thin fingers. "Yes, that's the one. She looks quite eccentric, but I must confess I found her personality to be quite ebullient."

Vivienne smiled knowing how much Harriet enjoyed using uncommon words to describe people and places. There wasn't a crossword puzzle invented that she couldn't solve. "Has she been in here recently?"

"She was, as a matter of fact. Wanted me to locate some books on myths and folklore." Harriet recalled. "I wasn't at all surprised at her request."

"I had a chance to talk to her and look around her shop. She's really making it a diamond in the rough, given the location."

"Magic and spells, just pure nonsense." Harriet's voice sounded like a school teacher correcting a student who completed a report with information from sketchy internet sources. "I don't know who in their right mind is going to shop at a place that peddles superstitious mumbo jumbo."

"Well, you just never know." Vivienne tried to be diplomatic. "So, you said she was looking for information on folklore. Did she say anything else?"

Harriet shrugged. "Not that I recall."

Vivienne had a feeling it may have been information on werewolf mythology. "Do you think you could locate that book for me too?"

"I could but I thought you were looking up medical information?" Harriet adjusted her glasses once more as they had slipped down the narrow bridge of her nose.

"I am, but you just got me thinking about adding in searches about folk remedies for accidental poisonings and such." Vivienne wished that Kathy could have been there to see how easily the lie had rolled off her tongue.

"Oh, that's a clever idea." Harriet clapped her hands together. "I'll go down and look it up."

Vivienne watched as Harriet pivoted on her flats

and hurried away, powered by the lure of chasing information. Seizing the moment, she crept over to the area where she was certain she had seen the other patron. She walked quickly between rows, looking left and right for any sign of the visitor or a fallen book that had made such a racket. She had nearly reached the far corner when another crash erupted from the genealogy area.

Her heart raced in her chest as she sprinted back hoping to catch the culprit. She nearly collided at the top of the staircase with Harriet, who herself had raced upstairs. "Vivienne, what are you doing up here?"

"It wasn't me." Vivienne protested. "I was over at the other end of the room looking for whatever made the sound the first time."

Harriet folded her arms across her chest. "Is this some kind of joke you're playing?"

"Harriet, I'd never do something like that to you."

Harriet was about to say something else when she pointed to the work stations and gasped. "Look at this mess." Vivienne's purse, the medical encyclopedia, several discs, and the chair were haphazardly strewn as if someone had just knocked everything off the table with a sweep of an arm.

Vivienne hurried over and began to pick up the items when her hand stopped over a book with a green cover and the title 'Mythology and folklore of early American settlers.' She quickly shoved it into her purse before Harriet could notice it and raise more questions. "I think it's some kids in here playing a prank."

"What is wrong with kids today?" Harriet spoke

softly as she surveyed the scene with a bit of anger. She placed her hands upon her hips and shouted in her best annoyed librarian voice, the kind she reserved for children's story hour whenever their attention spans waned. "Whoever is doing this is going to get a free ride to the Sheriff's office tonight."

"She's not joking." Vivienne added to the threat.

Harriet shivered suddenly. "Did you feel that? Is a window open up here?"

Vivienne shrugged. "I don't think so."

Harriet turned the chair back upright as Vivienne grabbed her purse and picked up the books and discs from the floor. "I think I'll close up early tonight."

There was another commotion from the lower level. A thud and the sound of paper scattering on the floor. Vivienne sprinted over to the staircase, slightly out of breath as she hit the middle landing.

"Do you see them?" Harriet called out.

"No, but the front door is open." Vivienne called out as she ran down the steps and was careful to avoid slipping on the papers blowing across the carpet as the winter wind blasted into the building. She reached the front entrance and stuck her head out the door. Other than a few cars passing by, not a soul was on the sidewalks as far as she could see. She pulled the door closed as Harriet joined her by the circulation desk. "I'm calling Sheriff Rigsbee about this."

Vivienne shook her head. "Whoever it was left in a hurry. We must have finally scared them."

"So we should just let these kids get away with it?" Harriet reached for the phone. "The need to see we've done something."

"We don't know who it was." Vivienne spoke quickly. "Besides, what can we tell them? Neither one of us saw anything to give a physical description."

Harriet paused for a moment and put her fingers on her temples. "I don't know about you, but given what's happened with those Bad Santa letters going up around here I'm more than a little nervous."

"Harriet, it was probably some young kids doing something foolish on a dare."

"You think so?" Harriet didn't sound all to convinced.

"Now that I think about it, the first time I thought I saw someone up here it looked about kid-sized." Vivienne lied again.

Harriet's face went from fear to anger in a few seconds. "They do like to pull stupid pranks like that."

"Exactly." Vivienne reasoned along with her. "They saw two women in here all alone and decided to have some fun. Kids do stupid things all the time."

"Oh, that just burns me up." Harriet bent over and started plucking the papers off the floor. "They have no respect for anything these days."

Vivienne helped her grab the last of the papers. "Are these the records I printed from upstairs?"

Harriet eyed the ones in her hands quickly. "Yes, everything prints at the front desk. It's a nickel a copy, but given what's happened they're on the house."

Vivienne smiled back. "You don't have to do that."

Harriet handed her the papers. "No, let's just call it a night and close up. I'll check the encyclopedia out to your library card in the morning."

"I'm fine with that." Vivienne agreed. "Let me get my purse from upstairs and we can go."

"I just want to get into my flannel nightgown, and curl up with a good book." Harriet's eyes narrowed. "If anyone else is in here, it serves them right to get locked in for the night."

Vivienne zipped upstairs, retrieved her purse, and returned slightly out of breath again. "Who needs a gym membership when you work here?" She teased.

"You're telling me." Harriet smiled.

"Thanks again for all your help, Harriet." Vivienne waited as she turned off the main light switches, and plunged the library into the dim shadow of dusk. She held the encyclopedia tight in her grip.

Harriet unlocked a desk drawer with a set of keys from her pants pocket and pulled out her small but sensible purse. "I'm glad you were here, actually. If I was by myself, I would have been scared to death." She retrieved her winter jacket from a set of wall hooks and slipped it on.

"Same goes for me."

As they walked out the front door, Harriet locked the doors with the keys and buttoned her coat up in the cold wind. "Well, I'll be keeping a sharp eye on any kids coming into the library from now on I can tell you that."

"Drive safe." Vivienne waved as they parted ways to walk to their cars in the parking lot.

"You too." Harriet slid into her little blue compact sedan and started the engine up.

Vivienne plopped into her Toyota and tossed her purse on the passenger seat. Impersonating a journalist, telling lies to avoid further police involvement, and now book theft. She was certainly racking up the points to a Bad Santa note. In fact, she wouldn't be surprised if the next one had her name on it, she thought as she turned the engine over and waited for the heat to blast from the vents.

CHAPTER 12

Vivienne scraped the last bits of rice left on the plate from her chicken and broccoli into the trash bin and rinsed it under a stream of warm water from the sink. "So, I managed to convince her not to call you guys after all." She confided to Joshua who was seated at the kitchen table finishing his cashew chicken.

"That's probably a good thing." He seemed tired and not quite there.

"Are you feeling okay?" She loaded the plate into the dishwasher rack.

"Yeah. It's just all this extra work is taking a toll on everyone at the station." He brought his plate over to her and kissed her on the back of the neck. "All this food doesn't help matters."

"We haven't done the fortune cookies yet." Vivienne reminded him of the little ritual they had started on their first date several months ago.

"I didn't see any in the bag." Joshua leaned forward and nibbled on her left ear. "I thought you pulled them out?"

"No." Vivienne pouted as she scraped his plate clean and rinsed it before loading it into the washer and closing the door. "Well, that's just great."

"It's just a cookie." He ran his hands along her hips. "No big deal."

She whirled around to face him. "We have no fortune."

"We don't need a cookie to tell us what's going to happen tonight." He gave her a friendly little growl.

She put her hands up on his chest. "I'm so full

right now and my stomach has been a little off the past few days."

"Come lay down with me. I promise you'll feel a whole lot better." He reached up and pulled her hands down.

She let out a little sigh. "If I lay down on the bed I'm going to fall dead asleep."

His steel-blue eyes narrowed slightly. "I'll make sure that doesn't happen.

"I was going to go onto the internet and do some more research too. Whoever it was in the library today sure seemed interested in what I was doing."

Joshua put his right hand over her lips. "I just want to relax with the one person in the whole wide world I most want to be with."

Vivienne decided to put off her research until a little later. Joshua looked quite tired and she was sure he'd fall asleep not too long after they had some quiet time together. She nodded and kissed his hand.

He led her out of the kitchen and up to the bedroom. Tommy danced around excitedly, clawing at the wall register vent which Vivienne called 'playing the harp', a strange habit he picked up recently. Joshua hurried him out into the hall and closed the door.

"He's going to claw at the door the whole time now." Vivienne warned.

"That cat takes my whole side of the bed far too often." Joshua said as he pulled his shirt over his head and revealed his furry chest.

Vivienne pulled off her wristwatch and set it on the bedside table. "He's stubborn."

"He's spoiled." Joshua stepped out of his trousers

and climbed into the flannel bed sheets.

Vivienne slipped out of her clothes, leaving only her undergarments on as she followed him into the bed. "I take care of my men." She cooed.

Joshua reached over and with polished perfection unhooked her bra which he gracefully dropped to the floor as he pulled her close to him. "For which the men in your life are most grateful for."

She kissed him on the lips, loving the prickly sensation from his beard as it caressed her cheeks. "You were right. I am feeling better now."

He pulled her closer into him, their noses barely an inch apart. "And you said we had no fortune." He kissed her once more.

* * *

A little while later, Vivienne slipped on her comfy white flannel robe and tied the belt at the waist. She stepped into a pair of pink scuff slippers and padded silently out of the bedroom, leaving Joshua to snooze with Tommy whom she allowed to sneak in.

As she crept into the living room, she stepped on the floor pedal that turned on the tree lights. The soft glow was all she desired, just enough light for her to find her way around the growing mound of wrapped presents that spread further out from the tree skirt each day. She eased herself in front of the computer to conduct a little more research since sleep was furthest from her mind. She was grateful that her business had taken off, but she rarely had late evenings to enjoy the blissful quiet anymore. There were no annoying calls from telemarketers, no unexpected knocks at the door from friends or neighbors. She could explore her curiosity freely without having to justify her reasons to anyone.

As the computer awaited her input, she pulled out the information that she had printed at the library from the desk drawer. It was at that moment she discovered what was missing. In her haste to leave, she had forgotten her yellow notepad back at the circulation desk. "Damn." She berated herself for leaving such sensitive information behind. She would have to return on Monday to fetch it when the library re-opened.

She began her search with the medical encyclopedia for hydroxybenzene poisoning and discovered that another more common name for it was carbolic acid. Upon further reading, she discovered it was quite a common item to be found in homes in the late nineteenth and early twentieth century. Carbolic acid, as it turned out, was used in soaps more often than not. Still, she couldn't imagine a sudden outbreak of soap-ingestion amongst the population of Cayuga Cove. There had to be another reason why so many had died.

As the minutes turned into an hour, her eyes began to bother her staring at the bright LCD screen. Despite her best efforts, she had made no further progress on finding a clue to crack the mystery of the flare up in reported cases. Until, she came across a name that rang a bell, Edgar Rothwell.

She was surprised to see that his wife, Hazel had died on September 22nd 1872 with the listed cause of death as 'accidental carbolic acid poisoning'. She was thirty-two years old and buried in the Cayuga Union

Cemetery two days later. Even more tragic, her children Jacob and Constance, both followed her to the grave less than a week later from accidental carbolic acid poisoning.

Edgar Rothwell did not pass away until the following December 21st of accidental carbolic acid poisoning, at the age of forty-two, upon which the Rothwell home fell into the hands of distant relatives who stripped it of the most valuable furnishings and left the empty shell to slowly crumble to a ghost of its former glory until the historical society purchased the building at auction in 1973 and had it refurbished.

She nearly jumped out of her chair when her purse tumbled off the end table, spilling the mythology and folklore book from inside of it. She quickly walked over and found it lying face down, about a quarter of the way open. She carefully lifted it off the floor and turned it over. The top right page was dog-eared under the entry 'Female Spirits; Banshee'. Vivienne scanned the entry and read it quietly aloud to herself. "A banshee is female spirit common in the mythology and folklore of early Irish-American immigrants. Known to haunt graveyards and battlefields, this fearsome specter often appeared to those about to face a violent death such as murder. It was also common for a banshee to attach itself to a family if a particularly tragic history unfolded."

Her thoughts drifted back to the Rothwell family and all the tragedy that befell them. If there was such a creature in Cayuga Cove, it would have certainly found the family a tempting target to latch onto. The question was, who exactly left this book for her to find in the library? Or was it a warning to stop poking her nose into what was going on? If it was that, she certainly needed more to be scared away from investigating. She reached down, retrieved her purse, and slipped the book back inside of it. She would hold onto it for a little while just in case.

Exhausted as the clock neared one in the morning, Vivienne finally put the computer into standby mode and walked over to the tree. She stared at the miniature lights and wished that life could be as idyllic as the little villages depicted on some of the ornaments hanging from the branches. There were no murders or poisonings happening inside the little homes that lined the cobblestone roads. No parents burying their children in the cemetery behind the stained-glass glow of the cathedral as a soft snow fell from the heavens. Nor were there invisible portals opened to other dimensions where dark things could sneak through and cause havoc. Each little scene on the ornaments depicted absolute peace on earth and good will toward men. She lingered for a moment before stepping on the pedal to turn off the tree.

As the lights went out, she heard the wind rattle the windows of the house. Bits of snow flew against the panes as the streetlight cast shadows of tree branches on the darkened walls of her living room. She heard the moaning sound again and froze in place. "Sally." A sepulchral voice called out from the freezing darkness. "Sally Rollins." It called out again as the windows rattled a bit more.

Vivienne moved to the window where she could get a better view of the moon. Sure enough, it resembled a grinning half-skull as dark clouds swirled around it. Vivienne turned to rouse Joshua from his sleep in the bedroom when she gasped. There were four shadows cast against the wall near her. Her own, that of a woman a bit shorter and heavier than herself, and the distinct shadows of two small children holding hands.

Vivienne watched in terror as each of the shadows, save her own, raised their arms upwards, pointing toward the window behind her. She felt a blast of bitterly cold air creep around her body as she slowly turned around. There, standing outside her window was a tall man with skin as pale as snow. His facial features were mostly hidden in the shadowy darkness, but as the moonlight faded in and out, she could make out thin lips around a mouth of chipped and rotten teeth. His arms were folded across his chest, as if he were lying repose inside a casket. His hands were lined with dark veins, fingers curled and gnarled like tree branches. Where his eyes should be, there were only two dark holes that seemed to pull the moonlight inside with some bizarre force.

She took a step backwards, unable to turn away. "Joshua." She called out, but her voice sounded hollow and weak. As if it were coming from across the street. She coughed and cleared her throat, but it didn't help.

The shadows of the woman and children melted like hot wax down the wall, slithered like snakes across the carpet, and climbed back up along the wall surrounding the window. The arms of both figures twisted around into strange positions, the sounds of bones snapping and popping out of joint as each one defied anatomical movement. When they stopped, they were each pointing to the man in the window.

"Joshua." She tried to speak again, only her voice was the faintest of whispers. The moaning outside grew louder as the man opened his mouth wide. His jaw continued to drop lower and lower, far beyond the normal range until it was nearly level with his chest. From inside his throat, she could see hands and arms reaching outwards in a frantic effort to escape.

She felt woozy, as the room began to slowly spin around her. The man moved closer toward the window, pressing the end of his nose against the cold glass. Her knees went weak and she struggled to remain standing. A line of frost shot across the windowpane, then another. Each one began to move of its own accord, until a few seconds later when the entire pane of glass was frozen solid.

Shielded from the terrible sight, she found her voice and cried out in terror. Her scream went higher and higher as a the shadows of the woman and children on the wall changed to skeletal forms and then crumbled into nothing.

"Vivienne." Joshua bolted out of the bedroom door.

She ran into his arms, sobbing. "Something was outside. A man."

He raced forward to the window near the Christmas tree. "Out there right now?"

"He's gone." She could see that the frost on the window had disappeared along with her stalker. "I don't think it was human."

"What was it then?" Joshua looked out the window and then pulled the curtains closed. "A ghost?"

"I don't know. But it felt evil." She took a deep

breath.

"What makes you say that?" He walked over to her and put his arms on her shoulders. "Wow, you're cold as ice."

She shuddered, crossing her arms across her chest to get warm. "There was so much hate inside that thing. It was overwhelming."

Joshua reached over to the loveseat and pulled a fleece blanket off the end. He wrapped it around her protectively. "It's not going to hurt you with me around."

She dropped her head on his chest. "I've never felt anything like this. It was like it was draining the life right out of me."

"I'm here now." He tried to soothe her.

"I heard a voice outside saying the name of Sally Rollins." Vivienne spoke. "I think she may be in trouble."

"The woman who lives out in the trailer park near Natalie?"

"Yes." Vivienne replied. "I have a bad feeling something's happened to her."

Joshua led her over to the loveseat and gently helped her sit down. He then picked up the phone and began to dial.

"Who are you calling?"

"Bill Collins is on the night shift tonight. I'm going to have him send a car out to check on Sally Rollins." Joshua explained.

Vivienne nodded. "Good. I won't be able to sleep until I know what's going on."

Joshua explained the situation as best he could to the night officer, but even he was at a loss for words to explain exactly what could be going on. He finally just asked for a favor and left it at that. He hung up the phone and sat down next to Vivienne. "It would be so much easier if they just knew about your powers as a witch." He spoke softly.

"Or yours as a werewolf?" She asked him.

"Right." He nodded. "That would not be good."

Vivienne began to feel the much needed warmth return to her body. "That's the price of magic." She added. "We have the power to change things, but we have to work harder than anyone else to explain how we did it in a way that makes sense and keeps us out of psychiatric wards."

"What were you doing up so late anyway?"

She pointed to the computer desk. "Research."

"On Eddie's case?"

"It started out with him, but then it lead to something else that concerns the entire town." Vivienne replied. "It involves the Rothwell mansion."

"Your gingerbread entry?" He looked at her with a puzzled look.

"The real thing." Vivienne went on to explain the carbolic acid poisoning of the entire family and several other cases within that two year span.

"Do you think it's something in the water here?" Joshua asked. "Perhaps the fracking for natural gas pockets has ruptured some old industrial waste site and contaminated the water supply?"

"They use well water out at the trailer park, don't they?"

Joshua nodded. "Yes, town services cut out just before the old cemetery."

"But how does that explain what I've seen

tonight?" Vivienne wondered. "Or the author of the Bad Santa notes?"

"I have no idea." Joshua replied as his phone rang. He answered it and then thanked the caller. "Jerry Parsons just took a cruise out to the Tall Pine Grove trailer court and everything is quiet. No trouble at all."

"What about Sally Rollins?"

Joshua shook his head. "He's not going to go knock on her door at one in the morning on a hunch."

"I know." Vivienne sighed.

"If there was a problem, he would have seen it immediately." Joshua reminded her. "Now, it's time to come back to bed."

"You're right." Vivienne pulled the blanket off herself and tossed it to the side of the loveseat. "Thanks for checking for me."

"I know better than to ignore your hunches." Joshua reminded her as he pulled her up . "Let's get some sleep."

She held his hand as they walked back into the bedroom, safe and sound inside her warm home. For the moment, she could rest. With the Sweet Dreams Bakery closed on Sundays, she would actually get to sleep in.

CHAPTER 13

Sunday, December 8th

Vivienne wanted desperately to return to the dream world as the shrill ring of the phone startled her awake. She couldn't recall all the details, but it involved her sitting on a lovely white sand beach as turquoise-tinged waves lapped the shoreline. As she opened one eye in the weak early morning light, she pulled the soft pillow over her head with a groan. The phone rang two more times before she felt Joshua's weight shift the mattress to his side of the bed as he finally answered the call.

"Say that again?" Joshua asked the early morning caller.

Vivienne's mind refused to allow her to drift back to the comfort of sleep. She pulled one end of the pillow up and gazed at Joshua who kept his voice low. "What's going on?"

He pulled the phone away from his face. "It's Bill Collins. He decided to swing by Sally's trailer one more time before his shift ended."

Vivienne tucked her elbows behind her and pushed herself back against the pillows. "Did he find something?"

Joshua put the phone back to his ear. "Yeah, I'm still here. Thanks for keeping me posted, Bill." He hung up the phone and turned to face her. "You were right."

"I don't want to be right about these things." Vivienne sighed. "It's never a good thing."

Joshua pulled the covers up to his chest. "Bill said that when he drove by Sally's trailer this morning he noticed her car had a fairly large dent near the front hood on the passenger's side."

Vivienne shook her head. "They think she was the driver who hit Eunice the other night?"

"He called it in and they're sending a few guys to comb it over for any evidence." Joshua replied.

"Why would she do something like that?" Vivienne asked. "Did they even know each other?"

"I don't know." Joshua snuggled closer to Vivienne. "If they find anything, she'll be brought in for questioning soon."

"This doesn't feel right to me." Vivienne squirmed in the sheets, wrapping her legs around the soft flannel as if she were a caterpillar spinning a cocoon.

"Nothing feels right with everything that's been going on here lately." Joshua reminded her. "Cayuga Cove is supposed to be a quiet town. People are supposed to be good hearted here."

"Nana Mary warned me that something has changed ever since Missy communed with dark magic." Vivienne said with a little sigh. "I don't know if it will ever go back to the way it was."

"Let's not focus on that." Joshua pulled her close to him and gave her a kiss on the cheek.

She welcomed his warm touch and nestled back against the pillows. "So we can still sleep in for a little bit?"

"We've earned it." He smiled and then reclined back, pulling her closer against his body. "Something tells me quiet mornings are going to be rare."

Despite the early morning call, they managed to sneak in another hour and a half of sleep before Joshua kissed her goodbye as he went in for the noon to midnight shift.

After opening a can of Tuna Delight only to have Tommy turn his nose up in disgust, she knew she had to get out of the house and accomplish something. "Two options, bud. Take it or leave it." She shook her index finger at Tommy who continued to stare at the plate of cat food with dismay. "You seem to forget how not too long ago you were eating out of dumpsters."

He gave her a half-hearted meow and batted a plastic ball with a bell inside. He went bounding away, claws scraping against the kitchen floor as he chased his prey.

After her own shower and depositing a load of towels into the washer, she pulled on a pair of comfortable jeans, a cozy yet faded grey sweatshirt, and a pair of faux-leather snow boots that she had found on clearance at the outlets last spring.

She decided it was a good day to finish off her shopping for holiday gifts, especially for Joshua as he usually followed her like a lost puppy through retail stores.

Bundled in her winter coat, she was pleased to see that the cold spell appeared to have broken as the temperature felt like it was in the upper forties. Even the overcast clouds were breaking up, allowing some much needed sunshine to brighten the morning. She unzipped her jacket and took in the fresh air. There was nothing like a free weekend day with an open agenda. She picked up the newspaper that was lying folded up on her steps and tossed it into the house. She didn't have time to clip coupons or scan sales flyers. This might be one of her last chances to shop before the holiday frenzy went into full swing.

As she zipped down Main Street, she was dismayed to see that none of the merchants had decided it was worth the time to start earlier Sunday hours yet. Store after store was dark and deserted, which left either a trip south to Ithaca or head north toward the outlets near Waterloo. She wasn't in the mood to drive either distance, but she had a feeling she'd find more of what she was looking for at the outlets. With the roads nearly empty, she turned onto Weyer Place to head north and spied Miss Octavia standing outside of her shop, Mother Earth Mercantile. The large display window was shattered into several sharp pieces and it looked as if someone had taken a baseball bat to the shelves and destroyed quite a bit of merchandise.

Vivienne pulled into a spot across the street and hurried over. "What happened?"

Miss Octavia seemed to be in shock. She just stared blankly at her shop, holding a broken goddess statue in her hands.

"Miss Octavia? Are you okay?" Vivienne waved her hands in front of her face.

This seemed to rouse Octavia from her trance. "I was asking for justice to smite whoever has done this."

Vivienne surveyed the scene with dismay. "I don't believe this."

"I was a fool to believe that things could be any different here than in a bigger city." Octavia sniffed back some tears. "Cities are full of criminals and mischief makers, they said. Small towns are safer, they said."

Vivienne put her arm around Octavia's shoulder. "Have you called the police?"

She nodded. "I was going to have an alarm installed next week."

"They should have someone coming any minute now."

Octavia glanced at Vivienne. "It doesn't matter. I don't have insurance to replace all that has been destroyed."

"When they catch whoever did this, I'm sure you'll be able to file a lawsuit for damages." Vivienne tried to cheer her up.

"All that I had was tied up in this business. I cannot afford a lawyer." She carefully set the broken goddess statue down on the sidewalk.

Vivienne could hear the siren of the approaching police vehicle. "We'll figure something out, Miss Octavia. I promise."

"It's hard to be optimistic when everything you worked so hard for is broken in pieces all over the sidewalk."

As the police vehicle pulled next to them, the officer stepped out carefully and approached. Vivienne recognized him as Kevin Lovell, one of the younger recruits added to the force and fresh out of college. "Which one of you called in the report?"

Miss Octavia raised her hand. "That would be me, the business owner."

Vivienne stepped aside as the officer approached Octavia. "Just answer with as much detail as you can." Vivienne encouraged. "It will help with the investigation greatly."

"Did you see the crime as it was happening?" Kevin asked.

Octavia shook her head. "I had just arrived to finish building a display for the tarot cards when I came upon this mess."

"Miss Finch." Officer Lovell stood ready with his notepad in hand. "How are you involved?"

"I'm not." Vivienne excused herself. "I was driving by on my way to the outlets when I came upon Miss Octavia standing on the sidewalk and stopped to see if she needed help."

He scribbled something down on his notepad. "You didn't see anyone fleeing the scene?"

"It had already happened before I arrived." Vivienne explained. "I wish I could be more help."

"Thank you Miss Finch. You're free to leave." Officer Lovell gave her a little smile.

Vivienne reached out and gave Octavia's hands a squeeze. "Give me a few hours and I'm going to round up some friends to help you clean up the store. We'll get this fixed up."

"Thank you." Octavia's voice quivered.

Not wanting to involve herself in any more police business, Vivienne turned to leave when a business card fluttered in the breeze and landed on her boot. She reached down to pick it up and noticed the emblem of a white cross with a foil-embossed fire behind it. 'Order of the Righteous Ministries, Pastor Seamus Kilpatrick'. Vivienne turned the card over and gasped. Printed in tiny lettering was a bible verse. 'I will set my face against anyone who turns to mediums or spiritists to prostitute themselves by following them, and I will cut them off from their people. - Leviticus 20:6'.

Vivienne considered showing her find to the officer Lovell, but thought differently. Once again, she felt as if she were being spoon-fed clues and it was starting to get on her nerves. She would not give whoever it was stalking her the satisfaction of helping to spread more panic and chaos. She tucked the card into one of her purse's many pockets and walked back to her car.

She had no sooner pulled out of her parking spot when her cell phone went off with another call. Thankfully, Joshua had upgraded her radio system with a hands free phone option so she could answer calls while driving. "Hello?"

"Oh my God, where are you?" Kathy's voice asked through her car speakers.

"I was on my way to the outlets this morning but then I got sidetracked." Vivienne answered.

"There are more Bad Santa notes this morning." Kathy spoke hurriedly.

"About Miss Octavia?" Vivienne filled in the blank confidently. "I was already over there."

"No." Kathy's voice went flat. "What happened to Miss Octavia?"

"Someone vandalized her store. Smashed the front window and destroyed lots of her goods. I'm going to organize a group of our Main Street business owners to help her clean up and donate some cash to get her back on her feet."

"I don't believe it." Kathy was quick to reply. "But count me in to help out."

"I know it's short notice, but I was hoping we could get started in about two or three hours."

"Sure, I think I can make some calls and get some more people to help out."

Vivienne smiled. "That would be a huge help."

"So, don't you want to know what the note says?"

"I was just downtown and I didn't see any notes floating about." Vivienne tapped her fingers on the steering wheel impatiently.

"It was tucked inside this morning's newspaper."

"I didn't even open mine." Vivienne felt foolish for not doing so. "Who are they targeting?"

"Tristan and Nathaniel." Kathy lowered her voice. "Oh Vivienne, it's very salacious. I feel terrible for them if it's true."

"Read it for me, word for word. Don't leave anything out." Vivienne replied as she turned a corner and headed for Main Street.

Kathy cleared her throat. "Sure thing. You better not pout!." She paused for a moment. "Our mysterious letter writer seems to think they're cute using the lyrics to that old chestnut."

"Kathy, normally I'd love your commentary but time could be of the essence here." Vivienne found herself making the 'speed it up' motion with her hand, a habit she tried often to break but somehow it always remained with her.

"Oh, fine." Kathy cleared her throat once again and continued where she had left off. "You seem the perfect couple, the very model of how love should be. Yet, one of you harbors a secret lover while the other turns a blind eye in the hopes it could turn into something more accommodating for three. Santa has been watching and is quite fed up with your hypocrisy. It's quite apparent your value in this town is decreasing. Clearly, you both are the lowest bidders when it comes to morality. Sincerely, Santa Claus."

"This is getting out of hand. The whole town is going to be at each other's throats if this keeps up." Vivienne reasoned.

"It's definitely sucked the joy out of the holiday season around here." Kathy agreed. "So do you think the break-in at Miss Octavia's is connected to this?"

"I don't think so." Vivienne spoke as she parked her car in front of Carriage House Antiques. She saw a hand pull back a curtain that was drawn across the main storefront window. "I've got an errand to run and then I'll call you back in a little bit."

"Are you investigating again?" Kathy asked with more than a hint of encouragement in her voice.

"I'm searching for the truth." Vivienne quickly answered. "You can quote me on that should the police ask you questions."

Kathy chuckled. "Talk to you later."

Vivienne stepped up to the door of Tristan and Nathaniel's business, which also served as their home, and rang the doorbell.

The door opened a sliver. "I'm sorry, Vivienne. We're not up for company today." Nathaniel's voice was soft and sullen.

"I know about the note and I'm here to help you fix things." Vivienne spoke up. "Please let me in."

There was a pause and then the door swung open to reveal Nathaniel, dressed in a robe and opera slippers. His ginger hair was disheveled and he looked even more pale than usual. "Come in."

She scooted inside as he shut the door rather forcefully and leaned against it. "How can you fix this?" He asked.

"You look terrible." Vivienne observed. "Why don't we go sit down and have some tea?"

Nathaniel sighed and looked at her. "You don't have an easy answer, do you?"

She shook her head. "Not yet. But I don't believe a word of that stupid note."

"Gossip travels fast Vivienne." Nathaniel led her toward the kitchen area near the back of the store. "We'll probably be out of business by week's end."

"I don't think so." Vivienne countered as they stepped into the kitchen. "We're going to sit down and figure this out."

Tristan climbed down the back kitchen stairs and paused at the landing. Normally the dapper dresser, this morning she was shocked to find him wearing only a pair of red flannel boxers and a simple white tee shirt. "Vivienne?"

"Hi Tristan." Vivienne sat down at the small farmer's table. "I know you've had a rough morning."

"That's the understatement of the year." He quipped back with much less zeal than she was used to.

"What did the paper say?" Nathaniel asked as he filled a kettle with water from the deep marble sink and placed it on the gas burner stovetop.

"It didn't come from them." Tristan replied.

"Of course it did. It was in every paper around town this morning." Nathaniel snapped.

Vivienne could sense an argument ready to erupt. "It's possible someone slipped them into the newspapers on the delivery truck or perhaps in some of the bundles that were dropped off at the carrier's homes during the night."

Nathaniel's face flushed red. "Whoever this is certainly has an ax to grind with a lot of the folks in this town."

"But why now?" Tristan asked the group. "What are they trying to gain from this?"

"That's true." Vivienne added. "These aren't blackmail notes asking for hush money. This is just someone getting some sort of retribution."

"But who?" Nathaniel asked as he pulled the steaming kettle off the stovetop. "It has to be someone who lives here to know the things they know."

Tristan buried his face in his hands. "I can't do this anymore."

Vivienne leaned forward at his outburst. "What's wrong?"

"Tristan, don't say it." Nathaniel's voice was stern.

"If you're holding something back, you need to tell me." Vivienne replied.

Tristan's shoulders began to heave as he started to cry. "I never meant for it to go this far. I tried to resist his advances, but he kept buying me drinks and before I knew it I woke up the next morning in the hotel room."

Nathaniel tossed his arms up in the air. "Well, now you've done it. The whole town is going to know about that stupid lapse of judgment that night in New York."

Vivienne felt terrible. "So there was an affair?"

"It was a lapse of good judgment." Nathaniel

corrected her. "An affair is mutual consent."

"I'm not judging you guys here." Vivienne was quick to speak up. "But I can't say the same for the people in town. After all these notes, I think everyone is on edge."

Tristan raised his head up and wiped away most of the remaining tears. "It was one night and it was months ago."

Nathaniel sat down next to him and draped his arm over his shoulders. "We've worked through it and we're fine."

"I'm glad to hear that." Vivienne felt a bit less awkward. "But the question remains, who else knew about it?'

Tristan took a deep cleansing breath and began to pull himself back together. "It was at the hotel bar in New York. There were people everywhere. It took a half hour just to get the bartender to get me a drink."

"Just for the record, I've never had any lapses of judgment on my end." Nathaniel added as the telephone rang. "I'll get it." He jumped up and dashed off to the living room to answer the phone. "If it's those idiots at the newspaper again I'm going to give them hell and the name of our lawyer."

Vivienne thought for a moment and decided to see for herself what had really happened. She had a gift. Magic was her ally. As Nana Mary had instructed her, she needed to use it more often to control it better. The first few times she had tried it, she was merely a passive observer. But, there was much more to the power which would prove itself to be more exciting than she ever could have dreamed for. Now, she was starting to learn how to interact with the memories. Ask questions and make conversation that perhaps didn't happen in the original memory. Granted, if she took the memory too far astray the person's sub-conscious would 'hiccup', as Nana Mary described, and kick her out which would end the spell rather abruptly.

She couldn't fully understand how she was able to step beyond the memory. She assumed that it was simply a matter of taking in all of the sensory details the mind recorded during a memory. Side conversations, pictures hanging on the walls, what the license plate number was on the car that left the scene. It seemed similar to how a hypnotist could coax vivid recollections out of willing subjects for police investigations. Still, magic was able to skirt the rules and it rarely had a logical answer. It just happened. She wondered if perhaps her gift was intertwined with time travel? Was she in fact moving into the past and poking around? Could she alter what had happened? Her grimoire at home had the answers inside the musty pages, but it would only reveal them when it knew she was ready to take the next step. For now, it was all based on faith.

There was no better time or place to give her spell work a try. She reached out her hands. "If there's anything I can do to help you guys, you know I will."

Tristan reached back and clasped hands with her. "Thank you."

There was a tingle of energy that zapped her, much like an unexpected static shock during the dry months of winter. She allowed the magical ability to transport herself into his memory work slowly. The room grew dark and swirled into blackness. When she could see again, there were lights everywhere. Bright lights, clanging of glasses, and loud conversation. She found herself at the hotel bar the very night Tristan made his mistake.

"What can I get you?" A handsome blonde man asked from across the illuminated bar top.

"A 7 and 7 please." Vivienne answered without thinking. The words just slipped out of her mouth.

"You got it." The bartender dashed away to make the drink. As he moved, Vivienne could see her reflection in the mirror. She was inside Tristan's body, yet she felt free to break free from the sequence of events that his memory recorded. Nana Mary had told her that the power would change and evolve the more she used it. It was an exhilarating yet terrifying feeling not to know where this would lead.

"I thought a handsome guy like you would be more creative than that?" A smooth tenor voice spoke from her left side.

Vivienne turned to see who it was. "I beg your pardon?"

The man was athletic in build, dressed in an expensive looking business suit that could have placed him as a hot-shot executive in any of the offices in Manhattan. His skin tone was a slight orange color that revealed itself as a possible salon spray tan. His dark black hair was slicked back and glossy, reflecting the lights from around the bar area. "I said I expected a hot guy like you to be more adventurous when it came to ordering drinks."

"Oh." Vivienne felt herself blush. "I'm sorry to disappoint you."

The handsome executive winked at him. "I can fix

that." He snapped his fingers and the bartender practically leapt to his call. "Cancel that previous order and get this handsome guy the house special and another for me."

"How do you know I'll like it?" Vivienne played along.

"Because it's like me. A little sweet, a little sour." The handsome executive pushed his bar stool closer to Vivienne. "But it goes down nice and easy."

She had to refrain from cringing at the horrible pickup line. "I guess I'll try it." She had always wondered how the gay bar scene differed from the heterosexual one. It turned out, they were both filled with lame pickup lines and promises that rarely lived up to their initial sell.

"I just realized I never introduced myself. I'm Robert." He offered his right hand.

"Viv..." Vivienne stopped just before she made the mistake. "Very nice to meet you. I'm Tristan."

"That's a sexy name." Robert moved a little closer as the bartender set down two drinks that were electric-blue in color.

Vivienne stared at the highball glass. "Thank you."

"So where are you from, Tristan?"

"A little town upstate. You've probably never heard of it."

"Try me."

She took a sip and nearly spit it out in surprise. It was potent. "Wow." She reacted. "This stuff should be fueling rockets for NASA."

"You're adorable." Robert raised his matching glass and downed a big gulp. "So where did you say you were from?"

"Cayuga Cove." Vivienne felt the burn of the alcohol as it slid down her throat.

"Get out." Robert slapped his hand on the bar. "I know that place."

"You're kidding?"

He shook his head. "My great-grandfather had a summer home way back in the olden days."

"In Cayuga Cove?" Vivienne was intrigued.

"Yeah, it's on the Eastern shore of Cayuga lake."

"I'll be damned." Vivienne had a ton of questions swirling in her mind. "So, when was the last time you were there?"

"About a year ago." Robert answered. "My family let the place go because no one wanted to move from the city to take care of it."

"Who is your family?"

"Don't judge me now." Robert smiled at her as he took a drink.

"What do you mean?"

"The Rothwells." Robert answered.

"Your great-grandfather was Edgar Rothwell?"

"I said don't judge." Robert smiled at her and took another large drink. "You're not a journalist looking for another angle on that golden parachute scandal that my father cooked up, are you?

"No. I sell antiques." Vivienne assured him.

"Good. Because I'm not like the rest of my family. I don't screw employees out of their retirement funds and bankrupt the place when my promises fail to deliver the results."

"Do you happen to know Samantha Charles?" Vivienne asked.

"The hotel heiress? We're both seasoned veterans of the charity fundraising circuit here in the city." Robert winked again. "Still, I'm old money and she is new. The two worlds never mix." He took another generous sip of his drink.

"I wouldn't know." Vivienne added. "I grew up without a trust fund."

Robert frowned. "Oh man. Now we're getting to the money part and this is where I start to get bored."

"I'm sorry." Vivienne took another small sip from her drink. "I've never dated anyone with significant wealth before."

"So we're dating?"

Vivienne shrugged. "I don't remember offering to do that."

Robert laughed, one of those drunk and getting drunker kind of laughs that seemed to go on for minutes. "You're so adorable."

There was a light from a cell phone on the bar in front of Vivienne. The phone vibrated and inched closer to her drink. She picked it up and saw Nathaniel's name on the caller display.

"Who's that calling you?" Robert asked.

"My husband." She spoke without thinking.

Robert raised an eyebrow. "Does he let you play when you come into the city?"

"I don't know." Vivienne replied as the call went to voice mail.

Robert put his arm around her shoulders and spoke into her ear. "I won't tell if you won't."

"Are you seeing someone?" Vivienne asked, feeling rather uncomfortable at the turn the conversation was taking.

"I have a girl, but she's not here tonight." He winked.

"Aren't you gay?" She asked.

"Oh, man. Enough with labels. You're starting to sounds like my parents and that's not a good thing." He pulled his arm off her and finished his drink. "If you're looking for a quote try this one on for size. Robert Edward Rothwell thinks that labels are best left for clothes." His eyes were slightly unfocused as he made 'air quotes' with his hands. "That should sell a few thousand copies."

"I'm not a journalist." Vivienne repeated. I'm an antiques dealer from Cayuga Cove."

"And I've got an enormous suite here at the hotel all to myself." Robert giggled a little. "It's got a hot tub that seats eight."

"Sounds like you could fit my hotel room in the hot tub." Vivienne quipped.

"Why don't we go upstairs and see?"

"I don't know if that's such a good idea."

Robert snapped his fingers as the bartender set another drink down in front of them. "It will be after you finish this." He smiled.

Vivienne felt dizzy as Tristan's memory began to fight back against her probing questions. She had gone too far and his mind was about to 'hiccup' and spew her out. "I think I better go back to my room and call my husband back." The room began to spin. "Thanks for the drink." Everything went dark as Tristan's mind ejected her.

She found herself back inside the kitchen of Carriage House Antiques a few moments later.

"Hey, can you hear me? You sort of faded out

there for a second." Tristan snapped his fingers in front of her face.

"I'm sorry." She found it was becoming easier to return back to the present without creating a scene. "My blood sugar has been all kinds of wacky this month." She lied. "Did I pass out?"

"Just for ten or fifteen seconds." Tristan answered. "It was like you were in a trance or something, your eyes never closed." He got up from the table and reached for a plate of blueberry muffins that was on the counter near the sink. "You better eat something."

"Thank you." She played along and snagged a muffin. "Hey, did I tell you that Samantha Charles called me the other day?"

"No. What did she have to say?" Tristan was happy to have the conversation be about someone else.

"She told me that she ran into someone at a fundraising event that has roots in Cayuga Cove."

"Anyone we know?"

"She said his name was Robert Rothwell." Vivienne slipped the name in. "He must be related to the family that built the mansion here in town."

Tristan's eyes narrowed. "You don't say."

"I've never heard of him. She said his family is old money." Vivienne continued.

"I've heard of him." Tristan spoke softly.

"You have?"

He nodded back. "He was the man I slept with in New York."

"Are you kidding me?" She played along as if shocked.

"He bought me a drink, a real strong one. Started talking about his family and how he knew about Cayuga Cove and it made me feel not so lonely."

"What are you saying, Tristan?"

"I'm saying that it really wasn't an alcohol-fueled lapse of judgment like Nathaniel keeps insisting it was. I knew what I was doing the whole time."

Vivienne could feel his shame as he bared his awful secret to her at the kitchen table. "I'm so sorry to hear about this.

"The truth is, I hate all the traveling. I hate the hotels, I hate the rental vans and dinners alone at chain restaurants." Tristan went on. "I just want to stay here at home and be a good husband. I just want to make a normal life here were we only travel on vacations together."

"That's understandable." Vivienne sympathized with him. "Have you told him about this?"

"We fought about it for months." Tristan revealed. "We don't have the money in the bank to make that happen. We're barely getting by as it is."

"I had no idea."

"We applied at the bank for a loan to help pay some bills but we got turned down." Tristan's lower lip began to quiver. "The worst part is that I know that Eunice Kilpatrick heard about it and she couldn't wait to start spreading the news."

"Eunice Kilpatrick knew about this?" Vivienne started to mentally connect some dots. Santa's naughty list was starting to look a lot less random. "Are you positive?"

"Yes, because this trailer trash woman came marching in here the other day trying to sell some cheap Hummel knock-offs for some quick Christmas cash." Tristan recalled. "I told her they weren't the real thing and she went ballistic, telling me that I was going to ruin her grandchildren's Christmas."

Vivienne wished she had brought a pen and paper with her to take notes. She had no choice but to just keep nodding reassuringly. "How does this connect to Eunice?"

"Because the woman went on to explain how the bank's loan manager was heartless, but a good Christian teller who worked there told her to come to our shop because we were flush with cash and always buying antiques."

"I thought you said Eunice knew you guys were having money trouble?"

"She did." Tristan hit the table with his fist. "She did it because she wants to see us go out of business."

"Why does Eunice have a vendetta against you two?"

Tristan took a deep breath before speaking. "Right after Halloween some relative of hers died and left her a supposedly antique pocket watch. She came in and tried to sell it for some fast cash, but I had to tell her it wasn't nearly as old as she thought it was."

Vivienne nodded. "So Eunice was on the receiving end of a bad deal?"

"She expected a couple of thousand dollars at least. I told her it was worth maybe two hundred at the most."

"Did she tell you what she needed the money for?" Vivienne asked.

"No, she was tight-lipped about her own business as usual." Tristan looked at Vivienne with new fear in his eyes. "So, now she's going out of her way to get everyone all riled up and mad that we won't buy their crap with all this supposed money we're sitting on. I thought maybe she was the one writing the Bad Santa notes, but when she got hit by that car I realized it couldn't be her."

"She's in a coma still." Vivienne added

"It's probably all planned by that religious-freak brother of hers. He wants to drive us out of town, and he's going to do it by making as many people hate us as possible."

Vivienne reached down under the table and pulled up her purse. She rummaged through it and then pulled out the business card she had found near Miss Octavia's store earlier. "Pastor Seamus Kilpatrick?"

"Why are you mentioning that name in this house?" Nathaniel returned to the kitchen.

"I told her the whole story." Tristan added.

"You what?" Nathaniel smacked his head slightly. "Why would you air our dirty laundry out like that? Isn't this letter enough shame for one day?"

"I'm tired of secrets and lies, Nathaniel. I can't do it anymore." Tristan began to break down.

Nathaniel rushed over to him. "We'll sell this place and move somewhere else. Get a fresh start."

Tristan shook his head. "Can't we do that here?

"I think our time in Cayuga Cove is over."

Vivienne interrupted. "Not yet it isn't."

"You've got a plan?" Tristan asked.

"Give me a few days." Vivienne asked. "Please."

Nathaniel nodded. "Can we help?"

"I'll let you know." She smiled back.

CHAPTER 14

Kathy rubbed her hands together in the cold air. "I'm still in shock someone would vandalize a store like this right here in Cayuga Cove."

Vivienne swept up some small shards of broken plate glass window into a dustpan. "There is something bad going on in this town and I'm going to figure out what it is."

Kathy looked around the interior of Mother Earth Mercantile. Although the vandal had done considerable damage to the front display, most of the store remained very much intact. "I'm just glad it wasn't as bad as it first looked."

Vivienne leaned against her broom. "Thanks to you and all the others who decided to lend out a helping hand today." She pointed to where Tony DiSanto, of The Leaning Tower of Pizza and Brian Amberry of Hummingbird Floral were nearly finished boarding up the broken window with some plywood. Miss Clara had brought in an thermal pot of coffee and some club sandwiches for everyone to eat while they helped clean up and secure he store. Even though she didn't have insurance through his office, Neil Harrison had brought with him some paperwork for Miss Octavia to fill out that would help with categorizing what had been destroyed should the police catch the criminal. He worked with her over at the table where she would conduct readings with her crystal ball and tarot cards with clients.

"I expected a lot more than this to show up to help, honestly." Kathy frowned. "I think some of the Main Street business owners are quite stuck in the past when it comes to how they treat people."

Vivienne really couldn't argue with her logic. She knew very well what it was like for a new business to deal with the merchants who had been in town for decades. "We can't discount these Bad Santa notes from having a negative effect on the town's morale."

"We are all potential targets." Kathy fired back. "None of us are saint material."

"That's true." Vivienne set the broom against one of the shelves stocked with books. "Let's grab a sandwich and some coffee."

"I thought you'd never want to take a break." Kathy followed her.

"Well, you two girls are sure to stay off that naughty list by helping out here." Clara noted as she began to pack up the few remaining sandwiches.

"Is there still a turkey on wheat left?" Vivienne asked.

Clara looked into the large plastic tote and rummaged around. "Yes, I saved one for you." She pulled it out and handed it to her. "Lettuce with light mayo."

Vivienne could feel her mouth water with anticipation. She had really worked up an appetite helping to clean the store up. "Split it with me?" She asked Kathy.

"Sure." Kathy poured herself and Vivienne a cup of hot coffee.

Vivienne unwrapped the cellophane from the sandwich and placed half on a napkin for Kathy. "Any thoughts from you on who our Bad Santa might be?" She asked Clara.

Clara shrugged. "I try not to get too involved

with things like that."

"Every time I think I start to unravel the mystery, it just gets deeper." Vivienne conceded. "I guess my sleuthing skills are not as sharp as I thought they were."

"Of course they're sharp." Kathy handed Vivienne a cup of black coffee. "You never would have solved Mona's murder otherwise."

Clara closed the lid on her container and made sure it was sealed tight. "I'm too old to go poking around town looking to solve murders."

"So I should just let things be?" Vivienne took a small bite of her sandwich.

"Heavens no." Clara grimaced. "I think you should keep poking around to see what you can stir up."

"Just don't get caught by Sheriff Rigsbee." Kathy added as she sipped her coffee. "He's not too keen on getting help from ordinary citizens."

"He's a stubborn old mule who knows his retirement isn't too far down the road." Clara warned. "So, don't take his gruff attitude too personal."

"I try not to." Vivienne sipped her coffee.

"So, what have you found out so far?" Kathy asked.

"Not too much, but I can tell you that these notes are starting to look much less random than we all thought."

Clara's eyes widened in surprise. "So, there is a method at work here. It sounds quite devious."

"Ladies, we can't forget that someone is dead because of these notes." Vivienne chided them. "Whoever it is doesn't seem to care if a life is lost as a result of their mayhem or not."

"Which makes them quite dangerous." Kathy finished her coffee and looked around the room. "For all we know, the letter writer could be in this store with us right now."

"Oh, Kathy." Clara picked up the tote in her arms. "I hardly think our killer is that casual."

Kathy put her hands on her hips. "Well, excuse me Miss Marple."

Vivienne stepped between them. "Ladies, please. We need to focus on the task at hand."

"I'm pooped from helping out here today. I vote we go back to our homes and curl up with a soft blanket and the television remote." Kathy stretched her arms in the air.

"I second that." Clara added. "Keep me posted on how the investigation is going."

"You got it." Vivienne finished off the last of the sandwich as Clara said her goodbyes to Miss Octavia and left the store.

"So, do you need me for anything else?" Kathy asked.

"What do you think about going with me to check out the old Rothwell mansion?"

"It's closed on Sundays." Kathy was quick to reply. "What does that have to do with anything anyway?"

"I can't tell you the exact details." Vivienne did her best to keep Tristan's secret. "But needless to say, one of the Rothwell family members lives in New York and has an interesting connection to someone here in town."

"You do know something big." Kathy gushed.

"Maybe or maybe not." Vivienne teased.

"So how do we get inside?" Kathy asked.

"With the keys, naturally." Vivienne winked.

"I don't have them."

"Not you." Vivienne pointed to Brian Amberry.

"Why would Brian have the keys to the Rothwell mansion?"

"Because he does all the floral and plant care for the historical society." Vivienne made sure to brush off any crumbs from the sandwich from her shirt. "How do I look?"

"Like a woman about to step once more onto the hot frying pan of life." Kathy smiled.

"That's why I want you to go with me. So you can play lookout while I snoop around."

Kathy shook her head. "I think I liked things better when you did all of this without me and told me the next day."

Vivienne rushed over to Brian who was helping Tony pack up the toolbox. "Hi Brian." She smiled warmly. "It was so nice of you to volunteer your time today to help Miss Octavia."

Brian set the hammer down in the metal toolbox and smiled back at her. "It's the least we can do to help each other out."

"That is the spirit of the season, isn't it?"

"I think it's more important than ever we do these things." Brian agreed. "Given the events the past few days."

"I couldn't agree with you more." Vivienne knelt down and handed him a screwdriver from the floor. "In fact, I was just thinking there was something else you could do for the town that just might help to bring the cheer back."

"I'd love to help." Brian chirped back.

"Great. Can I have the keys to the Rothwell mansion?"

Brian raised an eyebrow at her. "Why do you need to get inside?"

"Well, I've been sort of running my own little investigation into the events going on." Vivienne lowered her voice.

"I don't know, Vivienne." Brian shoved his hands into his pant pockets. "If anything happens I could lose them as an account."

"I promise I'll be super careful."

"How does the mansion fit into what's been going on?" Brian asked.

"I'm not entirely sure about that at the moment." Vivienne whispered. "But, I'm fairly certain there might be a clue hidden inside that will put me on the right track."

"I want to help you." Brian replied. "I really do."

"I know I'm asking for a huge favor from you, but in the long run it could help catch the person who is terrorizing the town." Vivienne reasoned. "Isn't that worth a little risk on your part?"

Brian reached into his pants pocket and pulled out a set of keys. He carefully removed a rather large brass key and handed it to her. "If it will help end this craziness, I'm all for it. The alarm code is 4037."

"Thanks, Brian." Vivienne gave him a little hug. "I promise I'll be careful not to disturb anything."

"Please do." Brian pleaded with her. "I'll need them back by tonight."

"I only need a little bit of time." Vivienne gripped

the key in her hand. "Wish me luck."

* * *

It was well after three in the afternoon when Vivienne and Kathy parked across the street of the Rothwell mansion that housed the town's historical society. The grounds would have looked quite bleak, were it not for the red ribbons and greenery that Brian had placed for the holiday season.

As they hurried to the front door, Vivienne looked up at the large structure and felt a slight chill. She could almost feel a pair of eyes watching from behind one of the many large windows that graced the structure.

"Can we go inside already?" Kathy moaned. "The wind is picking up."

Vivienne slid the key into the lock and opened the door. She moved to the alarm box just inside the doorway and put in the code Brian had given her as Kathy closed the door behind them.

"Did you ever notice how big homes like this smell different from our places?" Kathy asked.

Vivienne inhaled and nodded. The air smelled of old papers and books, wood oil, and just a hint of musty basement trailing through the floor vents. "It smells lonely to me."

"Lonely?" Kathy asked.

"Yes." Vivienne explained. "When a house is filled with a family it doesn't smell like this. There's perfumes and foods and laundry. It smells like life."

"You're right." Kathy smiled. "I never thought about it like that."

Vivienne looked around the entry foyer where a large oak desk was placed near the main staircase. It was filled with brochures for local businesses and landmarks for visitors to check out. "I never thought to come inside this place when we were scouting it for the gingerbread contest."

Kathy walked toward the formal receiving parlor past the staircase and stopped at the archway. "Okay boss, what are we looking for here?"

Vivienne shrugged as he put her hand on the carved oak banister of the staircase that led to the second floor. "I'm not sure yet." She glanced upwards at the paneled wall at a series of portraits of several Rothwell family members. "I was hoping for some information about the family history in this place."

Kathy marched over to the information desk and opened one of the brochures about the Rothwell home. "Let's see if there's anything like a map of what's in this place to help visitors." She scanned the brochure quickly. "Here we go. Learn about the Rothwell family history as you tour the splendor of their exquisite summer home." She turned the brochure around and frowned. "Okay, that's so not helpful."

"I guess we start down here and work our way up until we find something." Vivienne pointed toward the parlor near Kathy. "You take that side and I'll check over here."

Kathy folded the brochure back and set it back on the desk. "So we're looking for journals, newspaper stories, anything about the family?"

"That's a good start." Vivienne nodded. "If you find something like that let me know."

"You got it." She stepped into the parlor and whistled. "I'll say this, the rich sure know how to live. There must be enough molding in this place alone to build a new house."

Vivienne chuckled as she pushed open a swinging door. "As a confirmed member of the middle class, I wouldn't know."

"Me either." Kathy replied as she disappeared into the parlor.

Vivienne found herself inside the kitchen area of the home and found herself quite disappointed. She had expected a grand room filled with multiple stoves, rows of hanging pots and pans, and counter space to prepare meals for an army. Instead, the room was surprisingly narrow, compared to the more spacious layouts in modern homes. At most, Vivienne guessed one would be able to cater to a dinner party of no more than eight to ten people. An old wood-fired stove that looked to weigh at least a ton, took up most of the floor space near the center of the room. The behemoth had no dials or controls, it simply warmed up and cooked food. Back in the day, she imagined it probably was the envy of every housewife in Cayuga Cove. To the modern eye, it was simply a heavy iron eyesore.

Yet, there was something vaguely familiar about it. She stared at the scrollwork detailing, trying to recall where she had seen something like it before. Had it been in a magazine? Or had there been a smaller version in Nathaniel and Tristan's antique collection? She reached out and touched the handle to the oven door. The metal was cold, and it took more effort than she had imagined to yank the door open to get a peek inside.

She was surprised to see a single orange flame flickering feebly in the darkness of the oven. She was about to yell to Kathy to come take a look when her memory of just where she had seen the oven before returned with a vengeance. It had been in her vision of Natalie being attacked in the kitchen.

"Kathy." Vivienne called out.

The single orange flame swelled with a whooshing sound as the oven came to life. Vivienne quickly turned away and found Natalie standing behind her. Her hands shot out in surprise and passed through Natalie as if she were made of smoke.

CHAPTER 15

Vivienne felt woozy for a moment. It was as if her power to jump into memory had been activated, but once again it felt somewhat alien to her senses. She was detached from the action, as if a ghostly observer. She watched in silent horror as Natalie reached right through her chest and opened the oven door.

She was dressed in a rather somber black dress that nearly went down to her ankles. Her hair was pulled back into a conservative bun where a small white cap that an old-fashioned maid would have worn was pinned into place. Her face was devoid of emotion as she stared blankly ahead.

"Natalie?" Vivienne asked with bewilderment.

Natalie didn't appear to notice her at all. She simply closed the oven door, pivoted on her heels, and walked over a row of wooden shelves where several metal containers were neatly arranged.

"Is it too much to ask for supper to be served at the proper time, Miss Burdick?" A voice called out from somewhere on the first floor. Seconds later, a woman dressed in an old-fashioned burgundy dress with white pearl buttons sailed into the kitchen. "The children are starting to fuss and you know how my nerves have been lately."

Natalie quickly grabbed a dark green oval container from the shelf. "I apologize, Mrs. Rothwell. The hurrier I go, the behinder I seem to get." Her voice was steeped with an Irish accent that took Vivienne by surprise.

Vivienne stepped carefully away from the stove

and started to examine the kitchen which matched her earlier vision inside Natalie's head. "This can't be right." She spoke aloud to herself. "This must be more than a century ago."

Natalie pulled the lid of a large pot and stared at the contents inside. "I only need a moment to thicken the stew, Miss Rothwell."

"Well for heaven's sake please hurry. You've been working here for four years now, Miss Burdick. I think perhaps you've become complacent that your position here is quite permanent." The woman in the fancy dress put her hands on her hips as she surveyed the kitchen. "My husband is not paying you to keep a filthy kitchen either. I expect you will be up late this evening scrubbing it clean. If you can't keep up with the daily requirements of running this home, I shall not think twice about replacing you." She pushed the swing door and disappeared into the other room.

"Yes, ma'am." Natalie replied meekly as she opened a wooden drawer and pulled out a small wooden spoon. She dipped it into the container marked 'flour' and dropped several heaping amounts into the stock pot which hissed and bubbled.

'Could this be her great-grandmother?' Vivienne wondered. It had to be some sort of relative. She had never seen such a close match before except for twins. She then noticed a newspaper opened up on the floor near the sink. There were several piles of vegetable peels and a bucket on top of the pages, but she could make out the date quite clearly, September 15th, 1872.

Natalie returned to the stove and began to ladle out the portions of stew into some large serving bowls. "Angels, please let Mrs. Rothwell like the stew and make the children behave." She spoke softly as she positioned them on a silver tray and hoisted it to waist level. "Amen."

Vivienne followed Natalie through the swinging door into the dining room. She caught a glimpse of some people sitting at a formal table when suddenly the room swirled into darkness and everyone disappeared. She rubbed her eyes and a moment later the table was empty and a few sconces on the wall flickered with feeble candlelight. Natalie was down on the floor, with a scrub brush and a bucket cleaning the floorboards.

"Hazel and the children are asleep." The male voice she had heard in her earlier vision returned. Only it was not Eddie Robertson, it was Edgar Rothwell. He was tall and quite thin, dressed in a gray woolen suit that was well tailored to his trim figure.

Natalie did not look up from the floorboards. She continued to scrub the wood in gentle, even strokes. "I'm glad to hear that, Master Rothwell."

He walked over to her, his thick-soled shoes clopping loudly in the large room. "You don't need to be so formal now that everyone is upstairs."

Natalie plopped the brush into the bucket and looked up at him. "I'd prefer to keep things formal."

He knelt down and put his hands on her shoulders. "It breaks my heart to see a lovely young lass wasting her best years as a servant."

"I'm quite happy here, Master Rothwell." Natalie looked quite uncomfortable in his grip. "If you could be so kind as to talk to Mrs. Rothwell about how I've improved in my performance, I would be most grateful."

"Hazel doesn't pay the staff. Her opinion means nothing." Edgar leaned closer and put his nose against her dark hair. He inhaled deeply. "You smell like summer in the gardens. Fresh and full of life."

Natalie squirmed out of his grip and picked up the pail in her right hand. "You're too kind, Master Rothwell."

He reached out and gently took the pail out of her hand. "It's been so long, since I've smelled that."

"'Tis only the start of autumn. We've got some time before the lilacs bloom again." Natalie turned to leave but was held in place. "Spring will return before you know it."

"I love how innocent you are." He smiled. "Hazel is like winter. Dull and lifeless. She only delights when things wither and die under her cold demeanor."

"I wish you wouldn't speak ill of Mrs. Rothwell like that." Natalie pleaded. "It makes me uncomfortable."

He pulled her closer to him. "I need you, Natalie. I need you to bring me back to life again."

"No, Master Rothwell." Natalie tried to pull away. "I am not one of those kind of girls."

"Ah, but you are my dear and we both know it." He paused for a moment and then lunged at her, pressing his lips against hers.

She turned her head to the side, facing Vivienne. Her eyes welled up with tears which started to stream down her cheeks. "Please, Master Rothwell. I beg of you to stop this."

"I cannot." He dropped the bucket on the floor,

splashing sudsy water across the floor. "I need you Natalie. I must have you."

She tried to fight him off, but he easily forced her against the wall. "Please have mercy. I cannot do this."

He grabbed her chin and forced her to look straight into his eyes. "How is it you could spread your legs for some filthy gandy dancer laying track with his calloused hands?"

"It was a mistake." Natalie admitted. "I was not in my right mind then."

"Did I not help you out when you were with child down at the factory?"

Natalie nodded. "It was kind of you and Mrs. Rothwell to adopt my son as your own."

"Where would you be as an unwed mother? No good Christian woman would have you working in her home, soiled with the sin of pre-marital relations. You'd probably both be dead and buried in the ground by now."

Natalie's voice began to waver. "I will be forever grateful to you for giving my child the life I never could."

He smiled at her. "Then, I expect you to be grateful. I expect you to do as I command."

"Angels protect me." Natalie whispered as his hands began to undress her.

"Don't worry darling." He cooed in her ear. "This is only going to hurt for a little bit."

Vivienne rushed forward and tried to grab him, but she passed right through his body and fell forward. As she rolled across the floor the voices faded and the room faded to black.

"Help me." A female voice called out from the entrance foyer.

Vivienne groped her way through the darkened room and found the entrance foyer. The light changed back to a bleak daylight that somehow made the scene even more gloomy.

"Please help me." The woman's voice called from above.

Vivienne walked over to the main staircase and looked up toward the second floor. Hazel Rothwell was dressed in a long white nightgown, her hair in a single braid along her right shoulder. She stood at the edge of the bannister, her hands gripping the wood.

"Can you hear me?" Vivienne asked.

Hazel did not respond. She began to cough violently and lurched over the edge. Spatters of red dripped down her nightgown. "Lord, help me. Ease my suffering."

"Be careful." Vivienne tried to warn the woman.

"I was a good wife, taking in a bastard child as if he were my own." She coughed again. "Casting a blind eye while my husband ravished the help."

Vivienne raced up the staircase in a mad dash to help her. "If you can hear me, say my name. Say Vivienne."

Hazel coughed once more and then collapsed, her arms and legs sliding through the wooden posts. "Oh Lord, don't let me suffer like this. What have I done to warrant your wrath? Have I offended thee?"

Vivienne reached the top of the staircase just as Hazel disappeared and the light changed from day to night. The wall sconces flickered to life with dim candlelight once more.

"Is there nothing you can do, Doctor?" The voice of Edgar Rothwell sounded from a doorway nearby.

Vivienne followed the sound to a large double oak door that was half open. She peeked in and gasped.

Edgar Rothwell was standing next to a large canopy bed with another man dressed in a white coat whom she assumed was a physician. "Her appetite has diminished with each passing day." Edgar spoke softly. "She has been delirious most of the time. It pains me to say so Doctor, but she has made threats against her own life. She seems to think the good Lord is punishing her for her sins."

"Her mental health has always been fragile. I think it would be best to keep her here in the guest bedroom and away from the young children. She needs rest and quiet."

Vivienne stepped into the room and could now make out the form of Hazel reclined in the bed. Her lips were drawn tight against her face, her hair a tangle mess.

"I will keep her quiet and have the maid keep watch." Edgar nodded.

Hazel's eyes twitched and she suddenly lurched upwards in bed with a start. "Vivienne." She screamed and then reached out with a blue-tinged hand. "She is the angel of death come for my soul."

Vivienne stumbled backwards in shock. "You can see me?"

Hazel laughed maniacally and then dropped back down into bed. "Take him first, feast on his black soul to your heart's content. Let him writhe in the flames of hell."

"Hazel, who are you talking to?" The Doctor asked.

Hazel closed her eyes and said no more.

The Doctor leaned forward, putting his ear to her nose. After a few moments, he stepped away. "I'm sorry, Edgar. She's gone."

Edgar nodded solemnly. "At last she is at peace."

The room slowly darkened and the figures of all three dissipated like smoke. Vivienne stepped back out of the bedroom and found the light slowly changing back to daytime. From further down the hall she could hear the voices of children. She followed the sound to a small playroom. A young boy and girl, each with dark hair were playing with wooden toys.

Vivienne stepped into the room and nearly screamed. It was Connor, except the little boy's skin was pale blue, looking similar to a weak winter sky. His lips were drawn tight against his mouth, cracked and bloody. He pulled a small wagon around him, humming a merry little tune.

His sister, was propped back against a large trunk with a rag doll in her hands. She wasn't as blue as the boy, but her eyes were sunken in and lined with dark circles. She combed the doll's hair with a little brush and coughed. A spatter of crimson splashed across the doll's face.

"Oh children, what has happened to you?" Vivienne asked with a heavy heart.

The little girl looked directly at her. "We're sick."

Vivienne's heart raced in her chest. "You can see me too?"

The little boy stopped the wagon. His green eyes

glowing like emeralds. "And hear you."

Vivienne stepped closer to them. "How did you know your mother could see me?"

"She told us." The little girl giggled. "She still comes to tuck us in at night."

"Didn't she die?" Vivienne asked.

The little boy nodded. "She said she's waiting for us."

"Jacob. Mother said not to tell her about that part." The little girl chided. "Now she's going to be angry."

Jacob folded his arms across his chest. "She's going to be mad at you too, Constance."

"No one is going to be mad at anyone." Vivienne corrected them. "How long have you both been sick?"

"Since mommy fell ill." Constance replied.

"Where is Natalie?" Vivienne asked them both.

Jacob looked at Constance.

"Don't tell her."

Jacob looked back at Vivienne and shook his head. "I'm not supposed to say."

Vivienne knelt down in front of him. "Honey, it's okay to tell me."

"I can't." He replied.

"I'll tell your mommy it was my fault if she wants to blame someone."

Constance got up from the floor and pressed her right ear to the wall. "We were too loud. Daddy is coming."

Vivienne could hear the sound of heavy footfalls coming closer to the playroom. "Please children, you need to tell me where Natalie is."

Jacob pointed upwards to the ceiling.

"Is she up on the third floor?"

He nodded.

"No one is to ever go up to the third floor. Daddy forbids it." Constance whispered. "If you go up there, he's going to be very mad."

"So will mommy." Jacob added. "She doesn't like Natalie at all."

Vivienne straightened back up just as Edgar Rothwell's stern voice shouted into the room. "I told you children to stay in your beds."

The children screamed and their little bodies shattered like glass and disappeared, leaving the playroom empty except for the toys.

Vivienne stepped out of the playroom and back into the hallway. As she did she heard a crackling sound, dry and sharp. Out of the corner of her eye she saw the lid of the trunk slowly rising and a skeletal arm reaching upwards from inside of it. "Children?" Hazel's voice echoed.

The light faded back to evening as the candle sconces flared to life. Vivienne pulled the door closed and hurried back to the staircase. It was only when she reached the bannister she realized that they went no further up.

She looked at the ceiling and guessed there had to be an attic door with a pull cord either in the hallway or in one of the rooms. With her options limited, she started back down the hall. In the dim light, it was very hard to make out any details.

There was the muffled sound of a scream from the ceiling above her. Vivienne paused and listened. Footfalls creaked on the ceiling above her head and walked in the direction of the children's playroom.

She followed them and then turned the opposite way into a small office with a desk and a bookcase. The footfalls continued above her head and then disappeared beyond the wall past the bookcase.

She stepped lightly past the desk and listened once more. There was the muffled sound of two people, a male and female in some sort of conversation. She couldn't make out any of the words, but she was certain the female voice sounded very much in distress.

Her hands moved along the leaded-glass doors that kept the books safe from dust. She tried to pull it open but it was locked.

The murmur of the voices continued and she felt even more compelled to figure out where the attic entrance was hidden. She opened the desk drawers, searching for a set of keys. She found only bottles of ink, sheets of writing paper, and dust.

The voices stopped suddenly and Vivienne was enveloped in silence. She slid the desk drawers closed and turned around to give the lock on the bookcase another jiggle.

She came face to face with the angry face of Edgar Rothwell towering above her. "What are you doing in here?" He yelled at her.

Vivienne put her hands up in surprise. "I'm here to help."

His pale eyes turned dark black and he grabbed her roughly by her sweatshirt. "You were thieving."

Vivienne felt real panic as his form seemed as solid as hers. She reached up and tried to release his grip but was unable to do so. "I'm a friend, searching for Natalie."

"Lies. You women are nothing but deceit and lies. No better than Eve in the garden." He hissed. "Evil needs to be devoured."

Vivienne struggled to get free. "I'm not who you think I am."

Edgar pulled her closer and his breath smelled of musty earth and foul rot. She watched in silent terror as his jaw opened wider and wider, with a sickening crackling sound.

"Let me go." Vivienne screamed, kicking and pounding against him.

Edgar held her in place as his jaw lowered beyond his throat.

Vivienne saw movement from inside his mouth. A pair of fingers were reaching up from behind his tonsils, reaching out toward her. "I won't let you do this." Vivienne screamed once more as the fingers moved to the back of his teeth.

"Vivienne. Honey, can you hear me?" Kathy's voice called to her from somewhere in the distance.

"Help me." Vivienne screamed. "I'm in here."

The fingers shot forward and grabbed her around the throat. Vivienne gasped for air as they tightened and constricted her airway. She could feel them pulling her inside Edgar's mouth. A bitter, terrible cold enveloped her.

"Snap out of it." Kathy's face appeared inside Edgar's mouth.

Vivienne let out a scream of abject terror as the entire scene exploded with a deafening thud.

Kathy shook Vivienne firmly. "Vivienne, can you hear me?"

She was back in the kitchen of the Rothwell home,

lying on the floor near the oven. "Kathy?"

"Oh, thank God. I thought you'd gone insane." Relief washed over Kathy's face. "What the hell happened to you?"

Vivienne pulled herself up from the floor. "How long was I out?"

"Just a few seconds." Kathy replied. "I was about to explore the parlor room when you asked me to come in here because you found something."

Vivienne shook her head. "Only a few seconds?"

"Yes." Kathy confirmed. "I found you on the floor and thought you were having a seizure. I was about to call the paramedics when you came around."

Vivienne shook her head. "It wasn't a seizure. I tried to open the oven door and I must have slipped and hit my head on the darn thing."

Kathy clucked her tongue. "You need to be more careful." She offered her an arm and pulled Vivienne up to her feet. "Do you feel a bump anywhere on your head?"

"No." Vivienne gave her a little smile. "Just my ego is bruised I think."

Kathy folded her arms together. "This place sure got awful cold since we came inside."

"You feel it too?" Vivienne asked.

"Are you sure you want to poke around this place? It's kind of spooky."

Vivienne shook her head. "I think I've had enough for today. Let's return the keys to Brian and call it a night."

CHAPTER 16

Monday, December 9th

It had been a busy day for orders at the bakery, but Vivienne's head just wasn't in the game. She was fortunate enough to have Stephanie keeping track of everything. Under her watchful eyes, she made sure that dates were correct and double checked spelling of names on birthday cakes. As they finished the usual rush during the lunch hour, Vivienne fixed herself a cup of cinnamon tea and sat down at one of the bistro tables with her writing pad and pen. She jotted down as much as she could remember from her strange vision inside the Rothwell kitchen and began to list some of the strange questions that needed to be answered.

"Making out your Christmas list?" Stephanie asked as she placed a fresh batch of half-moon cookies into the glass display case.

"I wish I was that organized this early." Vivienne looked over in her direction and gave her a little smile. "I'm just trying to help some friends out."

"Anything I can do?" Stephanie closed the sliding door on the display case.

"Actually, would you mind running the store a bit for this afternoon?" Vivienne felt guilty pushing her business duties onto her assistant. She vowed then and there to up her Christmas bonus another twenty percent. "I'm going to check on Eunice at the hospital."

Stephanie walked over to the small closet where they stored the cleaning supplies and pulled out the broom and dustpan. "Not at all."

"I can't tell you how much this means to me."

Stephanie started to sweep the floor behind the counter. "I like it here." She gathered up some pieces of wax paper that had fallen during the lunch rush and dumped them into the waste bin. "It's never been just a job here. I love what I do."

"You're very good at running a business." Vivienne complimented her.

Stephanie paused for a moment, leaning against the broom handle. "It just feels right to me."

"I wouldn't be surprised to see you open a business right after you finish college."

"Maybe." Stephanie grinned. "But what would I open?"

"Whatever drives your passion." Vivienne replied. "When you follow your heart, you can't go wrong."

"Thanks." Stephanie went back to sweeping. "Speaking of hearts, I was sorry to see what happened to Nathaniel and Tristan."

"That note was terrible and it was written with nothing but malicious intent." Vivienne set the pen down on the table and took another sip of her tea.

"Any idea who the Bad Santa is?"

"I'm working on that." Vivienne nodded.

"Those two are the nicest guys, I can't believe how the town's just turned on them." Stephanie added.

"Joshua said they were keeping an officer out near the protesters in front of their store today. Just to be sure no one does anything stupid."

Stephanie emptied her dustpan into the waste

bin. "So who's this Pastor Seamus Kilpatrick?"

"He's Eunice Kilpatrick's brother." Vivienne confirmed. "He came into town right after she was hit by the car."

"It's like the whole town is suddenly going crazy." Stephanie remarked.

"I know how you feel." Vivienne added. "But I can tell you that Pastor Kilpatrick gathering a small group together to protest Nathaniel and Tristan's lifestyle isn't helping matters."

"Why don't the police just go out there and tell them to leave?"

Vivienne shook her head. "They have the right to protest peacefully.

"I wanted to yell at them when I drove by this morning, but I didn't." Stephanie confessed.

"You did the right thing. If you give them an inch of attention they'll run a mile with it."

"This Pastor Kilpatrick doesn't even have a church here, does he?" Stephanie asked.

"Not to my knowledge." Vivienne picked up her writing pad and slid out of the chair. "But that's part of what I'm going to find out today while you run the business."

"Go get them." Stephanie raised her broom up in the air with a grand gesture just as the telephone rang. She hurried over behind the counter and answered it. "Sweet Dreams Bakery, how can I help you?"

Vivienne walked over the display window that looked out upon Main Street. Inside her bakery, everything was peaceful. She counted her blessings that the Bad Santa hadn't targeted her yet, because she found it all too easy to imagine the protestors in front of Carriage House Antiques moving to her front sidewalk. Imagine if she were outed as a witch? Miss Octavia had her shop vandalized, but could an angry mob go even further and burn her bakery to the ground? The very notion gave her chills.

"Vivienne, it's Joshua on the phone for you." Stephanie called out.

"Joshua?" She turned around in surprise and hurried to the phone. "Thanks, Stephanie."

Stephanie handed her the phone. "I'm going to go out back and get a start on the inventory before you leave."

"Thanks." Vivienne put the phone to her ear as Stephanie graciously left to give her privacy. "Hi hon, what's going on?"

"Forensics has a match on Sally Rollin's car. She was the one who ran Eunice Kilpatrick down." Joshua explained.

"That doesn't make any sense." Vivienne clenched her teeth in frustration. "You know that Eunice tried to help her out not too long ago."

"Help her out how?" Joshua asked.

"She was at the bank applying for a loan and got turned down. Eunice told her that Nathanial and Tristan sometimes bought antiques and paid cash on the spot."

"Who told you this?"

"Nathaniel and Tristan." Vivienne explained. "But there's much more to that story."

"Sally Rollins is being brought in for questioning" Joshua offered. "Be careful you don't step on Sheriff Rigsbee's toes when you check things out. He's on his last nerve and not afraid to let anyone who gets in his way know it."

"I'm heading to the library, so I'll be far from the line of fire." Vivienne assured him.

"Any leads that your magic helped out with yet?"

Vivienne had wanted to tell him all about what had happened yesterday in the Rothwell mansion, but she could barely process the experience herself. She needed to verify information first, piece together what she had seen in her vision, and then formulate some sort of explanation that tied everything together. "I'm working on it."

"I wish I could talk longer, but I've got a meeting with Sheriff Rigsbee in a minute. Be careful." Joshua replied.

"You too." Vivienne wished that he could come with her. She always felt safe with him beside her. "I love you."

"I love you too." Joshua echoed back. "If you find out anything big be sure to call me right away."

"I promise." Vivienne hung up the phone and opened her display case. She pulled out two half-moon cookies and wrapped them in a small box. Delores would be thrilled to get the treat.

* * *

Vivienne's first stop was at the hospital to check on Eunice's progress and to say hello to Delores as she had promised. However, her plans changed slightly as she walked into room 508 and heard two familiar voices talking from behind the curtain, Eunice and her brother, Pastor Seamus Kilpatrick.

Delores, was fast asleep, her head tipped to the side as she snored.

"When did the doctor say you could leave?" Seamus' voice asked as Vivienne crept carefully closer to hear everything.

"Not for at least a week." Eunice's voice was raspy and sounded frail. "He says I might need some physical therapy first."

"Did you let him know that I could stay with you to help out?"

"I didn't know how long you were staying in Cayuga Cove for." Eunice replied. "Did you have a talk with Father William over at Our Lady of the Lake?"

"I did." Seamus replied. "He was happy to hear that I would be taking over the congregation at Shoreline Baptist while Pastor Green goes overseas on missionary work."

"So when you do start?"

"New Year's day." Seamus added. "That's when we start to clean up this town and put it back on the path of righteousness."

"Amen, dear brother." Eunice replied. "This town has been going downhill fast with the murder scandal, the opening of a witchcraft store, and those sleazy gays who run the antique store."

"I promised you that I'd fix things, sister. With the Lord on our side, how can we go wrong?"

Vivienne set the package of cookies on the bedside table and hurried away before she could be found. She didn't like the tone in Seamus' voice, but he was the least of her worries. At least Delores could enjoy the baked goods when she awoke. As for

Eunice, she could just stuff her face with communion wafers.

*   *   *

Harriet Nettles had been more than happy to once again assist Vivienne with research at the town library. She had felt quite free to express her own opinions on what was going on in town as she gathered the Cayuga Union Cemetery records for Vivienne upstairs in the library. As much as it pained Vivienne to think it, she had to admit that when it came to the stereotypical 'old maid' figure, Harriet fit the profile to perfection.

She had few friends, mostly keeping company with her books and the stray cats she fed outside her modest single bedroom home. She never expressed very much interest in getting married or starting a family, but that was where Vivienne had enormous respect for her. She was happy with her life and felt no need to justify her decisions to anyone. She was a collector of information and had a natural curiosity about the world. However, unlike Vivienne, Harriet was happy to explore from the comfort of her wingback chair with a hand-knitted blanket over her lap and a cup of chamomile tea on the side table.

As Vivienne explored the cemetery records she located the information about the death of the Rothwell family but could find no record of Natalie Burdick. It was as if she had never existed, yet her magical vision had told quite the opposite story.

Frustrated, she returned to the main desk where Harriet was busy gathering books that had been dropped off in the night return box. "Harriet, I have a question about the old Cayuga Union Cemetery that I can't find an answer to."

Harriet looked up from the desk as she scanned the books with a barcode device to log them back into the system. "I've given you everything I have on it."

"Do you know who the last caretaker was?" Vivienne wondered.

Harriet scratched her chin with her hand. "That's a good question. I wish I could tell you, but I have no idea. The records were stored here long before I assumed the job."

"Maggie Sandro died last year, so I can't ask her." Vivienne brought up the beloved former librarian that had served for nearly five decades.

"May she rest in peace." Harriet lowered her head for a moment. "You know Vivienne, I remember her talking about plans to fix up that old cemetery a few months before she died. She kept saying it was shameful to the memory of the civil war veterans buried there to let the place fade away."

"This could be very important, Harriet." Vivienne pressed. "Did she mention anyone she discussed this with?"

Harriet tried to pull up the memory but she simply shook her head in frustration. "I'm sorry, I just can't recall the details of the conversation."

Vivienne looked around the desk. The library was empty as usual. "It was worth a try." She looked down at Harriet's hands and noticed a charm bracelet on her right wrist. "Say, that's quite lovely." Vivienne pointed down.

Harriet smiled. "My bracelet? Why, thank you."

"Wherever did you find it?"

"It was on clearance at Meeker Jewelers last week for twenty-five dollars." Harriet beamed with pride. "I normally don't indulge in such things, but it was just so cute I couldn't say no."

"May I see it up close?" Vivienne asked.

"Sure." Harriet stretched her arm upwards at Vivienne's face. "I just love the simple elegance of silver."

Vivienne nodded and seized Harriet's hand in her own grip. "Think back to that conversation with Maggie Sandro. Back when she talked about the cemetery."

Harriet's face went blank as the magic worked through her mind. She let out a little gasp. "I miss Maggie so much."

"We all do, Harriet. But think back to the time when you and her talked about the cemetery."

Harriet nodded as her mind began to open to Vivienne. "Yes, what a shame it was to let it go." She murmured.

The library desk swirled away as Vivienne stepped into Harriet's memory. She felt more disconnected this time, as if she were more a silent observer than an active participant in the spell. When her vision cleared, she was standing in a charmingly-decorated room at the Whispering Oaks retirement facility. Vivienne knew the layout quite well from her many visits to Nana Mary's apartment.

Maggie Sandro sat on her blue-floral patterned loveseat with Harriet Nettles beside her. Her short white hair was neatly combed, her brown eyes still bright with the spark of curiosity that Harriet shared.

"I spoke with Mona Clarke about getting the mayor involved with rescuing the cemetery."

Vivienne was pleased to have the more unique view of a spectral observer than the more personal invasion of assuming the target's body. There was hardly any dizzy feeling or disorientation.

"What did she say?" Harriet asked.

"She said that her husband was a very busy man, having just taken office but that she would mention it to him." Maggie gave a little scowl. "I didn't find her very sincere."

"Well, she did come to Whispering Oaks to visit with the residents." Harriet replied. "That's something."

"It's the minimum she could do." Maggie spoke up. "She seems more caught up in the excitement of being first lady if you ask me."

"I can't argue with you on that point." Harriet chuckled. "Whatever made you take notice of the Cayuga Union Cemetery?"

"I know there are fewer days ahead than there are behind, Harriet." Maggie sighed.

Harriet reached out and took hold of Maggie's hands. "Oh, don't say such a thing."

"I've lived a very full life and I certainly can't complain for having eighty-nine good years to enjoy it with."

Harriet's eyes filled with tears. "The good Lord will bless you with many more I hope."

"Perhaps he will." Maggie agreed. "But, one last thing I hope to do before I go is have that old cemetery restored to a proper state."

"There hasn't been a burial out there for

decades." Harriet replied. "Does anyone even visit the graves? I never see any flowers."

"There probably aren't many living mourners alive anymore, but that doesn't mean they should be forgotten." Maggie spoke up. "There are quite a few union soldiers buried there, there's even a cannon and a stack of cannonballs up there."

"There is? I never noticed it."

"That's because the weeds and grass have taken over and hidden it from view." Maggie looked toward Vivienne for a moment, as if she noticed her.

"What's wrong, Maggie?" Harriet asked with a hint of concern in her voice.

"Nothing." Maggie shook her head. "Just a trick of the light."

"Just like in the library." Harriet nodded back. "You were so right about that when things are quiet."

"So, to make a long story short I asked this Mona Clarke to look into where the money for the perpetual care of the cemetery has gone to."

"Who was the last caretaker?" Harriet wondered.

"John Pagano, he retired about ten years ago."

"So he never had a replacement?"

Maggie shook her head. "The town took care of the lawn care for a year or two but then a mowing was missed, then another. Before too long, it was just forgotten and no one ever complained."

"That's a shame." Harriet agreed.

"Those folks buried out there deserve to be remembered." Maggie spoke softly. "I can't think of a worse fate than to simply be forgotten."

The room slowly faded away as Vivienne gently pulled away from Harriet's memory. There was a slight moment of dizziness as the spell effects diminished. Vivienne quickly worked to cover it before Harriet could ask questions. "You certainly snagged quite a bargain with that bracelet." She released Harriet's hand.

"I'm sorry." She blinked. "What did you say?"

"I said you sure snagged a bargain over at Meeker's." Vivienne smiled. "I never have luck like that with sales."

"Neither do I." Harriet took a deep breath and pulled her arm back down. "Oh, I hate that feeling."

"What feeling?" Vivienne felt a moment of panic build inside her.

"That feeling when someone walks over your grave." Harriet smiled. "I know it's just a silly superstition, but I can't help but think that whenever I get goose bumps."

"Oh, I wouldn't dismiss everything magical in the world." Vivienne played along. "There's a little truth to everything."

"I'm sorry I couldn't be more help to you." Harriet replied as she started scanning books again.

"Oh, don't worry about it. You gave me more help than I could have hoped for." Vivienne waved goodbye and stepped out of the library.

She retrieved her smart phone and activated the telephone directory app she had installed a few months ago on a lark. She typed in the name Pagano and found five residents in various locations around Cayuga Cove. John Pagano was listed as residing at 1435 Miller's Hollow Road.

She held the phone to her ear and activated the voice assist program. "Directions to 1435 Miller's

Hollow Road."

"Getting directions to 1435 Miller's Hollow Road." The digitized voice replied and displayed a map. Vivienne was pleased to see it was just on the northern outskirts of town, just off Route Ninety. She climbed into her Toyota and set the phone in a cradle on the dashboard to keep the map at eye level.

CHAPTER 17

John Pagano's two-story farmhouse seemed lonely sitting atop a small hill that was framed by a fee pine trees that swayed in the cold wind coming off the shoreline of Cayuga Lake. A small flower garden was barren, with pockets of snow scattered here and there between brown husks of hardy mums that had at last given up the fight against the coming freeze of winter. As Vivienne parked her car in the gravel driveway, she hoped that John would be feeling more hospitable than the residents of town.

The front door creaked open as a white-bearded face poked out to get a better look at his visitor. "Route Ninety is back the way you came. Take a left at the farm stand down the road."

"I'm not lost, Mister Pagano." Vivienne put on her friendliest smile and approached the front porch which had seen better days. The entire structure was slanted to the right. The roof was a canvas of moss-covered broken boards, some pulled apart to create openings where birds and squirrels made nests for their young. "I was hoping to talk to you about the Cayuga Union Cemetery."

John Pagano squinted and put his hand up to his eyes against the afternoon sunlight that broke through the clouds overhead. "The mayor's office finally decided to come around to that have they?"

Vivienne carefully walked up the wooden steps, the wooden boards bowing slightly with each movement. "I'm not working for the Mayor's office.

My name is Vivienne Finch and I run the Sweet Dreams Bakery on Main Street."

"You came all the way up here to drum up business?" He asked suspiciously.

"No sir." She reached the front door. "I'm a friend of Harriet Nettles and Maggie Sandro."

John's face was lined with deep-set wrinkles, a testament to all his years working outside under the sun. He would have been an inch or two taller than Vivienne, were it not for his hunched back. "Well, in that case I suppose it'd be rude not to invite you inside."

Vivienne nodded. "It's a little cold out here, for sure."

John opened the door fully and motioned for her to come into his home. "I'm afraid I don't entertain company much here anymore."

Vivienne stepped into the living room area of the home and her nose was assaulted with the unmistakable smell of a kerosene heater. "I won't take too much of your time Mister Pagano. I only have a few questions I hope you can answer for me."

John shut the door and kicked a draft blocker against the bottom. "Please have a seat and by all means call me John." He smiled, revealing a full set of yellow-stained teeth.

Vivienne quickly looked around the room. Like most older homes, the living areas were divided up quite small. There was a simple tan sofa with a multi-colored quilt draped over the upper edge of the cushions planted against the wall opposite the front door. The walls were covered with faux wood grain brown paneling that screamed vintage 1970's. She took a seat on the sofa. "Thank you."

John walked slowly over to her and sat down with a little bit of effort that revealed he most likely battled some form of arthritis in his back. "So what's a pretty young baker doing asking questions about an old cemetery?"

"Well, my research revealed that you were the last caretaker and I was wondering if you could shed some light as to why a replacement was never found." Vivienne asked.

John shrugged his shoulders. "The town never got around to it, I suppose."

"I thought the Cayuga Union Cemetery had perpetual care?"

"It's supposed to." John nodded. "Back when I took care of the grounds I used to go to town hall to get money for equipment and such."

"When did the town assume control of the cemetery?" Vivienne asked.

John paused for a moment in thought. "That would have been back in 1976. The town council wanted to load the cannons onto a float for the Bicentennial parade that July and they asked me to get it cleaned up as best I could."

"Did they do that?"

John shook his head. "No, they gave it a good try but that darn things were heavier than anyone thought. Snapped a few cables when the tractors tried to haul the first one out of the cemetery."

Vivienne hoped that her mind would be as sharp as John's when she reached his age. Despite his aged appearance, his recall was most impressive. "So, they abandoned the plans and left them alone?"

"Sure did." He chuckled. "I always thought it kind of odd how Union soldiers moved the cannons so easily back during the civil war, but all that modern equipment couldn't budge it an inch. Must be the ghosts didn't want it to leave."

Vivienne leaned forward. "Ghosts?"

He stared at her for a moment and scratched his chin. "I can tell from the look on your face that you believe in them too."

"Yes, actually."

"Well, working in that cemetery all those years I've seen and heard some things I can't explain." John revealed. "Does that scare you?"

Vivienne shook her head. "No. In fact, that was one of the questions I was going to ask you."

John let out a hearty laugh which turned into a coughing fit. He reached into the front pocket of his shirt and pulled out a handkerchief which he placed over his mouth.

"Are you ill?"

John waved her question off and recovered. "Just a tickle in my throat."

"I don't want to take your time if you're not feeling up to it."

"I'm fine, young lady." John straightened his posture a bit. "Now, do you want to hear about the ghosts up there or not?"

"Please continue." Vivienne said apologetically.

"Well, since we were talking about the cannons, I suppose I should start with the black widow."

"The spider?" Vivienne asked.

"No." John cleared his throat. "That's just the name I gave her. Late nights, usually around the beginning of fall I used to see her standing over by the civil war monument. She was dressed all in black, her head lowered as if she were mourning someone."

"Did she say anything?"

"She just walked real slow back and forth, looking at the cannons. I don't know why, but I always felt like she was real sad about something."

"How did you know she was sad?"

"She just kept doing this, over and over and then I heard sobbing." John acted out with his hand how he saw her caressing the cannons gently with her hands.

"That's amazing." Vivienne reached into her purse and pulled out her little note pad and a pen. She scribbled down John's story. "Did you get a good look at her ever?"

"Nope." John shook his head. "The few times I would walk closer to get a better view she would see me coming and then just disappear into thin air."

"Did you ever check the graves around the cannons to see if any women were laid to rest there?"

"I knew the names of most of the headstones like my own family." John explained. "When I'd be out there mowing, I'd be able to gauge my time by passing by certain markers."

"Are there any women around the cannons?"

"No." John replied. "It's all union soldiers."

Vivienne wanted to check it out on her own regardless and made a note to do so later. "So this black widow, what did she look like?"

"She was short and thin." John searched his memory. "It looked like her hair was pulled up into a bun in the back and she was dressed in this long black dress that looked real old-fashioned."

"So you think she was dressed in clothing from the civil war period?"

"Could be, but I'm no fashion expert." John chuckled. "So, why the big interest in ghosts?"

Vivienne felt her face flush warm at the question. "Well, I'm a bit of a ghost hunter in my spare time."

"Ghost hunter?" He smiled. "Like those fancy boys on the television shows?"

"Hardly." Vivienne smiled back at him. "It's just a hobby I like to engage in from time to time."

"I never talked to Harriet or Maggie about the black widow." John continued. "I never thought they'd believe me."

"I've got quite an open mind." Vivienne replied.

"Of that I have no doubt, young lady." John agreed. "So, are you going to go look for her in the cemetery?"

"I'm going to try."

"Well, you best watch where you step when you do." John warned her. "There are plenty of old graves that never had burial vaults put in them. When the wooden casket rots away, it leaves a big gap in the earth. You step on one of those and you could end up six feet under."

Vivienne shuddered at the gruesome thought. "Thanks for the warning."

"Happened back in the early eighties once. A young couple went to the cemetery to make mischief. The boyfriend decided he wanted to try and load a cannon ball into one of the cannons and pried the protective cap off the end with a crow bar. When he went to get a cannon ball from the pile, he got pulled into the ground and I had to rescue him." John recalled. "He damn near suffocated but we got to him in time."

"John, you said earlier that you know most of the headstone names in the cemetery." Vivienne interrupted.

"Sure do."

"Can you recall seeing the name Natalie Burdick anywhere there?"

John paused again in thought. "Burdick." He glanced upwards toward the ceiling in thought. "Burdick."

"She would have died sometime in the late 1800's, maybe the early twentieth century." Vivienne tried to help him out.

"I don't think that name is in there." John replied. "But, it could be one of the stones that is so far eroded you can't read it anymore."

"I checked the records at the library and I didn't find any mention of her." Vivienne sighed.

"Well, those records aren't complete. The city hall fire of 1932 destroyed some of them."

"I didn't know that." Vivienne perked up. "So it's possible she is buried there."

"Do you think she's the black widow?" John asked.

"What makes you say that?"

"You ask me about the ghost, give me a name." John smiled. "I may only have an eighth grade education, but even I can figure that out."

"I think it's a possibility." Vivienne conceded.

"Well, if you find out will you promise to come back and let me know." John asked.

"Sure." Vivienne agreed and pulled herself up from the sofa. "Thank you again for being so kind and sharing your stories."

John nodded. "Before you leave, would you go over to the hutch and open the right drawer?"

Vivienne glanced at the simple hutch that was covered with dust and piles of junk mail. "Did you need something?"

He nodded. "In the drawer there's a cigar box. Could you bring it over? My back gets a little testy when I sit for any length of time."

"Of course." She did as he asked and found a small vintage Cuban cigar box right where he said it would be. She picked it up and brought it over to him. "Would you like me to help you stand before I leave?"

"No need to trouble yourself." He smiled as she handed him the box. "I just wanted to give you this." He flipped the top of the box open and revealed a silver brooch. With a shaky hand, he gave it to her. "It was something I found years ago mowing the lawn near the cannons."

Vivienne shook her head. "Oh, I couldn't accept this."

"I thought it might help you find the black widow." John spoke up with a glimmer of excitement in his tired eyes. "Those boys on television always say having an object usually gets the ghost's attention."

"Do you think it came from a grave?"

"No, if I did I never would have taken it with me." John replied. "I think someone wanted me to find it."

"The black widow?" Vivienne raised an eyebrow.

"You said it, not me." John chuckled. "You're a brave soul, I'll give you that."

"Thank you." Vivienne slipped the silver brooch into her purse and glanced at her wristwatch. "I really must be going now, but it was a pleasure talking with you."

"The pleasure was all mine, young lady." John smiled back. "Don't forget to let me know what you find out."

"I promise." Vivienne smiled back.

CHAPTER 18

As she was driving out to the Cayuga Union Cemetery, she decided against her better judgment to just go to Natalie's trailer and look for some answers directly. After all, she was practically there by the time she reached the cemetery anyway.

She knew that if one of Sheriff Rigsbee's officers found her there, she would be in a heap of trouble, but it was Joshua she was more concerned about. She had kept some of her findings from him because she didn't want him to worry. He had enough on his mind with everything going on in town.

As she pulled into the trailer court she was relieved to see no patrol cars parked anywhere. She carefully navigated the road, avoiding some new potholes that opened up, pulling alongside the trailer where she had watched the entire saga unfold not too long ago.

Natalie's trailer looked dark inside, and there were no footprints in the snow to indicate anyone had been there for quite some time. Vivienne stepped out of her car and charged forward toward the front door. As her feet crunched in the snow, she heard a voice call out.

"She's not home. Why don't you vultures go chase another story?"

Vivienne turned toward the voice and saw a man dressed in a puffy blue winter jacket with an orange hunter's cap on his head. "I'm not with the media."

The man tipped his head to the side. "Then what are you doing poking around this trailer court?"

Vivienne pointed to Natalie's trailer. "I was hoping to visit with my friend. She's had a rough time of things here lately."

The man walked toward her, his boots crunching the snow with his heavy steps. "I know that. I'm here neighbor."

Vivienne searched her memory quickly. Sally Rollins had mentioned a neighbor that had heard a gunshot the day Eddie was attacked. His name was on the tip of her tongue. "Of course, Sally Rollins mentioned you." She stalled for time.

"I don't associate with her kind." The man stopped in front of her and wiped his red nose with his gloved hand. "Always sticking her nose in other people's business."

"You're Gus Holt." Vivienne snapped her fingers.

"I am." He eyed her suspiciously. "And you are?"

"Vivienne Finch. I own a bakery down on Main Street in town."

Gus nodded. "I've heard about you. You were part of that whole Mona Clarke murder mess a while back."

Vivienne gulped. "Well, a small part."

He sniffed the cold air. "Like I said, ain't nobody been home for a few days now."

"Do you happen to know where they are staying?" She asked.

"I don't stick my nose into other folk's business." He folded his arms.

"Mister Holt, mind if I ask you a question about the day Eddie Robertson was attacked?"

"Shot." Gus corrected her. "I know a gunshot when I hear one."

"But the medical staff found no evidence of a bullet wound on Eddie anywhere." Vivienne explained. "How can that be?"

Gus shook his head. "I only know what I know. I told the police and I'm telling you that I heard a gunshot that day and no one is going to convince me otherwise."

"Do you think maybe it was someone's television turned up loud? Those home theater systems can really surprise you."

Gus scoffed at her theory. "You sound just like those Keystone Cops downtown."

"I'm just trying to figure out the truth of what happened here." Vivienne pleaded. "For Natalie and Connor's sake."

"That's all well and good, but I don't have any other answers for you."

Vivienne wanted to go snoop around the trailer for clues, but that wasn't going to happen with Gus standing guard. "Well then, I guess I wasted some gas coming out here for nothing."

"Sorry I can't help you, Miss Finch." Gus apologized and glared at her. "Was there anything else?"

"No." Vivienne gave him a little smile and headed back for her car. "Thank you for coming out to let me know she wasn't here."

"Anytime." Gus waved and stood his ground.

Vivienne pulled away, wishing she had a spell handy to make nosy neighbors disappear. She'd have to ask Nana Mary about one the next time she saw her.

As her car rounded the corner onto Cemetery

Road, Vivienne spied a little kid running across the road. She slammed on her brakes, as the car skidded sideways off to the side and hit a small snow bank.

The little kid laughed and threw a snowball at her windshield. Vivienne gasped when she recognized the little imp. It was Connor. Dressed in a little black coat with a white hat and mittens, he gave her a smile. "Hey, don't run off." She yelled and exited the car. Connor turned around, giggled at her, and ran up the snow bank and into the Cayuga Union Cemetery.

"Connor." Vivienne yelled after him. "I need to talk you."

There was a faint giggle as a reply. Vivienne locked her purse in the car and gave chase through the snow. "Connor, I need to talk to you and your mom. Please come back."

"Hide and seek." Connor squealed with delight. "Come and find me."

Vivienne hurried up through the main gate of the cemetery expecting to see Connor's white hat bobbing along the headstones. She paused for a moment to listen for his footfalls, but was greeted with silence. Thankfully, the snow was a little deeper out here in the countryside and she was able to easily track his little boot prints. "Connor, I don't have time to play a game today. Can you tell me where your mommy is?"

There was no answer. The late afternoon sun was hanging low in the western sky, the shadows from the tombstones grew long against the white snow on the ground. Vivienne followed his twisting little path without much effort, stepping further and further upwards toward the civil war monuments and the cannons. "Hey Connor, I bet you can't find the big cannons in here. I'll bet you can't find them before I do."

Suddenly, she saw the white hat leap upwards from behind a large marble stone and run off toward the cannons. "Yes I can." He yelled back.

Vivienne charged ahead, careful not to trip on any of the smaller stones that had fallen over onto the ground. At last, she could see the large cannons looming ahead, their capped nozzles raised skyward. Connor was standing between them, he giggled and pointed at her. "Slowpoke."

"You won, Connor." Vivienne managed to speak between breaths as she trudged through the uneven ground. "You beat me fair and square."

"I won." He jumped up and down with excitement.

Vivienne was only a few steps from him when suddenly she felt her legs give out unexpectedly. She threw her hands upwards in shock as the ground disappeared below her and she was swallowed up into the cold darkness. With a muffled scream, she tumbled downward into a sinkhole where a forgotten grave had been.

*   *   *

She awoke inside a room that smelled of old wood and lavender. It was dark, but there was a sliver of light peeking out from behind some boards that covered a small window. Her senses told her that she was in the throes of one her memory trips into the past.
Unlike the last time, she felt more grounded and part

of the memory.

"You shouldn't have come here." A familiar voice spoke softly from the darkness. "You were not meant to see this."

Vivienne coughed in the stale air. "Where am I?"

"My prison." The voice replied. "The place where I was strangled to death by Edgar Rothwell."

"Who are you?" Vivienne coughed again and pulled herself up from the cold floor.

A pair of slender white hands slid under her arms and helped her to her feet. "It's me."

Vivienne pivoted around to come face to face with Natalie Burdick. "Natalie."

"You shouldn't have come here." She spoke softly.

"What happened to me? I was just in the cemetery with Connor." Vivienne felt disoriented and weak.

Natalie glared at her with cold, dark eyes. Her features were gaunt, her pale skin pulled tight against her skull. Her dark hair was a tangled mess that cascaded over the familiar dark uniform she had seen her in during her vision in the Rothwell mansion. "Now you are here."

"Where is here, exactly?" Vivienne looked around the barren room. She could see peaks where the roof angled upwards.

"The Rothwell mansion." Natalie replied. "In the attic. After Edgar strangled me, he stored my body up here until he could find a proper hiding place for his crime."

"I couldn't find the attic." Vivienne explained. "Is it one of the secret entrance deals?"

"He had it covered up, after my death. He didn't want any evidence to be found." Natalie stepped aside and revealed a blue-tinged figure wearing the same dress as her, tied up in a wooden dining chair. Streams of old blood, dried black, crusted her face. "He left me here for two days before he retrieved my corpse and stuffed me inside the old cannon in the cemetery."

Vivienne gasped. "Why did he do it?"

Natalie walked over to her corpse and gently caressed the strands of hair that began to fall out in clumps. "He killed all of us because of my son."

"Jacob?"

Natalie's face contorted into one of great pain. "His real name was Connor, after my father."

"When the Rothwells adopted him, they named him Jacob." Vivienne followed along.

"They stole my child from me along with his rightful birth name." Natalie's voice cracked. "Stole the life of the great man my son was to become." She broke down into frantic tears. "Poisoned by the father he loved unconditionally."

"Why did Edgar kill all of you?" Vivienne demanded.

"Because Connor was his own flesh and blood." Natalie dropped to her knees and began to cry. "He blamed that poor soul that worked on his railroad to cover up the fact that we had improper relations."

"It was consensual?"

"I was young and stupid. I believed him when he said we could start a new life together somewhere far away from Cayuga Cove."

Vivienne walked slowly over to Natalie. "He

couldn't leave his wife or daughter."

Natalie shook her head. "I spent four years being a servant to that evil woman. Guarding my tongue when she scolded and threatened to fire me. Scrubbed every inch of her home until the skin on my hands was so raw and cracked that they bled daily."

"His frustration at the situation turned to contempt." Vivienne nodded. "Contempt turns to rage."

"He raged at the world. He raged at the church which taught him his sin would damn him to burn in the lake of fire. He raged at the wife whom all love was drained long before I came into their lives." Natalie continued. "He raged at the lack of control that a man of his means should have. In the end, he raged at all of us and destroyed himself in the process."

Vivienne couldn't help but think of the symbol of evil, the snake eating its own tail. "I'm so sorry."

"They're not sorry." Natalie looked up at Vivienne.

"Who are you talking about?" Vivienne wondered.

"All of them in the town. Those that keep secrets and act as if they are pure as snow."

"You're talking about Eddie Robertson, Eunice Kilpatrick, Nathaniel and Tristan?" Vivienne took a step back. "What do they have to do with what happened to you?"

Natalie sprung forward like a cat and knocked Vivienne to the floor with a thud. Her eyes were dark as the night sky and her smile twisted upwards almost to her ears. "I cannot rest, so I will make them all pay for the sins of the past. Why should I alone be made to suffer for eternity?"

Vivienne tried to fight her off, but the weight on her chest was unbearably heavy. "I can give you peace if you let me."

"Peace?" Natalie cackled maniacally. "It's too late for reparations. For too many years I have haunted the streets from the shadows, unable to do anything but observe. But, thanks to the witch that opened the portals, I now have the power to walk among you and punish the guilty."

Vivienne gasped as the weight of Natalie began to push the air from her lungs.

Natalie threw her head back and let out a scream that roared like the wind in a winter storm. The room began to shake, the boards rattling as her crescendo rose higher and higher.

A bright light exploded from the attic roof above. "Vivienne? Can you hear me?" Joshua's voice echoed faintly.

"No." Natalie screamed in frustration as more light poured into the attic.

Vivienne could see a hand inside the center of the light. A warm, flesh-colored hand that seemed more real than her surroundings. She reached upwards and clasped onto it. The attic dissolved away, revealing a wall of earth surrounding her.

"I've got her." Joshua's voice filled her ears.

She felt herself rising into the air, as Natalie grabbed onto her legs and tried to pull her down. Vivienne started to kick in frustration.

"She's fighting me." Joshua's voice returned. "Don't let go of my hand." He ordered.

"This isn't over, witch." Natalie hissed. "I'll take them all to the grave before this Yuletide."

Vivienne felt the grip on her legs loosen. One of her boots slipped off as she was pulled out of the ground. Her eyelids fluttered for a moment and then she saw the cemetery.

"Oh, thank God." Joshua leaned forward and swept the dirt off her face. "Can you breathe okay?"

Vivienne blinked, the bright light began to fade to a more tolerable level. She coughed up some dirt that tasted terrible in her mouth. "Water."

Gus Holt stepped forward with a small thermos. "I have some hot cocoa in there. Give her some of that."

Joshua twisted the top off and poured a small amount into the little plastic cup. "Drink some of this."

She did as he asked, coughing again. She spit out the first mouthful, hoping to get rid of the dirt that had fallen in. "More."

Joshua poured another cupful and she swallowed a little bit without coughing. "How did you find me?"

"You can thank Gus for that." Joshua wrapped a warm blanket around her. "He was heading down into town and recognized your car in front of the cemetery."

"You fell into a grave." Gus added. "This old cemetery is full of sink holes."

Vivienne noticed the paramedics working their way through the headstones. "Why are they here?" She croaked.

"Because you almost suffocated." Joshua assured her. "We're going to have you checked out."

Vivienne shook her head. "I'll be fine." She coughed again, a little more violently.

"Sure you will. After you go to the hospital and have everything checked out."

The paramedics stood over her. "We'll take it from here, Deputy Arkins."

Joshua easily lifted her off the ground and the paramedics guided her onto the stretcher. "Easy now."

Vivienne weakly reached out to him. "I need to tell you something important." She coughed again.

"Let them help you." Joshua ordered.

Vivienne tried to clear her throat. "It's about Natalie…" Her voice gave out.

The paramedics carried her swiftly down through the cemetery. She coughed again and again, spitting out bits of dirt. It was no use. She'd have to wait until later to tell him. With her energy fading, she closed her eyes as they loaded her into the back of the ambulance and into the warmth.

CHAPTER 19

Friday, December 13th

Vivienne had never been so happy to walk into her front door. Tommy Cat bounded at her with a concerned meow as Joshua helped her inside. She had been in the care of the staff at Cayuga Memorial Hospital for the past four days. Of course, she only could recall the past two days, as she was informed she had lapsed into a mini coma on her ambulance ride in on Monday afternoon.

During her stay, Stephanie had taken over the bakery on a limited hour basis and kept things moving smoothly. Kathy had stopped in to visit, informing her that Eunice Kilpatrick had been discharged from the hospital and that Sally Rollins was formally charged with hit and run.

"Now don't jostle her too much." Nora appeared from the kitchen wearing a festive snowman apron which was splattered with red tomato sauce.

Vivienne took a seat on the sofa. "I'm fine, mother. My oxygen levels stabilized."

"You had a collapsed lung from nearly suffocating in that sinkhole." Nora chided her. "You still need to take it easy."

"She's right, sweetie." Joshua agreed.

Vivienne fought the urge to roll her eyes. "I must be dead if you two are agreeing with each other."

"Don't say such a thing." Nora clucked her tongue. "Now, I made your favorite spaghetti and meatballs with my special sauce." Nora smiled and returned to the kitchen humming a cheery Christmas carol.

"Family recipe?" Joshua asked.

Vivienne chuckled. "Only if our last name is Prego."

"I'm glad to see you back in fighting form." He smiled and sat down next to her.

"So the big question, why did Sally Rollins run Eunice Kilpatrick down?" Vivienne asked.

"Turns out she's quite the alcoholic. The team went out there and found bottles hidden all over the trailer." Joshua explained. "She was cursing up a storm when they brought her in, blaming Eunice for blabbing her secret vice."

"You mean before she was run down?"

"Yes." Joshua added. "Eunice smelled alcohol on her breath many times at the bank and she reported it to social services who removed her grandchildren from the trailer after they investigated the claim."

"So, she goes on a binge and gets in the car to run Eunice down as payback?" Vivienne shuddered. "I don't know about this. I was in her trailer before and I never saw any bottles or smelled alcohol."

"I'm just telling you what the team has in the report." Joshua interrupted.

Vivienne leaned close to him. "So, what did your background check on Natalie turn up?"

"Nothing." Joshua frowned. 'The same thing with Eddie Robertson "It's as if they both just fell into Cayuga Cove out of thin air."

"They exist." Vivienne pointed out. "We've all seen and interacted with them."

"Are you sure it's not some sort of spell?"

Vivienne shook her head. "I'm positive. Magic

can fool the eye for a short time, but not that long."

"Natalie and Connor have both been missing since Monday. Sheriff Rigsbee wanted to ask her some questions about Sally Rollins but she hasn't been back to her trailer. You were the last one to see Connor, actually."

"You saw the boot prints."

"We found yours, mine, Gus Holt and the paramedics. None of them were child-sized." Joshua reminded her.

"She must have erased them."

"With magic?"

Vivienne shrugged. "I guess that's possible. But I can tell you for certain that I was not chasing a ghost that left footprints."

"So what the hell is she?" Joshua asked.

"If I had to guess I would say we're dealing with a banshee."

Joshua whistled. "Great. Another supernatural creature to try to wrangle in."

"Natalie isn't a ghost because too many people have seen and touched her. She has a physical form, she walks in daylight, and she has been exposed to the most brutal tragedy."

Joshua shifted uneasily on the sofa cushions. "So, what about Connor?"

"She must have found a way to bring him back from the dead. Who knows what powers she has now. I wish I had the answers, but I'm afraid Natalie is the only one to give them up."

"Is she writing the Bad Santa notes?" Joshua wondered.

"I think she is and she's using magic to circulate

them." Vivienne deduced. "She told me herself that when Missy Collins opened the dark portals, it gave her energy to leave the graveyard and start interacting with everyone in town."

"But what's the reason for the notes?"

Vivienne thought for a moment. "She was lied to and had no one to come to her defense when she was alive. She had to sit back and take every bad thing that came to her without complaining."

"So, when she gained this new power to work dark magic, she decided to start dealing out punishment to those whose deeds she had witnessed first-hand." Joshua added. "Writing Bad Santa notes to stir up the town and get everyone as upset as possible."

"Misery loves company. She must have felt a great deal of satisfaction having such power for the first time."

"What about the vandalism at Miss Octavia's shop?"

"Yes, I think she did that and planted Pastor Kilpatrick's business card at the scene in the hopes to stir up more trouble."

"But you told me that you overheard his conversation with Eunice at the hospital. They wanted to clean up the town and get rid of certain people."

"I did, but that's the most sloppy way possible, wouldn't you think?" Vivienne shook her head. "She has an ax to grind with Pastor Kilpatrick, but I don't know exactly what it is."

Joshua scratched his chin. "You're right. People like that cover their tracks much better."

"I think it's more likely that Natalie overheard Eunice and Sally's conversation at the bank and decided to target Nathaniel and Tristan."

"You witnessed Tristan having an affair with that guy in New York when you slipped into his memory. How is that connected to Natalie?" Joshua asked.

"That man was a relative of dear old Edgar Rothwell. What better way to deal with family sin?" Vivienne reached out and gave Tommy a pat on the head as he smelled her hair. "You know, being stuck in the hospital all week gives you time to really think things through."

"So how do we deal with a banshee?"

"I had a folklore book in my purse." Vivienne started to get up from the sofa when Joshua stopped her. "You stay put. Let me get it."

She nodded back. "It was in the car the last time I saw it."

Joshua nodded. "It was, but I took it out and put it into your bedroom when we brought your car home Monday night." He wandered off to get it.

"Do you feel like garlic bread, my darling daughter?" Nora popped back into the living room.

Vivienne smiled at her. "Can you make it extra cheesy?"

"Sure can." Nora waved the wooden stirring spoon in her grip like a wand and wandered back into the kitchen. "Dinner will be ready in about fifteen minutes." She called out as the doorbell rang. "Are you expecting company?"

"No." Vivienne shook her head.

Nora walked over to the front door and opened the peephole cover. "Who is it?"

"Delivery from Hummingbird Floral." The voice replied from behind the door.

"Oh." Nora replied with excitement as she unlocked the door. "How lovely."

Vivienne could see a tall high school boy, dressed in a heavy jacket and a woolen hat hand a large fruit basket to Nora. "Happy Holidays." He smiled.

Nora accepted the big basket and waved at him. "Happy Holidays young man." She then shut the door in his face.

"Mother." Vivienne scolded her. "You were supposed to tip him."

"For what?" Nora asked as she walked the basket over to Vivienne and set it on the coffee table. "Doing his job?"

"It's customary." Vivienne sighed. "He's just a poor high school kid working part time."

Nora clucked her tongue. "I swear, everyone doing anything these days feels they need a tip for doing the job they're getting paid to do."

"Never mind, I'll catch up with Brian downtown and make it right." Vivienne admired the brown wicker basket. It was filled with apples, oranges, kiwi fruit, plums, and a large pineapple. Wrapped in a festive red and green cellophane, an envelope dangled from the curled ribbon tied on top. "I wonder who sent it?"

"Open the card and see." Nora rubbed her hands together.

Joshua returned with the library book in his hand. "Who sent that?"

Vivienne opened the envelope and pulled out the card. "Heard about your accident and hope you are on the mend. Give me a call when you feel better. Cheers, Samantha Charles."

"Such a lovely young woman." Nora gushed.

"I wonder who told her?" Joshua asked.

"It must have been Kathy." Nora guessed.

"Probably." Vivienne smiled.

"I better check on dinner." Nora dashed off.

Joshua handed Vivienne the book. "Here you go."

Vivienne opened it to where the pages were dog-eared. "Okay, so it says here that holy water is an effective way to drive the creature away when under attack."

"Anything else?" Joshua asked as Tommy jumped onto his lap and began head butting him while purring.

"This isn't a hunting manual." Vivienne winked. "We're going to have to wing most of this."

"That's assuming we can find her."

That won't be a problem." Vivienne interrupted. "Despite the fact that she can roam the entire town, there is one place that she always will appear."

"The graveyard." Joshua snapped his fingers.

"There's something buried there that keeps her anchored. We need to find out what it is."

"You're in no shape to go back there right now." Joshua put his arm around her.

"Nor do I want to." She agreed. "What about the Rothwell mansion?" Vivienne asked. "Did you find the attic?"

"Brian Amberry knew about the attic. He stores some of the seasonal décor up there."

"Did you check it out personally?"

Joshua nodded. "It was empty, except for the

decorations he told us about. There wasn't a skeleton tied to a chair." He took a deep breath. "But, when I ran the ultra violet light up there I did find some residual blood spatter on some of the floorboards."

"I knew it." Vivienne snapped her fingers. "So Edgar did murder her up there."

"There wasn't enough blood to indicate anything like that. It was just a few stains here and there."

"Still, that proves that what I saw in my vision was true." Vivienne nodded.

"But that's your magic at work." He whispered quietly. "We need solid proof for anything to be verified."

"I think we need to set a banshee trap." Vivienne's eyes sparkled. "Bait it with something she can't resist."

"And what would that be?"

Vivienne glanced at the Christmas tree that sparkled in her living room. "I'll bet Miss Octavia might have a suggestion. I'll go see her tomorrow morning."

"I don't know why, but I have this feeling we're missing this one thread that connects everything together."

"Me too." Vivienne agreed.

Nora called out from the kitchen. "Dinner is ready everyone."

Joshua helped Vivienne to her feet. "After you."

She winked at him. "Such service. Why don't we dine here more often?"

"Joshua, would you be a dear and fetch me some antacid tablets from the bathroom medicine cabinet?" Nora called out again. "This sauce is going to give me trouble, I can tell just from the aroma."

Joshua lowered his head. "Probably because the staff can drive you crazy."

Vivienne gave him a light tap on the arm. "Now dearest, she means well."

"Anything but the cherry flavored ones." Nora corrected. "For some reason they don't seem to work as well and the flavor is just dreadful."

"You're right." Vivienne smiled. "It's the staff."

CHAPTER 20

Saturday, December 14th

Miss Octavia stared at Vivienne as if she were rambling some arcane spell incantation. "You want to run that by me again?" She asked with her charming tropical accent.

"Do you have any charm bags or herbs that would be effective in repelling a banshee?"

"I didn't realize that your unfortunate accident at the cemetery affected your mind." Miss Octavia put her hands on hips.

"I'm serious." Vivienne replied as they sat at the reading table inside Mother Earth Mercantile.

"Child, if you're serious than you have some cuckoo problems going on up there." Miss Octavia tapped her index finger on her head.

Vivienne grimaced. "Look, I'm coming to you as a trusted friend."

Miss Octavia raised an eyebrow at her. "If you are a friend, then you will allow me to test that."

"Test?"

She got up from her chair and walked over to a set of shelves were various glass bottles of liquids were neatly displayed. She retrieved a small clear vial of prismatic cut glass and pulled off the rubber stopper. "You will drink this."

Vivienne stared at the vial. "What is it?"

"As I said, it is a test." Miss Octavia handed her the vial. "If you want my help with such a matter, I need proof."

"Why do I suddenly feel like Alice?" Vivienne

took the vial from her. "You don't have a white rabbit carrying a stopwatch hopping around in the back room, do you?"

"Drink." Miss Octavia ordered without even cracking a smile. "Or leave my shop."

Vivienne took a deep breath. "To friendship." She raised the vial and then slurped the contents. She wasn't sure what she expected to taste, but whatever it was had no flavor.

Miss Octavia eyed her carefully. "How do you feel?"

Vivienne set the vial on the table. "Fine."

"I'm just giving it a moment to work." Miss Octavia replied.

"Can I ask what is it now that I've imbibed?" Vivienne smiled.

Miss Octavia nodded and then a big smile appeared on her face. "Of course, child. I had to make sure you were who you said you were."

"Well, what did I drink?"

"Holy water." Miss Octavia replied as she retrieved the vial from the table. "I couldn't take any chances."

"So you do believe in magic?" Vivienne felt relief wash over her that she hadn't sent snake venom or some other poison down her gullet. "May I ask why you thought I wasn't me?"

Miss Octavia returned the vial to her collection. "While you were in the hospital, I got a surprise visit from you."

"I don't understand."

"You came to see me on, let me think, Tuesday evening I believe." Miss Octavia sat down across from

Vivienne and rested her hands upon the crystal ball that was between them.

"I was in a coma then." Vivienne explained. "I didn't wake up until Wednesday afternoon."

"That's what I found out, after the fact." Miss Octavia explained. "You see, this banshee you are worried about has some powers she shouldn't."

"Obviously."

"When you fell into that grave you must have lost some kind of personal object. Something that would allow her to assume your form using her dark magic."

Vivienne thought back to that horrible moment and gasped. "I lost a boot when they were pulling me out."

"And that is all she needs to assume your form."

"Why would she want to become me?"

"She warned me that Pastor Seamus Kilpatrick was on the warpath and wanted to get rid of me. So, she asked me to craft a potion that she could spike Our Lady of the Lake's annual holiday bake sale items with that would sicken a great number of people in town. She would then create some evidence and use Joshua to plant it ensuring that the preacher man would be brought to swift justice."

"That's diabolical." Vivienne gasped. "I would never do such a thing."

"Which is the point at which I became suspicious of her identity." Octavia continued. "I played along and thanked her for looking out for me. I then asked if she would like some tea and she said yes. I went into the kitchen and boiled some holy water to use for the drinks. When I brought it out, she took a tiny sip and then she excused herself, saying she forgot she had an order to work on back at the bakery and that she would return for the potion on Sunday morning."

"The holy water sickened her?" Vivienne asked.

"It must have. She couldn't get out of my shop fast enough." Miss Octavia sighed. "Dark magic is powerful, but it is easily disrupted when you know the proper counter measures."

"The holiday bake sale is Sunday afternoon, so she must plan on spiking the baked goods in the morning during Sunday mass."

"That was my guess as well. I'll craft something for her, but it won't be what she thinks it is."

Vivienne shook her head. "She knows me well. Sunday mornings Joshua and I always sleep in late, usually past eleven."

"So she's able to assume your form and walk in carrying donated baked goods without anyone thinking twice."

"How is she going to frame Pastor Kilpatrick?"

"I don't know yet." Miss Octavia continued. "She is drawing on some sort of dark magic source that is nearby." Miss Octavia continued. "Cayuga Cove is a nexus of magic activity. Do you know what that is?"

"A nexus means a center focal point." Vivienne replied. "I got a pretty high score on the verbal portion of my S.A.T."

Miss Octavia nodded. "I've been to some magical places in the world, but I've never felt anything like this before. It's practically broadcasting a signal to those who are able to hear it."

"I believe you." Vivienne let her guard down. "I've felt it too."

"You are a child of the Goddess. I could tell the night I tested you in the library."

"That was you?"

"I had my suspicions, but I couldn't be sure. You moved around too much for my crystal to get a good fix on your aura." Octavia smiled. "Finally, I just gave up and decided to leave the book out for you to find."

"Which I did and started me on the path leading to Natalie." Vivienne took a deep breath.

"I didn't mean to scare you like that, but I've never been any good at sneaking around."

Vivienne smiled. "You were right. I am a witch." She put her hands over Octavia's. "But you can't tell anyone about this. No one knows, not even my mother."

Miss Octavia smiled. "I understand. A small town. Small minds. They are not ready for such knowledge."

"That's it exactly." Vivienne nodded. "If word got out about what I am it could destroy everything."

"We are bound by honor never to reveal our sisters and brothers to the ordinaries."

"Are you part of the Elder Council?" Vivienne asked. "Did they send you to help me?"

"No, my child. I work best alone." Miss Octavia revealed. "I was curious as to what I would find so near a powerful source of magic."

"It wasn't always like this." Vivienne explained. "A few months ago, there was another witch in town who violated the sacred oath and began to work with dark magic. Her reckless actions opened some portals that we won't be able to close, until the Elder Council figures out some kind of solution."

"There is more to the story than you know." Miss Octavia interrupted. "There is a history here in town, a magical history that explains why we are drawn here to this spot."

"I think it has to do with the refugees that fled from the Salem colony during the witchcraft hysteria."

"You're on the right track." Octavia affirmed with a gentle squeeze of Vivienne's hands. "The Elder Council brought me here as a freelance witch to help them with the portal problem. I specialize in stitching together the fabric of history through my visions and working the tarot cards."

"How come Nana Mary doesn't know about you?" Vivienne asked. "She didn't even sense you."

"I am able to shield my power from everyone. That is my unique gift. The ultimate undercover witch for hire." Miss Octavia nodded. "Like you, I must ask that you not blow my cover. Not even your Nana Mary can know about my true nature or my mission here in Cayuga Cove."

"Why did you trust me?"

"Because, telling you is the only way I can save your life." Miss Octavia spoke softly. "I've seen you die several times during my card readings."

"I'm going to die?" Vivienne's voice cracked.

"The night of the full moon, I'm afraid." Miss Octavia explained. "The readings revealed one solitary time when you do manage to outsmart the banshee that haunts this town. One possible path to escape the dark fate she has planned for you."

"What do we do?"

"We start by arming you with the very things you

asked me for when you first came in tonight. You need to set a banshee trap and you need a way to drive her away forever. I can help you with that, but we haven't much time."

Vivienne felt a sense of panic rising inside her. "How much time?"

"She will carry out her plan when her power is at its zenith. The full moon."

"That's three days from now." Thanks to Joshua's lupine nature, she knew the moon phases by heart.

"I had a feeling you keep careful track of that." Miss Octavia smiled. "He's a good one, your man. Very non-typical of werewolves."

"Yes he is." Vivienne agreed. "But, when he's in wolf form he's at a disadvantage when it comes to helping me out."

"As I said, our foe is very intelligent." Octavia echoed. "We have quite a battle ahead."

* * *

Normally, on a Saturday afternoon Vivienne would be hard at work in the kitchen of her bakery, but Stephanie insisted she take the weekend to recover and report fresh on Monday morning. Vivienne began to feel as if she were the part-time employee in her own shop, but then she realized she was just lucky to have an amazing employee like Stephanie to keep the fires burning without missing a beat.

So, she found herself with a free afternoon thanks to the lucky combination of Joshua working a twelve hour shift while Nora was busy hosting a clutter-free seminar at the Whispering Pines home.

As she drove back to her home with an assortment of magical items to use in defense of Natalie's attack, she decided to follow up with a thank you. She pressed the telephone button on her stereo system. "Call Samantha Charles."

"Calling Samantha Charles." The monotone automated voice crackled through the speakers.

The phone rang three times before Samantha answered cheerfully. "Vivienne Finch, am I glad to hear your voice."

"Hi Samantha. I just wanted to thank you for sending that gorgeous fruit basket. You really shouldn't have."

"It was the least I could do. How are you feeling?"

Vivienne stopped at a traffic light and watched a group of children carrying sleds cross the intersection toward the school playground. "I'm back to normal, thank goodness."

"I must say, when Kathy told me how you fell into an old grave I was quite shocked."

"It's not as uncommon as you think." Vivienne felt a little twinge of terror, recalling the feeling as the ground gave out beneath her. "Just my dumb luck, I suppose."

"Well, I hope you stay out of old cemeteries for some time." Samantha joked.

"Oh, that's something I plan on doing." Vivienne accelerated as the light turned green.

"Oh, Vivienne." Samantha chuckled. "I miss our chats."

"You're a busy executive now. Your time is gold."

"I miss Cayuga Cove and the quiet peace that you all take for granted. The city is just mobbed with tourists this time of year." Samantha's voice lowered. "I actually thought of taking a little holiday getaway there and checking on the progress at the house."

"I've seen the renovations crew working. They're really doing an amazing job."

"Hey, that's part the reason I wanted to check in with you." Samantha interrupted. "Has the Rothwell mansion been purchased from the town yet?"

"What?"

"I'll take that as a no." Samantha sounded relived. "Good, because I didn't want to be neighbors with that smarmy Robert Rothwell. He's going to ruin the town with his gas fracking plans."

"Back up a second. When was he supposed to buy the mansion?"

"Oh, quite some time ago. I saw him at a fundraiser and he kept trying to impress me with talking about his old family home in Cayuga Cove and how he was going to buy it back to show his father how he was going to take their family fortune into the future with natural gas fracking."

"Samantha, I need to know the exact day that fundraiser was held." Vivienne turned onto Meier Drive.

"I have it in my phone, let me pull it up." Samantha went silent for a moment. "It was on June 7th, over six months ago."

"That was when he must have met Tristan in New York." Vivienne pulled her car into the driveway of her home.

"Who's Tristan?" Samantha asked.

"He runs an antique store here in town." Vivienne answered. "There was a bit of scandal with him having an affair with Robert around the time of that fundraiser."

"So he is bisexual." Samantha added. "I had a feeling he had to be."

"What do you mean?"

"Oh Vivienne, he has a girlfriend, but let me tell you she was such an obvious prop. Plain and just so mousy. I can't even fathom why he would have looked at her twice."

"Did you get her name?" Vivienne asked.

"Um, she didn't say much. Just sort of hid by the potted plants. I think a few people assumed she was the help and gave her their empty glasses." Samantha recalled. "I think her name was Natalie."

"Oh my Goddess." Vivienne put her hands up to her mouth. "Short stature, dark hair pulled up in a bun. Pale complexion."

"Yes." Samantha confirmed. "You know her?"

"Oh, I know her." Vivienne could barely get the words out of her mouth. "Have you seen her lately?"

"No, in fact I was going to say that she and Robert disappeared from the scene right after that."

"What does Robert look like?" Vivienne asked.

"He's tall, athletic-type of build. Very easy on the eyes. Of course, when he opens his mouth it all falls apart." Samantha sighed. "The very definition of narcissism."

"Can you email me a picture?"

"Sure." Samantha confirmed. "I have some right here on my phone, one with him and Natalie actually. I'm so glad he hasn't had a chance to buy property in town yet."

"Yes, you mentioned that earlier."

"He's tied in with one of those shady companies fracking for gas deposits." Samantha explained. "I'm sure he wanted to get cozy with the locals so he could throw gobs of money at them until they sold their mineral rights."

"We've had some debates here about it." Vivienne recalled. "I hate to say it, but money would win out over ecological safety issues for most working families around here."

"This isn't a reputable company, Vivienne. This is a get rich quick scheme by Robert to fleece Cayuga Cove. They don't drill safely. They poison the water supply. If they get their claws into the town, they will turn it into a poisoned wasteland." Samantha's voice took in a tone of urgency. "I've had a legal team putting a case together to use against them when Robert makes his move on the town council."

"Thank you for looking out for us." Vivienne's head was spinning. "I think you just saved the entire town by telling me what I needed to know."

"Really?" Samantha asked. "I'm going to send you all the information on that bogus company that I have."

"Thank you so much." Vivienne finished. "I have some very important errands to take care of."

"Let me know how things turn out. Miss you Vivienne." Samantha hung up.

Vivienne turned the car off and sat inside, letting the silence clear her head. She had to see the picture of Robert and Natalie and then she had to find Joshua.

Once her computer booted up, she opened the email that Samantha had sent. The picture confirmed that Natalie was indeed the woman who haunted Cayuga Cove. There was a hollow darkness to her eyes, a deep sadness that reached out from the confines of the digital photograph. But it was the picture of Robert that disturbed her more. His face was so familiar, yet so alien. She was transfixed by the image of the robust and healthy man before her. She could see why Tristan had been attracted to him. But as she squinted and the image blurred, the answer came. "Oh, no she didn't." Vivienne gasped. "How could I miss something so obvious?" She had found the thread that pulled the whole tapestry of tragedy together and it was a bigger threat than either of them could have imagined.

It was nearly an hour later after reading what Samantha had sent about the gas drilling that the picture became clear. She combed over the emails, pulling out what she needed to explain in the most logical order.

Her fingers dialed Joshua's work number. "Honey, it's me. I've got one hell of a bombshell to tell you."

"I was just about to call you." Joshua's voice was uncertain. "Tristan and Nathaniel have been admitted to Cayuga Memorial. It looks pretty bad, Vivienne."

CHAPTER 21

As they sat in the waiting room in the emergency room at Cayuga Memorial Hospital, Vivienne and Joshua held hands. The trauma team was working somewhere behind the automatic doors, trying to bring them back to health.

"This isn't right." Vivienne shook her head.

"They were targeted by the Bad Santa note like everyone else." Joshua gave her hand a gentle squeeze.

"We're so close to solving this." Vivienne felt tears well up in her eyes. "This town is falling apart at the seams."

"They're still sorting out the details of what happened, but apparently Nathaniel confronted the protestors outside of their store and someone threw a punch." Joshua shook his head. "It turned into a free-for-all fight right afterwards."

"Did you round up all the protestors?" Vivienne sniffed.

"Most of them took off when the first cruiser arrived on the scene." Joshua explained as he used his free hand to gently rub her back. "But we've got a pretty clear statement about who started it."

"Who was it?"

"His name is Neil Carter and he's a gas worker from a company called R.N.G incorporated." Joshua sighed. "He doesn't even live here. He's just one of the workers that's driving those big equipment trucks up and down Route 90 to the different drilling sites."

"R.N.G." Vivienne repeated. "Rothwell Natural

Gas."

"That's right."

Vivienne stood up from the uncomfortable chair. "We need to go somewhere private where we can talk."

Joshua joined her. "The cafeteria?"

"The chapel." Vivienne answered.

"This is a surprise."

"I think it's off limits for her." Vivienne explained as she guided him into the hallway. "At least, I hope so."

Joshua simply nodded and followed her down the mostly empty hallway.

As they entered the small chapel that was decorated with a few red and white poinsettias, they nearly ran into Pastor Seamus Kilpatrick. "Oh, pardon me." He apologized, his grip on a small bible tight in his right hand.

"Pastor Kilpatrick?" Vivienne blinked in surprise.

"Yes. Have we met?" He asked her.

Vivienne looked at Joshua and shook her head. "Not in person. I'm Vivienne Finch, I run the Sweet Dreams Bakery downtown."

Seamus winked at her. "Oh, I've heard quite a bit of good things about your baked goods."

Vivienne gave him a little smile. "Thank you. How is Eunice?"

"My sister is doing better each day, praise the Lord." He smiled. "Are you two friends?"

"We know each other, but just casually." Vivienne answered. She gestured to Joshua. "This is Deputy Arkins."

"Deputy, it's always a pleasure to meet a man of

the law." Seamus passed the bible to his left hand and offered his right hand. "We must keep the flame of the righteous burning bright against the darkness."

Joshua gripped it tight and gave him a vigorous shake. "Thank you, Pastor."

"Are you here to say a prayer for a sick friend?" Seamus asked them.

Vivienne nodded. "Two friends, actually."

"I'm sorry to hear that."

"Nathaniel Schroeder and Tristan Carr." Vivienne revealed.

Seamus' face paled. "I see."

"What's the matter, Pastor Kilpatrick?" Vivienne pressed. "Are you troubled by the fruit that your seeds have wrought?"

"I beg your pardon." Seamus straightened his posture.

"You were the one responsible for organizing the protestors after the Bad Santa note hit town, were you not?" Vivienne asked matter-of-factly.

"Vivienne, this isn't the place." Joshua gently put his hand on her shoulder.

"Cayuga Cove is a small town, Pastor. I suggest not talking about how you intend to clean up the sin in this town in such a public place. The walls have ears, you know." Vivienne finished.

"I have no idea what you're talking about, my child. But I will pray that the anger inside you goes away."

"Why don't you go down to the emergency room and pray that those two gentlemen down there don't die from being beaten to within an inch of their lives by a bunch of moral cowards?" Vivienne brushed past him and stepped into the chapel.

"She's an angry woman." Seamus whispered to Joshua.

"Hell hath no fury." Joshua replied as he followed Vivienne into the chapel.

Vivienne took a seat on the front bench. "I'm sorry." She took a deep breath. "I didn't mean to go off on him like that."

"Oh, he deserved every word you gave him." Joshua sat down next to her. "I'm proud of you."

"Well, he's not going to be very happy with me after that."

"I don't think he's happy with many people living here in Cayuga Cove." Joshua added. "But, he's not our problem."

"No." Vivienne positioned herself to face Joshua. "I've figured out what's going on and I've only got three days to stop it before I die."

"What?" Joshua leaned forward. "Did someone threaten your life?"

She nodded. "Natalie."

"You saw here again?" Joshua asked.

"No." Vivienne had to choose her explanation carefully. She would tell him everything she knew, while keeping Miss Octavia's secret. It wasn't going to be easy, but she had no other choice.

* * *

It was well after eleven in the evening when Vivienne and Joshua returned to her home. The trauma team managed to stabilize both Nathaniel and Tristan, but their recovery was going to be rough.

More importantly, she had been able to explain the entire plan to Joshua and although she could sense that he was edgy about the threat to her life, he remained rational and in control.

Vivienne pulled up the email photograph of Robert and Natalie. "It's impossible for a non-witch to see through magic of a glamor spell."

"I don't see it." Joshua admitted.

"Robert Edward Rothwell is Eddie Robertson, and vice versa." Vivienne pulled up the newspaper obituary picture from online and placed the two together on the screen.

"But why did Natalie do that?"

"She needed to bring him to Cayuga Cove in order to carry out her plan, but he was far too visible as Robert Rothwell." Vivienne explained as best she could. "As Eddie, he was just some low life creep that no one would pay much attention to. Except, to feel sympathy for her as the abused girlfriend and mother."

"So, Robert Rothwell was going to bring in his R.G.E. company to set up shop drilling gas and inflating his family fortune?"

"Right." Vivienne clicked on a separate email and brought it up on the screen.

"How the heck did the two of them hook up in the first place?" Joshua asked.

Vivienne pulled up the email from Samantha Charles with the information that her legal team had collected over the past few months. "Well, it was an unfortunate twist of fate that did it. He was in town over a year ago setting up a survey team to look at gas deposit prospects under Cayuga Cove, starting at the most promising location."

"The Cayuga Union Cemetery." Joshua caught on.

"Exactly." Vivienne pointed to the screen. "This is a funding query a team of geologists sent out about two years ago. In the fall of 2011, they detected a large pocket of gas in the farmlands surrounding the cemetery while conducting a geographic survey for a now defunct energy company. Lacking the monetary capital to explore drilling options, they had no choice but to shelve the project until additional funding could be secured." Vivienne pulled up another email on the screen. "Well, at some point these geologists approached Robert Rothwell while cold calling various wealthy individuals and when they mentioned his family's hometown, he couldn't get his checkbook out fast enough."

"So he buys the survey information and creates an new company to explore these drilling options." Joshua followed along. "Eventually, he makes a personal visit here to see how things are going."

Vivienne nodded back. "When I traveled into Tristan's memory, I remember Robert telling him he had traveled to Cayuga Cove about a year ago which would work out to be around the summer of 2012."

Joshua pulled a pillow behind his neck as he sat on the sofa staring at the monitor. "So, Robert was visiting the fields out here and comes across the cemetery."

"John Pagano told me stories of how he used to see the black widow, that's what he called Natalie, out by the old civil war cannons. It's not a stretch to think that Robert had an encounter with her as well at some point."

"You're positive that the black widow is Natalie?"

Vivienne opened a drawer on her computer desk and pulled out the silver brooch that John had given her. "John found this near the cannons. It's engraved." She handed it to Joshua.

Joshua turned it over. "Never a time apart, love is eternal." He handed it back to her unimpressed. "I don't get where you find a link to Natalie."

Vivienne turned the brooch inscription toward him. "Look at the first letter of each word."

"N-A-T-A-L-I-E". Joshua blinked. "Vivienne, you're brilliant."

"Old Edgar couldn't go out and have her name engraved, not for a secret mistress in a small town."

Joshua smiled. "So, Natalie finds Robert visiting the cemetery and must have sensed that he was a Rothwell family member. From that moment, she at last had a chance to take revenge."

"How could she not? She'd been trapped out in the cemetery for over a century, unable to seek vengeance against the man who murdered her and her child. Now, all during this time this is going on we had Missy Collins working her dark magic in her plot to take down Mona Clarke." Vivienne placed the brooch back in the desk drawer. "Unbeknownst to her, she was opening dark portals which fed new energy to Natalie and allowed her to do so much more than simply kill Robert Rothwell for his family sins. She would be able to seek vengeance against the entire town of Cayuga Cove for celebrating the life of Edgar Rothwell and his family's charitable donations over the years."

"So, she casts a spell on him and controls his mind?" Joshua asked.

"We know she can glamor, so my guess is that he only saw a knockout beauty who made his heart skip a beat. He tells her about his soon to be big fortune, because as Samantha Charles told me, he loves to brag to everyone about it."

"They both travel back to New York to secure the plan to harvest the gas from Cayuga Cove and make his family richer than they ever had been."

Vivienne nodded back. "So, after getting the funding in place, it's time for Natalie to seek her vengeance. I also guess that the time away from the dark portals was taking a toll, so she has to return to Cayuga Cove to boost her power in keeping all the magic spells she cast in place." Vivienne pointed to her grimoire resting by the computer. "In order to do that, she combines a glamor spell with a mind alteration spell, changing Robert physically into Eddie, while blocking all memory of his former life."

"Whoa." Joshua stopped her. "How did you figure that out?"

"It's in my spell book." Vivienne opened her grimoire to the proper page. "An individual with a mind block spell will become more agitated and aggressive with each passing day as the mind fights the spell to restore balance. Sounds like the Eddie we encountered, doesn't it?"

"You have never used that, have you?" Joshua asked her with concern.

"I don't think I ever will. It feels too dark, at least to me." She reassured him and closed the book. "We witches have to be aware of both the light and the dark magic, in order to work to the optimum potential."

"So how did Natalie get these spells?"

"When we cast spells, they are sent out into the world free to travel without boundaries. From what I understand, certain spirits are more adept at capturing that energy and using it for their own purpose."

"Like when a haunting suddenly gets more active because someone used a Ouija board to try and contact the ghosts? Joshua's blue eyes flashed with excitement.

"I can't tell you everything, sweetie." Vivienne warned him gently. "We have our secrets for a reason."

"I know."

Vivienne walked away from the computer and sat on the arm of the sofa next to him. "So, they move back to Cayuga Cove and she gradually recoups her power while the Rothwell Natural Gas Company proceeds with the plan to start getting the mineral rights to start drilling."

Joshua reached up and caressed her arms with his hands. "They moved into the trailer court at Tall Pine Grove where at some point she must have brought Connor back from the dead."

"Connor has always been a lost soul, just like Natalie. He just couldn't take physical form like she was able to do." Vivienne felt a moment of pity. "She helped him by casting a risky spell."

"Why?"

"There's no greater tragedy than a young life cut short." Vivienne mused. "When I had the vision with her in the attic, she was most troubled about Connor not living the life he was fated too. Using dark magic, she was able to correct that mistake on her own."

"So why not bring herself back from the dead and just go start a new life far away?"

"I don't know much about resurrection spells, only that they are the most dangerous to cast. One little slip up and the witch can end up as dead as the person they are trying to bring back."

"Natalie has nothing to lose." Joshua quipped. "Why not cast it on herself?"

Vivienne shook her head. "I don't know the specifics. When I asked Nana Mary about it she said it only worked on a victim who was cheated out of their natural fate. Something that rarely happens."

"So Natalie was fated to die at the hands of Edgar Rothwell, but Connor wasn't?"

"That's a good guess." Vivienne replied. "We may never know why, that's what makes working with dark magic such a risky proposition."

"Still, this seems like an awful long-term plan to slowly let Cayuga Cove get strip mined into oblivion." Joshua remarked. "How could she be sure everything would work out to that end?"

"This company takes short cuts and the men are paid extra money to do so. They don't need to follow the rules."

"So they still need time to get all the mineral rights from the property owners and such." Joshua argued.

"No. That was Robert's plan to make money." Vivienne interrupted. "Natalie's plan only needed one parcel of land to start drilling. Gus Holt's."

"The same Gus Holt who saved you from suffocating in a sunken grave?"

Tommy meowed and emerged from the bedroom, his yellow eyes blinking in the bright light. Vivienne reached down and ran her hands along his back as he rubbed against her legs. "While they lived in the trailer park, she still had access to all the information Robert's company had accumulated."

"I'm following you." Joshua replied.

Vivienne pulled out an email she had printed from Samantha's legal team's research. "One of the tactics this shady gas company uses is scouring the newspaper legal section during tax time when all the delinquent property owners names are published for not paying on time. They match up the property addresses with their gas deposit research and look for any matches."

"Gus Holt has one of those delinquent properties." Joshua added. "He charges hunters a fee to use the land during deer season. A couple of the guys at work do it every year."

Vivienne pulled up the title search and printed it out. "So he makes maybe one or two hundred dollars off of that, but it's not nearly enough to pay the full taxes."

"That sounds logical." Joshua nodded.

"Natalie finds this property deed with Gus Holt's name on it and now she has a motivated seller. She tells him about this new company paying top dollar for mineral rights. As a renter on the Tall Pines Grove property, they have no legal claim to any royalties earned by gas production. But to a property owner, it could be like a lotto jackpot win."

Tommy moved over to Joshua's legs and rubbed against them. "So he sells his rights and the company starts drilling out in his field where very few people will see what is going on." Tommy jumped up onto his lap and head butted Joshua. "Natalie starts up these Bad Santa notes exposing the town's secrets to keep everyone from paying attention to what a shoddy job this company is doing."

Vivienne took a deep breath. "The company started the exploratory drilling process just the other day and are expecting to hit the gas pocket on December 24th."

"Christmas Eve." Joshua looked at the calendar.

"The last thing Natalie told me was that everyone here would be dead before Yuletide." Vivienne shivered. "The company breaks into the gas pocket, Natalie sabotages the equipment, and the entire town is blown to bits from an explosion of hellfire."

"Not on my watch." Joshua stood up, placing Tommy onto the sofa. "We're going to make some calls and get a safety inspection team out here pronto."

"I'd feel better if we could get them and their equipment out of town for good." Vivienne sighed. "We also have to stop her from setting another sabotage up with the bake sale tomorrow. If lots of people get sick, we could have chaos break out."

"We're going to fix that too, before she can light the fuse."

Vivienne picked up her phone and started to dial. "It's time we let Miss Octavia in on this plan."

"You trust her with that kind of information?"

"She has the tools we're going to need to stop

Natalie." Vivienne reminded him. "And you're going to need her help to catch her."

"I trust her if you do."

Vivienne winked at him. "Miss Octavia, it's Vivienne Finch. Let's have a talk about setting a banshee trap. Sure, we're free tonight if you are."

"I better get the coffee maker going." Joshua smiled at her. "It's going to be a long night."

CHAPTER 22

Sunday, December 15th

The bake sale at Our Lady of the Lake Church consisted of ten folding card tables that were setup in the lower level reception area where weekly bingo games were held.

As she moved past the gaggle of church parishioners vying for a peek at what goodies were most likely to sell out first, they barely paid her any attention. Most of the glances, she suspected, were directed at the foil-covered plate in her hands. Was she bringing the highly coveted no bake cookies? Even though they were perhaps the easiest item to make, none of the women could ever find time in their busy schedules to make them at home. Thus, they gained a prestigious value at the bake sale. A sort of sugary holy grail that everyone quested for.

"Vivienne, so nice to see you out and about after your misfortune." Suzette Powell smiled broadly at her.

"Thank you." She replied.

"I brought my famous peanut butter thumbprints." Suzette pointed to a large oval platter where bags of four were neatly tied up with red and green curled ribbon. "I would just love to make something more challenging, you know. Like a Neapolitan mile high cake, but when the public demands a favorite, I just hate to disappoint."

"That's true."

Suzette reached for the foil covering her plate. "So, what did the famous baker of Main Street bring today?"

She gently slapped her hand away. "It's a secret."

Suzette's jaw dropped slightly in annoyance. "Oh, Vivienne Finch, I was only kidding."

"I really need to set up at the table in the corner, please excuse me." She pushed her way past Suzette and disappeared behind a quartet of blue-haired ladies in purple choir robes who were admiring a joyously decorated yule log cake.

Suzette turned to Clara Bunton, who had just arrived with two coffee cakes in her hands. "Someone is in a snit this morning."

"Who are you talking about?" Clara asked.

"Vivienne Finch." Suzette waved in the direction of the choir ladies. "You'd think she has gold from Fort Knox under that foil."

"Well, she had quite a bad week." Clara rationalized. "You try falling into a grave and see how you feel afterwards."

Suzette shook her head. "Boy, there's no shortage of nastiness in town lately."

"She saved you from getting wrongfully jailed not too long ago. Where's your gratitude?"

"I have thanked her numerous times, Clara Bunton, and you know it." Suzette's hands went to her hips. "As I told Vivienne, we have to keep friendship and business in two separate worlds."

"Is that what you're going to write in the next Bad Santa note?" Clara quipped.

"How dare you." Suzette reached upwards with her right hand to strike Clara across the face, until the sudden hush of the crowd brought everything to a standstill.

Clara blinked in surprise. "I'm sorry, Suzette. I

don't know what came over me."

Suzette lowered her hand. "No, it was my fault. I suddenly just felt so angry inside."

The general murmur of the crowd struck back up.

"I blame it on an early morning and not enough coffee." Clara tried to lighten the mood.

"I wish I could blame that, but I've already had two cups here this morning." Suzette relieved Clara of one of the cakes in her arms. "Let me help you with that."

The organist started the first hymn, announcing that the doors to the sanctuary had been opened. The crowd began to file toward Father William who stood at the entry way shaking hands and welcoming them to morning mass.

* * *

Carlton Jones smiled as he passed through the crowd to locate the cash box inside the church office. As he turned the corner past the restrooms, he nearly ran head first into Vivienne Finch. "Oh, pardon me." His reading glasses slipped from his jacket pocket and skidded across the slick floor.

"Let me help you." She reached down and snagged the glasses in her grip.

"Thank you, young lady." He reached out for them only to have her plunge her ice-cold hands around his neck. Unable to cry out, the older man fell against the wall and slumped slowly to the floor as his oxygen ran out.

"You're welcome." She hissed and dragged his body into the men's room.

She dropped the glamour spell, as her power was fading faster than she could keep up with. After leaving him inside one of the stalls, she hurried out into the hall to rest a few minutes more and compose her energy.

"Vivienne Finch." Suzette Powell's eyes widened. "I'm sorry, I thought you were someone else."

Natalie, caught off guard, lowered her head, allowing her hair to hide her face. "The restrooms are closed while I clean them. One of the toilets overflowed."

"I wasn't going to use the restroom." Suzette replied. "I was looking for my friend."

"There's no one in here." Natalie spoke quietly. "Just me."

"Do we know each other?" Suzette puzzled. "You look sort of familiar to me."

Natalie shook her head. "I don't think so."

"Do you know Vivienne Finch?" Suzette asked.

"No." Natalie answered.

Suzette folded her arms across her chest and sighed. "She's not inside for service and I know I saw her come down this hallway just a bit ago."

"Maybe she went home after she dropped off her baked goods?" Natalie asked her.

"Could be." Suzette acknowledged. "How did you know she had baked goods?"

"Uh." Natalie stammered. "Most of the women down here were bringing things to the bake sale."

"Are you sure you haven't seen her?" Suzette pressed. "Is she trying to avoid me now?"

"I'm just the cleaning lady." Natalie averted her gaze from Suzette.

Suzette exhaled in frustration. "Well, I was woman enough to try to find her and apologize if I said something to offend her. But I'm not going to chase her down."

Natalie shrugged. "I have to finish cleaning."

"Of course." Suzette turned around and walked away, muttering under her breath.

Natalie slipped back into the men's room and pulled out the reading glasses from her pocket. She concentrated, wringing all the dark magic she could muster to change into the image of Carlton Jones. She dropped down to one knee, as casting the spell sapped her strength. She would need something other than her hands to carry out the next part.

* * *

Joshua Arkins pulled his Jeep into the parking lot of the church and chose a spot far in the back area.

"Are you sure this is safe?" Miss Octavia asked.

"Just stay down and keep out of sight until I need you." He instructed. "Are you sure you have everything you need to trap her?"

"She assumed Vivienne's form just as we thought this morning." Miss Octavia surveyed the parking lot full of cars. "Spirits don't like chaos, they are definitely creatures of strict habits."

"So what did you end up giving Natalie when she showed up this morning?"

"A harmless blessing potion. It's supposed to soothe the nerves and calm the spirit."

Joshua nodded with agreement. "Smart move. Given the mood of everyone here, that could be extra helpful."

"That's the general idea." Miss Octavia cracked the passenger side window as the sun warmed the interior. "Wasn't there a shady spot to park in?"

"Not this far back in the lot." Joshua replied as he glanced at his watch. "We don't want to take a chance on Natalie spotting you before we can act."

"The things I do for magic." Miss Octavia chuckled.

"The things we both do." Joshua lowered his window a tad and gave a listen. As the full moon was approaching, his wolf senses were coming into bloom. His sense of smell and hearing increased with each passing day. "They've started."

"Good." Miss Octavia replied. "She won't be anywhere near that sanctuary while the mass is going on. It would drain her energy quickly."

Joshua stepped out of the Jeep and gave one last look at Miss Octavia, hunched down in the back seat with a two way radio in her hands. "Don't use that unless it's an emergency. It could blow our cover."

"Right." She clicked the two way on and kept it close to her ear. "Just tell me when to come and I'll be there in a flash."

"Affirmative." He closed the door and walked the distance across the parking lot to the entrance of the church. The sound of his boots, echoed between the rows of cars all lined up for morning mass. It felt strange to be dressed up in a suit and tie, but he had to blend in with the others as he targeted Natalie.

As he pulled the main door open, he gave one last look at the Jeep and took a deep breath. He hoped the plan would work and that everyone would be back to normal by nightfall.

"They've just started." An older man dressed in a dark suit approached him with a flyer announcing the bake sale in his hand. "There are some open pews along the back right side."

"Thank you, but I must use the restroom first." Joshua smiled.

"Deputy Arkins, I hardly recognized you." The older man's eyes widened. "I didn't know you were Catholic?"

"I'm not." He felt his cheeks redden. "I was up early and since it's so close to Christmas I thought I'd like to enjoy some of the spirit this morning."

"Why yes, you've come to the right place." The man handed him a bake sale flyer. "You know about this bake sale after service, don't you?"

"I do." Joshua replied. "It's a shame Vivienne couldn't be here to see..." His voice trailed off the moment he realized his mistake.

"Miss Finch was here earlier bringing something delicious." The older man cocked his head. "Didn't you know that?"

"I did." Joshua chuckled and patted the man on the shoulder. "I had to work the night shift last night, so I didn't have a chance to see her this morning."

"Of course." The older man chuckled. "Playing with your sleep schedule like that is bound to make it hard to remember things. Just wait until you're older like me." He adjusted his reading glasses on the bridge of his nose.

"You're sharper than I am this morning, that much is for certain." Joshua hoped his cover up was enough. "Where is the restroom again?"

"It's downstairs, past the kitchen and to your right. You can't miss it."

"Thank you. I'll see you inside." Joshua smiled and headed for the stairs as the usher returned to his post near the sanctuary doors.

As he reached the bottom level of the church, his sense of smell was assaulted by the row upon row of sugary treats readied to sale. He usually never went to Vivienne's bakery this close to the full moon because the overwhelming sweetness made him a bit nauseous.

As he walked past the kitchen, the restrooms were located just ahead and to the right. He stepped into the men's room and noticed one of the stalls was occupied thanks to the pair of black oxfords straddling the toilet. Once he secured the door lock, he reached into his suit jacket and pulled out a coiled length of silver thread that Miss Octavia had blessed to keep Natalie bound securely. Once under control, he'd radio for Octavia to come find them and cast a silencing spell upon her mouth and throat, allowing them to quietly make an escape to the cemetery and perform the banishing ritual.

The door to the bathroom opened as a single set of footfalls echoed inside. A lonely melodic tune was whistled as the bathroom visitor waited patiently for his turn.

Joshua slipped the items back into his coat pocket and flushed the toilet. He unlocked the stall door and opened it to find the older man with the reading glasses blocking the door.

"You found it." The older man smiled and then swung a heavy wooden baseball bat at his head.

Joshua dropped to the cold floor with a thud. He groaned and reached for the radio that was hidden on his belt behind his suit coat.

"You think I'm stupid?" The older man laughed. "I know all about your plan." He swung once more.

Joshua saw stars and then everything went dark.

*   *   *

Miss Octavia waited patiently in the back of the Jeep with the radio. It had been nearly a half hour and still she hadn't heard a peep from Deputy Arkins.

Her fingers hovered over the talk button to ask Joshua if he was still okay, but she thought better of it. If he happened to be sneaking up on Natalie at that exact moment, it could ruin the entire plan.

She would try to focus on something pleasant as she waited. The warmth of the Jeep in the sunlight reminded her of the carefree days growing up on Barbados as a child. She could picture the clear blue ocean beneath her father's glass-bottom boat, as he took her out when tourist excursions weren't scheduled. She would always ask him to try to find the mermaids hiding beneath the waves and he would tell her stories of how he saw a few just the other day with a boat full of tourists. How they waved to him and then disappeared beneath the surface to frolic amongst their coral playgrounds.

She missed him so. He had left this world more than a decade ago, but still her heart ached as if it were yesterday.

The shrill blare of sirens interrupted her nostalgic trip into memory. She remained hidden, waiting for the radio to tell her it was time to take action with her magical spells to restrain Natalie and force her to leave for good.

There was a knock at the window and she slowly pulled herself upwards to see who it was. Much to her surprise, a police officer in full uniform was standing outside the car. He knocked again on the window and gestured for her to get out.

Not wanting to disobey, she did as he wanted and opened the door. She reached to the floor to grab the radio when suddenly he yelled at her. "Hands up right now."

Octavia changed her mind and raised her hands up. "It's just a radio. I was waiting for Deputy Arkins to signal me. We're working together."

The policeman opened the Jeep door and grabbed her roughly by the upper arm. "Get out of the car, nice and slow."

"There must be some kind of mistake here." She spoke softly upon exiting the vehicle.

"Put your hands on the back of your head and turn around slowly." The policeman ordered as a second police car came screeching into the church parking lot.

"Yes sir." She did as he asked. "May I ask a question?"

"Shut up and stay still." He ordered.

"Yes sir."

The newly arrived officer on the scene flanked the first one. "Have you found Deputy Arkins yet?"

"I imagine he's inside for Sunday mass." The first officer replied.

Miss Octavia shook her head. "He's in trouble,

that's what I've been trying to tell you."

The first officer raised his voice at her. "Now take your hands and place them apart on the roof of the car."

"Yes sir." Miss Octavia complied.

He started to frisk her, working his way from her upper shoulders, patting down her midsection until he stopped at her waist where her the pockets of her winter jacket were stuffed full of magical spell supplies to take care of Natalie once they caught her. "What have you got in your pockets?"

"Charms." She replied. "Little trinkets I use for my work."

He reached into her pocket and pulled out a small bottle of holy water. "Alcohol?"

"Holy water." She corrected him. "Like I said, just little charms I use to do my work."

He reached into her pocket again and pulled out a small purse gun with a polished pearl handle. "Is this one of your tools you use for your job?"

"That's not mine." She protested. "Where did that come from?"

He handed it to the second officer who looked it over as he pulled out a small hand-mirror, some dried rose petals and foxglove blooms, five small birthday cake candles, and a plastic baggie filled with dirt. "Just what exactly is your job?"

"I am Miss Octavia and I am in the business of helping those who seek answers from the spirit world."

"It's loaded, Hank." The second officer confirmed.

"So, you were planning on surprising him after

church?" The officer named Hank asked her.

"Please, you must listen to me." She continued to plead with him.

"That's all we needed." Hank produced a pair of handcuffs and pulled her arms down behind her back. "Miss Octavia, or whatever name you do business under, you are under arrest for threatening the life of Deputy Joshua Arkins."

"What?" Octavia's voice jumped up and octave. "Now just a minute."

He snapped the cuffs onto her wrists and spun her around. "You have the right to remain silent." He continued reading her the Miranda Rights, ignoring her requests to speak with Joshua.

"Do you understand these rights?" He asked.

"Yes, but if you'll just get Deputy Arkins out here I'm sure he'll be able to explain everything."

"We're taking you down to the Sheriff's office where you will be provided with the opportunity to speak with a lawyer." Officer Hank replied as he escorted her to the second officer's police vehicle.

"Joshua." Octavia yelled out as loud as she could. "Can you hear me?"

Hank opened the back door and shoved her inside. "Take her down to the station. I'm going inside to inform Deputy Arkins what has taken place." He informed the second officer as he slammed the door closed.

"Shall I call for more backup?" The second officer asked.

"There's no need to get the whole church riled up. I'll sneak in and get him nice and quiet. You head back to the station."

"Affirmative." The second officer climbed into his car and sped away with Miss Octavia.

Hank glanced at the pile of items that he had pulled out of Miss Octavia's pockets. He snatched the plastic baggie with the dirt inside and opened it. He took a long smell and smiled. "Graveyard dirt. How thoughtful." He reached in and grabbed a handful just as the glamour spell dissolved away to reveal Natalie's true form.

She turned back to face the church and listened to the sounds of the mass. She dropped a handful of dirt into her mouth and chewed it slowly. The dark energy stored in the cemetery dirt revived her, repairing the toll being on holy ground had taken.

She climbed into Joshua's Jeep, pleased with how easy it had been to subdue and tie up Officer Hank. Lucky for her, she had flagged him down from the street only a few blocks away from the church on his standard morning patrol.

Having recognized her from the missing person fliers, he had been more than happy to give her a ride. Away from the holy ground, she had felt her dark magic return. As she distracted him with a bogus story about her disappearance, she snagged his Taser gun and fired. A short drive later to the wooded area behind River Road, she handcuffed him to a tree and cast a sleeping spell on him. He'd be out of her way long enough to finish her task.

As Natalie turned the Jeep on, she focused her energy and assumed the form of Vivienne Finch once more. She stepped on the gas pedal and pulled out of the secluded parking spot.

Suzette Powell came running out from the front

entrance of the church and waved her arms wildly as the Jeep sped by with Vivienne behind the wheel. "Vivienne." She called out as the vehicle made a right turn and disappeared into traffic, oblivious to her pleas. "Don't be childish."

She turned to go back into the bake sale when a flyer on the church bulletin board caught her eye. It was a photograph of a woman and a child and the police phone number was listed below to call if anyone had seen either. She pulled the handle on the door to go inside when she suddenly placed the face. "Oh, my God."

She rummaged through her purse to find her cell phone.

"Did you find Vivienne yet?" Clara asked as she emerged from inside the church. "We need her to help setup the hot drink station downstairs."

"Clara, I just found that missing woman." Suzette grabbed her found and called the number. "I found Natalie Burdick."

Before the two women could say another word, a blood-curdling scream erupted from inside the church.

"What in heaven's name is going on in there?" Clara asked Suzette.

They both dashed inside as several parishioners pushed past them with their cell phones held close to their ears in conversation.

"Edith? What's going on?" Clara asked one of the choir ladies.

"Two men have been attacked downstairs. Blood everywhere they say." Edith wrung her hands nervously. "Who would do such a thing?"

CHAPTER 23

Vivienne dreamt that she had the power to fly, just like the birds. She simply flapped her arms and with a sudden jolt she was soaring over the tree tops and feeling the breeze blow against her face. She climbed higher into the blue sky and then soared toward the ground with an exhilarating rush, watching the buildings below become larger.

Suddenly, she found herself entangled within a flock of wild geese, honking and pecking at her furiously. She tried to shoo them away, but they did not scare off.

The honking became a shrill ringing. She covered her ears but it wouldn't go away. The ringing continued over and over until at last her eyes sprung open and she bolted upright from the sofa.

It was her cell phone that had stirred her from her deep sleep. She clumsily grabbed at it, trying to focus on the name and number displayed on the screen.

With a swipe of her fingers, she answered it. "Hello?"

"Vivienne. Where are you?" Kathy's voice was filled with concern.

"I'm at home." She croaked, her throat dry. "I dozed off waiting for Joshua to call me."

"You need to get yourself over to Cayuga Memorial right now."

"What's going on?" She shook the sleep off.

"Joshua was hurt over at the church bake sale along with one of the church ushers." Kathy explained. "Hasn't anyone called you?"

Vivienne snapped awake. "What do you mean he's hurt?"

"I don't know anything else." Kathy replied. "Clara searched the church high and low but couldn't find you."

Vivienne glanced at the wall clock. It was nearly half-past two in the afternoon. "No one called me." She jumped off the sofa, still groggy.

"Why did you go home?" Kathy asked.

"I thought I could sneak a quick nap in before the bake sale." Vivienne lied.

"You better get over there and find out what's going on. Do you need a ride?"

"No." Vivienne raced out into the living room and grabbed her winter coat off the wall rack. "I've got my car here." She stepped into a pair of beat up sneakers and grabbed her keys. "I'm on my way."

"I'll let Clara know you've been found."

"Thanks for letting me know." Vivienne hurried out the front door and nearly tripped as she hurried to the car. "I'll call you back when I get some more information."

The drive to the hospital was a blur, but somehow she managed to get there safely. After a frantic conversation with the admissions desk, she was given access to Joshua's room on the fourth floor.

As she entered, she was relieved to see that he had no roommate to share it with. Sheriff Rigsbee was sitting in the visitor's chair next to the bed where Joshua was reclined with his eyes closed.

Most of his head was wrapped in bandages, an IV dripped pain medication into a vein on the top of his left hand. His face looked puffy and swollen.

"Joshua." She could barely get his name out of her mouth.

Sheriff Rigsbee stood up from the chair and walked over to her. "Vivienne, I'm glad you're here."

"What happened to him?" She asked.

Zeke Rigsbee was dressed in his full duty uniform, but today he looked less than happy to be wearing it. "Someone attacked him and Carlton Jones in the men's room at Our Lady of the Lake." Zeke turned back to get another look at his bruised and battered body. "They used a wooden baseball bat from the church's recreational supply room."

"Carlton is in better shape. He's unconscious, but expected to recover."

Vivienne felt her lower chin quivering as she stared at Joshua lying so helpless in the soft light of the hospital room. "Who did this?"

"The last person anyone would suspect."

"Natalie Burdick?" Vivienne asked him.

"Why do you suspect her?" Zeke asked.

"It's a long story." Vivienne shot back.

"Natalie and Connor Burdick are still missing persons at this point." Zeke spoke softly. "But if you have some information that might lead to their whereabouts I'd like to hear it."

"I don't know where they are." Vivienne wiped the tears that started to flow from the corners of her eyes. "Who do you have in custody?"

"The woman known as Miss Octavia."

"What?" Vivienne shook her head. "No, she wouldn't have done this."

"My officers found her hiding inside Deputy Arkins' Jeep in the church parking lot this morning.

She was carrying a gun."

"No, you've got it all wrong. She was helping him to capture the person who is responsible for everything that has been going on." Vivienne tried to explain.

"Perhaps you and I should take a ride down to the station and you can tell me whatever it is that you've been holding onto." Zeke offered her his hand.

"If it will free Octavia, I'll go." She replied. "But, I need a few minutes with Joshua first."

"Of course." Zeke nodded. "Would you like me to wait?"

"No, you go on ahead." Vivienne walked over to the bedside table and stared at Joshua. "I'll drive down in a little while."

Zeke gave her a reassuring smile. "Joshua is a strong man. He'll pull through this."

Vivienne reached out and stroked his left arm gently. "Yes, he is."

"I look forward to hearing your story." Zeke quietly stepped out of the room.

"Joshua, I don't know if you can hear me but I'm going to talk to you anyway just in case you can." Vivienne sat down in the chair and listened to the rhythmic monitoring devices that beeped and chirped in the quiet hospital room.

"We really underestimated her power, but she's not going to get away with this. I'm going to go down to the station and set things right." Vivienne waited for some sort of sign that he heard her. She stared as his chest would rise and fall with each breath.

"Open your eyes, Joshua. Please, let me know that you're still in there." Vivienne grabbed his hand in hers and squeezed it. "Give me a sign that she didn't destroy your mind with a spell." The tears dripped from her face and splashed onto his blanket.

"Please come back to me. Come back to us. Come back to the life we've just begun to start making. I don't want to walk another step without you by my side."

She stared and waited for a sign, but there was none. He remained motionless. "I know you're still in there. I can feel it." She spoke softly. "You need to reach deep down inside yourself and find that will to come back."

One of the nurses, a kind looking woman with very short hair stepped into the room. "Excuse me, I need to check on his wound dressing."

Vivienne sniffed back the tears remaining. "Of course."

"I'm Carol, the evening nurse for Joshua." She walked to the other side of the bed and gently tipped his head to the side. "A little bit of bleeding, but not bad. I expected to see worse."

"Really?" Vivienne felt a little bit of hope flare up inside her.

"Given the severity of the injuries, he's recovering remarkably fast." Carol crossed over in front of Vivienne and checked the flow rate on the IV monitor. "He must have some angels watching over him."

"I know he does." She smiled weakly. "Has he woken up at all?"

"My shift just started a half hour ago, so I haven't been here." Carol reached into the pocket of her scrub coat and pulled out a tablet device. "Let me check his chart and see what we find."

"Thank you."

"He's remained unconscious since he was transferred up here from emergency." Carol gave a quick check to make sure the IV site wasn't irritated. "Don't give up hope. He's definitely a fighter."

"Are you going to be here all night?" Vivienne asked.

"I'm here until seven in the morning."

"Will you give me a call if he happens to wake up?"

Carol nodded and tapped the tablet with a plastic stylus that was hung around her neck with a little chain. "I'm assuming your Vivienne Finch."

"Yes, I am."

"You're listed as his third emergency contact, behind Sheriff Rigsbee and his brother, Hunter Arkins." Carol confirmed.

"His brother?"

"That's what it says here." Carol put the tablet back into her pocket. "I'll call you the moment he wakes up."

"Thank you, Carol. It really means a lot." Vivienne slowly pulled herself up from the chair. "I need to go down the Sheriff's office and take care of some business."

As Vivienne stepped out of the hospital she heard the whine of an ambulance siren and then another. She was really starting to hate that sound and part of her just wanted to run home and put a pillow over her head and be done with it. It was the sound of terror and death. The sound of pain and loss.

Pulling out the parking lot she watched as the

first ambulance sped toward the emergency entrance with lights flashing.

As she drove along Maple Street, she had to pull off to the side to let another ambulance speed past her on the way to Cayuga Memorial.

When she arrived at the Sheriff's office, she walked into the sights and sounds of complete pandemonium. Desk officers were swamped with phones ringing off the hook, people shouting and nearly running into each other as each tried to be louder than the other.

Vivienne walked past the information desk and headed down the all-too-familiar hallway that led to Sheriff Rigsbee's office.

As she passed the water cooler, she was pulled to the side by one of the officers whose name she never could seem to remember. All she could recall was that his pencil-thin black mustache looked like a pathetic attempt to appear older and have authority, but it failed to work on both attempts. "You?"

"I'm sorry, it's been a long day." Vivienne apologized. "I can't remember your name."

"She's here." He shouted to the others and then spun her against the wall roughly. "I got her."

"What the hell is going on?" Vivienne screamed in frustration.

"You must be crazy to come strolling in here after trying to poison half the town." He quickly snapped some handcuffs on her wrists.

"What are you talking about?" She asked as he spun her around to face him.

"Vivienne Finch, you're under arrest for multiple counts of attempted murder." The officer was joined by several others who looked at her as if they had just caught Jack The Ripper.

"This is a mistake." She sputtered.

"You have the right to remain silent." The officer continued.

CHAPTER 24

Monday, December 16th

It felt like time had come to a complete stop. Not that she would have minded such an event happening, as the past week had been exhausting both emotionally and physically. She sat alone in Sheriff Zeke Rigsbee's office, having just endured the unpleasant task of standing in a police lineup.

She did have an ace up her sleeve. She only hoped that her single allowed phone call would yield the desired result.

As the sheriff stepped into his office, he closed the door behind him and folded his arms across his desk. "In all my years serving this town, I never would have believed you capable of such a heinous act."

Vivienne lowered her head. "I know this doesn't mean much, but it wasn't me."

He walked over to his desk and sat down to face her. "Thankfully, my faith in humanity has not been completely destroyed this year."

"What?" Vivienne lifted her head to face him.

"You are a very lucky woman to have such good friends to cover your back." Sheriff Rigsbee leaned back in his chair. "Kathy Saunders dropped this off the moment she heard about your arrest." He lifted a thick manila folder off the desk.

"Thank you, Kathy." Vivienne felt an enormous weight suddenly leave her shoulders.

"Yes and you are darn lucky that she did." He

spoke softly. "Your notes proved quite useful."

"So you read it?"

"I have here the information that one Samantha Charles has forwarded to you about the R.G.E. Company and the plans to start drilling in Cayuga Cove." He tapped the folder.

"Then you know about Robert Rothwell and Natalie Burdick too?"

"I just got off the phone with Miss Charles. We had an interesting conversation about Natalie's tenure in New York." Zeke's usual poker face was devoid of any emotion.

"Natalie wants the drilling to start at any cost." Vivienne's voice gained a sense of urgency. "Joshua and Miss Octavia were trying to stop her."

"I've had an interesting talk with Miss Octavia as well. She's a strange bird, but her story matched up with the information in here. I may not believe in her magic mumbo jumbo, but I do believe that she was setup in an attempt to keep this department distracted and unaware of what really was going on out by the cemetery."

"She's a very dangerous woman." Vivienne interrupted.

"She was also spotted at Our Lady of the Lake today, after the attack on Joshua and Carlton Jones."

"Spotted by who?"

"Suzette Powell. Oddly enough, she was searching for you when it happened."

"Yes." Vivienne worked fast to cover the fact that it had been Natalie impersonating her inside the church. "During my investigating, I became aware that Eddie Robertson had died from poisoning."

"No one outside of this department knows that, but I'm willing to overlook Deputy Arkins' lack of judgment in sharing that with you given the circumstances." Zeke cast a wary eye at her. "Please continue."

"So, I started to wonder if maybe she was one of the gold digging black widow characters you see on those true crime shows." Vivienne felt quite proud of the little white lie that was covering all her magical bases. "It made sense that in order for her to get in on the family money, she had to bump off Eddie first. In order to create a diversion, she came up with the plan to use the Bad Santa notes to stir up dissent amongst the townspeople. After all, this is a small town. If someone just opens their ears in the right place, you'll learn more than you ever thought possible."

Zeke nodded in agreement. "You'll get no argument from me there."

"So, you've found other poisoning evidence?" Vivienne hoped.

"Someone poisoned all the baked good with hydroxybenzene." Sheriff Rigsbee revealed to her.

"So how did you figure out Natalie was behind it?" Vivienne asked.

"You can thank Suzette Powell for that. She picked you out of the lineup."

"I don't understand."

Zeke leaned back in his chair. "You were placed at the bake sale this morning along with several other women from the town. Suzette Powell told one of the investigating officers that she had a small confrontation with you before mass started."

"Oh." Vivienne had no idea what her imposter

had done, but she had to play along. "It was nothing."

"Oh, it was more than that." Zeke continued. "That little spat happened to be your key to freedom."

"Really?" Vivienne smiled. "I need to have words with friends more often."

Zeke cleared his throat. "Getting back to business, she informed me that after your spat, she lost sight of you in the crowd getting the baked goods ready downstairs."

"I had been up late baking and wanted to get a quick nap in before it started so I snuck home." Vivienne put her cover story in place.

"Which your friend Kathy was able to verify when she called to inform you about the attack on Joshua." Sheriff Rigsbee nodded. "Those smart phones you own all have GPS location devices and the cellular carrier was able to verify your phone's location during the call this morning."

"Thank goodness." Vivienne sighed. "So how does this all link to you suspecting Natalie? She's been missing for days."

"As soon as the morning service started, Suzette thought she saw you in the back corridor near the restrooms. She followed up and discovered a strange woman who claimed she was the church's cleaning lady."

"Natalie." Vivienne nodded.

"Standing right outside the crime scene at roughly the same time we assume the attacks happened." Zeke finished. "Suzette informed me that the woman had her hair in her face and avoided eye contact, but she still looked familiar. It wasn't until later on when she happened to glance at one of the missing flyers on the church bulletin board that she made the connection and called the station."

"Thank goodness." Vivienne sighed. "So when did you catch her?"

"We haven't." Zeke's posture tensed up. "I have a missing officer whose last known location was the church and a bad feeling that she's behind it."

"I'm sorry, sheriff." Vivienne lowered her head. "What about the bake sale poisonings? Is everyone okay?"

"They're very sick at the moment but the medical teams are dispensing medication to counter the lethal effects. Her choice of poison is most peculiar."

"I think she was obsessed with using hydroxybenzene because the original Rothwell family members were killed off by the same thing." Vivienne added. "It's rather obscure now. Most likely if she killed with it, there was a good chance it would not get picked up on a basic autopsy.

"Unless someone suspected otherwise." Zeke concurred.

"Think about it. After she married Robert Rothwell, she could poison him with the same thing. If someone became suspicious, it wouldn't have been very hard to dump an amount into the waste water generated by the drilling company and blame it on accidental exposure while visiting the site in person." Vivienne finished. "The black widow kills her final victim and walks away with a large chunk of the Rothwell family fortune."

"Not if we stop her."

"Vivienne, it's time I fill you in with the plan we have to catch this Natalie in the act." Zeke announced.

"She's very intelligent." Vivienne spoke up. "You better have a good trap."

"It's one we think she can't resist." Zeke tipped his hat at her. "You."

There was a knock on the door as one of the officer's stepped inside. "She's back from her supply run."

"Send her in." Zeke nodded.

Vivienne looked up as Miss Octavia stepped into the room with a large silken bag in her grip. "Am I glad to see you."

"I told them you needed my help." Miss Octavia smiled. "Even if they don't believe in 'mumbo jumbo'. She glanced warily at Sheriff Rigsbee.

"I don't care what you use, I want her stopped." Zeke folded is arms across his chest. "You can employ Santa Claus for all I care."

Both Vivienne and Miss Octavia groaned in response.

* * *

"We are asking all of our responsible citizens to help us out in capturing this dangerous fugitive." Zeke spoke to the press outside the Sheriff's office. "If you spot her, please don't try to detain her. Call the police right away and tell them as much information as you can."

"How did she escape?" One of the reporters asked.

"I am not at liberty to discuss that." Zeke scolded the intrusive reporter. "Our priority is not to assign blame, but to ensure that Vivienne Finch is brought to justice and made to answer the charges against her."

Kathy turned to Clara who was standing in the throng of concerned citizens gathered to hear the press conference. "Good thing we're in on this or I'd be hopping mad at him."

Clara nodded. "You? If they hadn't told Nora she'd have had a stroke by now."

"I hope she's careful." Kathy worried.

"She'll be okay. She's our Vivienne. One of the smartest cookies we know." Clara whispered back. "Let's get out here and hope it ends soon."

* * *

Thanks to a secret ride in a patrol car, Vivienne and Miss Octavia had been safely transferred to Gus Holt's land where the drilling equipment was quiet and shut down for the evening.

Their protector, officer Jeff Waverly, was hiding off to the side behind a large tanker of waste water that the drilling process had generated. Both Sheriff Rigsbee and Vivienne had agreed that only one officer be posted to ensure Natalie would not spot the trap too early by mistake. It was a risk, but one that needed to be taken.

As agreed to, Vivienne decided to start the dialogue that she hoped would draw Natalie to her while Miss Octavia and Officer Waverly remained hidden. "Okay Natalie, you've won. You can come out now and finish this."

There was nothing but silence. Vivienne had to force herself not to look in the direction where her surprise party was hiding. Seeing that her words were not enough, she decided to make it more personal. She retrieved the silver brooch from her purse and held it tightly in her palm. "Natalie, the police know all about your plan to destroy the town. It's not going to work."

A gentle breeze blew along the snowy field but Vivienne remained alone. As she carefully crunched across the snow, she noticed the fresh set of little footprints. She thought for a moment and decided to take the biggest gamble of all. Before leaving the Sheriff's office, she had stopped at the vending machine and purchased a pack of chocolate chip cookies to snack on as her stomach growled incessantly with hunger pains. Thankfully, she had been too nervous to eat them. She pulled the cookies out of her jacket pocket. "Connor, I have cookies. Just like I promised. Do you want some?" She called out.

A moment later, Connor stepped out from his hiding place behind a large trailer that had sections of metal piping strapped down. "Cookies?"

He bounded toward her, a look of pure joy upon his face. "They are all for you, sweetie."

He stopped at her legs and gave her a little hug. "I love you Miss Vivienne."

Her heart melted and she fought back a flood of tears. She knelt down to embrace him. "You poor thing, caught in the middle of this vicious plot."

He took the cookies from her hand and began munching on them. "I don't like staying at Uncle Gus' house. He won't let me play in the cemetery like

Mommy does."

"Where is your mommy?" She asked.

"Right here." Natalie's voice called out from behind her. "Using my son to get my attention. Have you no shame?"

"It's over, Natalie." Vivienne spoke quietly. "It ends here."

Natalie raised her arms into the air as the wind picked up to a howl, scattering snow in a crazed fury. "Yes it does."

"Don't move another inch." Jeff jumped out from his cover with his gun aimed in Natalie's direction. "Stay right where you are."

"I intend to." She yelled back to him and then waved her left fingers.

A piece of metal pipe tore off the water tanker and smacked him in the back of his head. Jeff dropped to the ground, unconscious. "Now, we finish this."

"Yes, we do." Vivienne directed the large piece of silver rope to snake up behind Natalie and wrap itself tightly around her body.

"Connor." Natalie cried out. "Help mommy get out of this."

"No Connor, don't listen to her." Vivienne warned.

"Mommy?" Connor appeared confused and remained frozen in place.

"Good work, Vivienne." Miss Octavia stepped out from the shadows of the drilling equipment. "That will hold her for now."

Natalie struggled and squirmed, falling to the ground with a thud. "No." She turned her head to face Miss Octavia and opened her mouth. A great wind blasted her backwards, forcing to put her hands up against her face to fight off the icy blast.

Vivienne cleared her head and recited the silence voice spell that Octavia had faxed her at the Sheriff's station.

Natalie's wind died off as suddenly as it started. She turned to Vivienne in anguish. She mouthed words, but no sound left her lips.

"I'm sorry." Vivienne spoke back.

"Mommy." Connor ran over to Natalie and tried to touch the rope, but the silver rope shocked him and he tumbled away into the snow.

"Quickly, we must get her to the cemetery before the spell wears off." Octavia ran over and grabbed hold of Natalie who continued to scream at them silently.

With Vivienne's help, they loaded her, Connor, and the unconscious body of officer Jeff Waverly into the patrol car and sped across the field to the Cayuga Union cemetery. "How long is the spell going to hold?"

"Not long." Miss Octavia yelled back as they bounced along through the snowy field.

Vivienne spied the main gates, which were closed and appeared locked with a chain. She gunned the accelerator. "Hold on."

The patrol car smashed through the gates, knocking them off the rusty hinges. Vivienne turned sharply to the right, narrowly missing taking out a large marble obelisk. The path to the cannons was barely visible in the fading sunlight, as they roared uphill and came to a halt just shy of the monument.

Vivienne and Octavia jumped out of the car and dragged Natalie to the space between the cannons.

"What do we do now?" Vivienne asked.

Octavia pulled out her supplies from the deep pockets of her jacket. She pulled the stopper of the vial of holy water and drizzled it onto Natalie.

The water bubbled and steamed as Natalie found her voice again. "I'm not ready to go yet." She screamed. "You must not do this."

Octavia hurled a bottle of silver powder to Vivienne. "Walk a circle and keep it tight around her."

Vivienne pulled the stopper off the powder and poured the silver powder onto the ground. She walked quickly in a tight circle around Natalie, trapping her inside the magical boundary.

"Blessed be the light that draws you near." Octavia spoke in a monotone voice. "With love and reverence, we bid thee spirit farewell." Octavia raised her hands upwards and closed her eyes. "Your business here amongst the living is done. Feel the burden of sorrow no more."

Natalie shook violently and then arched her back, as a bolt of white energy crackled out of her mouth like lightening and struck one of the cannons.

Vivienne covered her ears as the wind roared around them. "Is it working?"

"You tell me." Octavia looked at her in surprise. "I've never done this kind of thing before."

A thick, black smoke poured off the ground between the cannons and coalesced into the spectral image of Edgar Rothwell. He appeared even more fearsome than Vivienne remembered. His blue-tinged flesh was pulled taught against his skull, eyes sunken deep and glowing like two red-hot coals. Vivienne stood frozen in terror as he stepped toward them. "You've done well, witches."

"Leave them alone." Natalie cried out. "This is between the two of us."

Edgar raised his palms in the air and then flipped them upwards in a jerking motion. "You are correct."

Both Vivienne and Octavia dropped over backwards, pressed to the cold ground by his magical force.

Natalie squirmed inside the circle. "I tried to destroy him before he could walk the earth." She yelled to Vivienne.

"You were going to kill all of us." Vivienne yelled back, still pinned to the ground. "I couldn't let that happen."

"I will have your silence." Edgar glowered at them both. "You women are always at the root of corruption."

"You haven't been a paragon of virtue yourself." Vivienne spat back. "Murdering your family because you felt guilty after being rejected by your maid."

Edgar howled with rage.

"Big man you are." Vivienne mocked him.

"You shall pay for your insolence." He pointed at her.

"Come and get me." Vivienne challenged.

Edgar charged at her with murderous intent, stepping onto the silver circle which encircled Natalie. A split-second later, he was on fire, screaming in agony as his spirit form was disrupted by the sacred barrier.

"You should look where you step." Vivienne felt the pressure holding her down release. She sat upright as he continued to burn, the flames ripping his spectral body apart piece by piece. "You're not human anymore, silver is like poison."

"I'll kill you all." He cried out in defiance. "Witches." He screamed and writhed in agony and with a sudden popping sound dissolved into a wisp of dark smoke. It snaked upwards, curling toward the vortex that hovered about twenty feet over their heads.

"One of the portals." Vivienne gasped and helped Miss Octavia to her feet.

"It's pulling the dark energy back in." Octavia nodded. "We have to destroy it."

"But how?" Vivienne wondered. "I don't have a spell prepared."

The portal swirled faster and faster as a jet of black smoke-like energy hurled to the ground.

"He's re-forming again." Vivienne cried out.

"Untie the silver rope and I'll destroy the portal." Natalie spoke up.

"No, Vivienne. Don't trust her." Octavia warned.

"Please, let me right these wrongs so that I might rest in peace." Natalie begged. "I give you my word."

"What should I do?" Vivienne asked Octavia, casting a wary eye on the smoke that began to take Edgar's spectral form again.

"Whatever it is, you better do it fast." Octavia shook her head. "This is your moment."

Vivienne looked into Natalie's eyes. "Swear on Connor's life."

"I swear."

Vivienne darted into the circle and began to untie the silver rope around Natalie. As she did, Natalie's physical body went limp as her spirit form soared upwards.

"I hope you're right about this." Octavia replied.

Natalie's spectral form drifted over to the now almost fully formed figure of Edgar and embraced him. "Tie us up." She yelled. "Hurry."

Vivienne dashed over to their location with the rope in hand. She made a loop and tossed it over Edgar's head where it came to rest at the base of his neck. She then ran quickly around them, binding them tightly.

"Don't worry darling. This is only going to hurt for a little bit." Natalie hissed at him.

"You wretched fiend." Edgar's voice boomed. "What have you done."

"What should have been done long ago." She looked at Vivienne one last time. "Now toss the end up toward the portal and run as far as you can."

"Thank you Natalie." Vivienne tossed the rope upwards where it was caught in the vortex around the portal. It grew taught and yanked both Natalie and Edgar upwards.

Vivienne and Octavia ran as fast as they could to the other side of the patrol car and ducked down as the forms of Natalie and Edgar were sucked into the portal. There was a popping sound and then a blast of wind as the silver reacted to the dark energy. Like a great wheel on fire, the portal spun wildly in the air and then imploded, disappearing into the night sky with a thunderous boom.

After a few moments, the two women peeked

over the car and found the cemetery dark and empty once again.

"It worked." Vivienne smiled. "She sealed the portal."

"One down." Octavia nodded. "Goddess knows how many more to go around here."

"One less entry point into Cayuga Cove." Vivienne smiled. "I'm happy with that."

"I wanted to say I'm sorry." Natalie's voice startled them from behind.

"Natalie." Vivienne gasped. "I thought you were destroyed when the portal sealed."

"The dark magic that allowed me to leave this cemetery has been sealed." She spoke softly. Her visage was serene. "I've returned to ask you for one last favor so that I may cross over."

"What is it?"

She floated through the car and stood between the cannons. She passed her hand through the cannon on the left. "When Edgar murdered me, he hid my body in the cannon to deny me a proper burial."

Natalie paused for a moment and turned her face toward the sky. "I only knew bitterness and anger as the years went by and we were forgotten."

"It is time to rest." Octavia spoke softly. "You are free now."

"Where are we going mommy?" Connor bounded from the patrol car and held tight to Vivienne's legs.

"I'm going someplace far away, my love. Far beyond the stars."

"The stars." He smiled and stepped toward her. "Can I go to?"

"Not yet, my sweet darling." She kissed him on

the head. "Be a good boy and mind your manners." He closed his eyes and fell to the ground in a deep sleep.

"He will have no memory of these events. Will you see that he has the chance to live a full life?" Natalie asked.

"I will." Vivienne replied.

As the wind died down, Natalie faded away into a wisp of fine smoke that loaded itself into the cannon where her remains were interred.

Natalie's cannon craned upwards slowly as a bolt of blazing energy erupted from the cannon, burned cross the sky and headed for the gas equipment. A few seconds later, an enormous explosion rocked the ground as the tanker and drilling equipment was destroyed in a massive fireball.

There was a groaning sound as Natalie's cannon dropped the protective cap and lowered to the ground.

Vivienne watched as a pile of bones tumbled out onto the snowy ground. "It is done."

"Yes." Octavia nodded back solemnly.

"But what will we tell people?" Vivienne worried.

Octavia walked over to the area where Natalie's physical body was huddled next to a faded headstone. A bottle of hydroxybenzene and a note lay on the ground next to her. "She wrote her own ending."

Vivienne picked up the paper and read it. "It's a suicide note, explaining why she did everything."

"It's more than that." Octavia pointed to sky. "Look up."

A single star was just visible in the evening sky. It

winked and then disappeared as a mass of winter storm clouds swirled overhead. Thick, puffy snowflakes began to fall to the ground, but when they hit the ground they sparkled like fireflies. Each snowflake lattice connected to the other and in a few moments the entire cemetery was pulsing with a warm, golden light. The bones of Natalie Burdick dissolved away as the energy flared brighter than the fire over at Gus Holt's drilling site.

"What is it?" Vivienne shouted.

"An early Christmas gift." Octavia beamed. "Or a miracle?"

The golden glow enveloped them both in a warm cocoon, as the magic pulsed and raced into the town of Cayuga Cove.

The residents could only stand and watch in amazement as the glowing snowflakes danced through the air, passing through homes and buildings with ease.

All of the hatred and bad feelings that had plagued the town was washed away as the spell Natalie had cast dissipated. In the silence of the winter night, peace returned once more to Cayuga Cove.

Afterwards, there were all kinds of guesses as to what the glowing snowflakes had been. Most believed what the media had reported, it had been an adverse chemical reaction from the fire out by the drilling site. A rare scientific reaction that created a localized 'aurora borealis' effect over the town.

"Connor?" Gus Holt's voice called out from the darkness. "It's time to come home. You know I don't like you playing in the cemetery."

Vivienne approached him. "That won't be happening anymore, Gus." She pointed to where Miss Octavia had Connor wrapped in a blanket to keep him warm on the snowy ground.

"What's going on here?" He asked angrily. He moved toward them and stopped when he saw the crumpled body of Natalie. "No." He cried out. "What happened to her?"

"She confessed to everything." Vivienne spoke softly as several police cruisers pulled into the cemetery entrance. "I think Sheriff Rigsbee is going to have a lot of questions for you to answer."

He dropped to his knees at Natalie's side. "I just wanted to help her out. I was just being a good neighbor."

After the patrol cars reported to the scene, Vivienne handed the suicide note to Sheriff Rigsbee and directed him to the body of Natalie. They explained how Gus Holt had been hiding Connor for Natalie and he was arrested for interfering in an ongoing police investigation.

Sheriff Rigsbee informed Vivienne that a new press conference was scheduled that evening to thank the newest local hero for her efforts, explaining the elaborate ruse and clearing her name in the process.

"I won't feel better until my good name is restored." Vivienne said as she and Miss Octavia rode back with Sheriff Rigsbee in his vehicle.

"Until then, please try to remember what this feels like Miss Finch." He replied.

"I won't soon forget it." Vivienne agreed.

"Good." Sheriff Rigsbee replied gruffly. "So maybe you'll think twice about staying out of police business and focus on your own from now on?"

"Yes sir." Vivienne gulped.

Miss Octavia held Connor in the back seat. "At least Connor isn't harmed. That's a certified Christmas miracle in my book."

"I don't believe in miracles." Sheriff Rigsbee replied as he followed the convoy of patrol cars back to town. "What I do believe is that his crazy mother had enough sense to drop him off before killing herself."

"So what's going to happen to him now?" Vivienne asked.

"Our investigation found no other living relatives, so child protective services is taking him." He explained.

"He's an orphan." Miss Octavia sighed.

"But at least he's alive. He has an entire life to experience." Vivienne nodded as the lights of Cayuga Cove appeared in the distance.

"I hope you don't mind another pit stop." Sheriff Rigsbee asked them.

"What's one more tonight?" She shrugged.

"Someone at Cayuga Memorial is asking to see you, Miss Finch."

"Joshua?" She hoped.

"He's made a remarkable recovery. They're at a loss to explain it. They're going to release him tomorrow morning."

Vivienne looked up as the nearly full moon peeked from behind the clouds. "Sometimes, you just don't need to know why. You just accept it and say thanks."

"Now that, ladies, is what I believe to be a true

miracle." Zeke smiled. "And you can quote me on that."

CHAPTER 25

Tuesday, December 24th

Joshua poured Vivienne a cup of eggnog. "I can't believe Christmas is actually here."

"It seems like it was only Thanksgiving the other week." Vivienne marveled. "Of course, it was quite a roller coaster ride to get here."

"Alive and well." Joshua raised his glass to her. "Thanks to you."

Vivienne clinked cups with him. "Well, I may have had a small part in saving the entire town."

"Which is why I love you all the more." Joshua gave her a kiss.

Tommy sat curled up by the fireplace, he opened one eye and meowed to let everyone know he was present and then went back to his sixth nap of the day.

"We're not under the mistletoe." Vivienne pointed to the archway on the opposite end of the living room.

"So let's change locations and fix this grievous lapse in holiday protocol." He wrapped his arm around her waist.

"Sounds like a plan."

Joshua walked by the Christmas tree and pointed to the ornament of the little drummer boy. "Is Connor really alive or is he some kind of powerful spell?"

"He's as real as any of us." Vivienne nodded.

"That doesn't really answer my question." Joshua reached out and lifted the drummer boy ornament into hand. "Is it really that easy to bring someone back from the dead with a spell?"

"Don't go thinking that bringing the dead back to life is common for witches." Nana Mary shook her right index finger at them both. "It's one of the most dangerous spells out there and there are strict coven laws about using it."

"I understand, Nana Mary." Vivienne agreed. "It violates the flow of natural time."

"There are usually terrible consequences for even attempting it." Nana Mary explained. "A mother's enduring love mixed with all that crazy portal energy. It was a one in a million shot but for some reason it worked."

"I still say it was a Christmas miracle." Vivienne argued.

"Given the circumstances surrounding his unusual resurrection, the Elder Council saw to it that a proper paperwork history was created to allow him to slip back into society." Nana Mary smiled.

"I never would have guessed that Samantha Charles would volunteer to be a foster mother." Vivienne added. "Although I'm sure she's doing a fantastic job."

"So, how is he doing?" Joshua asked Vivienne.

"He and Samantha are doing well. He's adjusting to his new life in New York, but the amnesia is still a bit of challenge." Vivienne sipped more of her eggnog.

"It's probably for the best that he not remember anything about what happened." Joshua added. "As we found out, the past can be something dangerous."

"Samantha is going to be bringing him here for the summer when the house is completed." Vivienne spoke up. "So he can enjoy Cayuga Lake and make some new friends."

"You don't think having him here will draw Natalie back from the grave, do you?" Joshua worried.

"She's at peace." Nana Mary answered for them.

"Did I mention that I ran into Tristan the other day when I stopped by the hospital to visit Delores?" Vivienne spoke up. "He looks much better, just some residual bruises and a broken arm. He told me Nathaniel is healing up quite nicely and is expected to be released tomorrow morning."

"Thank the Goddess." Nana Mary smiled.

"I can't believe that Nora is running so late." Joshua looked at his watch.

"It's definitely not like mother." Vivienne agreed.

"She'll be here." Nana Mary smiled. "Now stop worrying and just relax and enjoy the holiday." She reached into her pocket and pulled out a little flask. "Can I Irish that eggnog up for either of you?"

"Nana Mary," Vivienne laughed. "Do you know something about why Mother is late?"

"So what if I do?" She dumped some of the flask into Vivienne's cup. "Just relax and enjoy the holiday."

"Good advice." Joshua lowered his cup toward the flask. "I'll drink to that."

"Good man." Nana Mary winked at him.

The front door opened as Nora hurried inside with a large basket in her arms. A festive red and green ribbon was tied on the top handle. She bumped the door closed with her rear and smiled. "Merry Christmas everyone."

"Merry Christmas." Nana Mary replied. "You're late."

"You didn't tell them, did you?" Nora asked as she stepped forward.

"Not a word." Nana Mary smiled. "So, what are you waiting for?"

"What's going on?" Vivienne asked with a slight hint of concern.

Nora set the basket on the floor as a tiny orange tiger kitten clawed his way to the edge and meowed. "You always say you don't need anything, but I found someone who needs a mommy and daddy and I couldn't think of two nicer people who fit that mold."

Vivienne rushed forward. "Oh, he's adorable. Where did you find him?"

"He was living out by Whispering Pines. Poor thing was eating birdseed he was so hungry." Nora smiled. "My plan was to take him to the shelter, but I just couldn't do it."

Vivienne picked him up as Tommy strolled over to see who the new visitor was. He meowed loudly.

"Looks like you've got a new brother, Tommy." Joshua laughed.

"What are you going to call him?" Nana Mary asked.

"I suppose having four-legged grandchildren isn't so bad." Nora smiled. "It's good practice for when the real thing happens."

Vivienne giggled as the orange tiger kitten crawled on top of her shoulders and meowed at Tommy down below.

Tommy meowed back and then walked over to

Joshua where he sharpened his nails on his right leg.

"Ouch." Joshua jumped back. "This wasn't my idea, buddy." He pulled Tommy's claws out of his pants and lifted him up to get a better view of the kitten. "Say hello to your new little brother."

"Another furry in the family." Nana Mary winked at Joshua.

Vivienne scooped the kitten up in her hands, feeling his little body shake as he began to purr loudly. He sniffed the air with his little pink nose. "You look like a Sam to me." She cooed as the kitten reached out with his little paw and touched her nose in response. "Welcome home, Sammy Cat."

VIVIENNE'S FAMOUS TREAVIS CAKE

(This recipe, created by Virginia Treavis, was a top prize winner at the Cayuga Cove Summer Fair for many years. It is one of the Sweet Dreams Bakery's top sellers.)

1 box of yellow cake mix
1.7 oz. box of instant pistachio pudding mix
4 large eggs
1 cup sour cream
½ cup vegetable oil
½ teaspoon almond extract
4 drops of green food coloring
½ cup granulated sugar
1 teaspoon of ground cinnamon
½ cup chopped nuts
Confectioner's sugar (for garnish)

Preheat oven to 350 degrees. Combine yellow cake mix, pudding mix, eggs, sour cream, oil, extract, and food coloring in a large bowl. Beat with an electric mixer on medium speed for two minutes. Grease and flour a Bundt cake pan.

In a small bowl, combine the granulated sugar, cinnamon, and chopped nuts. Stir together until well mixed and set aside.

Pour half the batter into the prepared cake pan. Sprinkle the cinnamon sugar nut mixture on top. Pour the remaining cake batter over the nut mixture and bake for 50-55 minutes.

Allow to cool for 15 minutes, then remove from pan onto a cake plate. Dust with the confectioner's sugar.

Coming Soon!

Body Bags & Blarney:

Book Three of the Vivienne Finch Magical Mysteries

After a long winter season, Vivienne Finch and the residents of Cayuga Cove are just itching to put away the snow blowers and shovels for good and welcome the return of spring. With preparations underway for the annual Saint Patrick's Day Parade and Luck of the Irish Carnival, members of the Shoreline Baptist Church prepare their own counter celebration with a weekend of faith-based activities they hope will turn hearts and minds away from the green beer and bar hopping. The charismatic new preacher, Seamus Kilpatrick, warns the town that such alcohol-fueled debauchery will only lead to retribution for their wicked acts.

As the first crocus buds push up from the frigid ground, the weather service issues a warning for a historic Nor'easter to strike the East Coast with Cayuga Cove in its crosshairs. Preparations are made to deal with the coming onslaught of snow, but no one is prepared when Father William is found drowned in the baptismal pool at Our Lady of the Lake Church. Sheriff Rigsbee investigates what he believes to be a case of unfortunate bad luck, while Pastor Kilpatrick believes it is a call to arms to wage spiritual warfare against those who revel in sin, leaving Vivienne Finch to see only cold-blooded murder. With the storm brewing and tempers rising, Vivienne must search for the killer before the only thing found at the end of the rainbow is her own grave!

ABOUT THE AUTHOR

J.D. Shaw is a 2008 graduate of the prestigious Odyssey Writing Workshop run by Jeanne Cavelos, former senior editor at Bantam Doubleday Dell. During his six weeks in the program, he worked alongside such award winning authors as Barry B. Longyear and Nancy Kress.

He resides in Elmira, NY with Sam, an indoor orange tiger cat who seems to think that sleep is just wasted time between feedings and spending quality outdoor time with his pal, the neighborhood stray, Mister Tommy Cat.

This is the second novel in his ongoing supernatural cozy series *The Vivienne Finch Magical Mysteries*. He is hard at work on the next book in the series.

'Like' *The Vivienne Finch Magical Mysteries* page on Facebook and stay informed on all the latest news, contests, and book signing events.

Be sure to visit his web site, **JDSHAWBOOKS.COM**, to discover more about the author and the series.

J.D. loves to hear from his readers. Email him at **AUTHOR@JDSHAWBOOKS.COM**

Made in the USA
Charleston, SC
02 December 2013